Tangled Magic

Regency Magic Book 2

Margaret Ball

Galway Publishing

Also by Margaret Ball:

The Regency Magic series
Salt Magic (Book 1)
Tangled Magic (Book 2)

The Applied Topology series

A Pocketful of Stars (Book 1)
An Opening in the Air (Book 2)
An Annoyance of Grackles (Book 3)
A Tapestry of Fire (Book 4)
A Creature of Smokeless Flame (Book 5)
A Revolution of Rubies (Book 6)

The Harmony series

Insurgents (Book 1)
Awakening (Book 2)
Survivors (Book 3)

Other books

Disappearing Act
Duchess of Aquitaine
Mathemagics
Lost in Translation
No Earthly Sunne
Changeweaver
Flameweaver
The Shadow Gate

Tangled Magic

A Regency fantasy romance

Chapter 1

I had been waiting ten years for Richert Dalkey to notice that I was a personable young female and to pay court to me. When I was twelve and he eighteen that might have been an unreasonable expectation; at twenty-two, with my red hair tamed and my adolescent chubbiness conquered and the best dressmaker in Din Eidyn helping me to select the fabrics and cuts that best displayed my complexion and figure – well, at twenty-two I felt the visit he paid me that morning was long overdue.

But that was nothing to the way I felt when I understood the object of his "courtship."

We had been in Town a month already, and Richert had done no more than pay us a formal courtesy call lasting all of fifteen minutes. I was beginning to despair of ever awakening him to the deep bond that I knew existed between us. Naturally my mother was no help; as always, she was much happier interfering with the servants by taking over the stillroom than shepherding her youngest and most difficult daughter through Din Eidyn society. Go to parties? She was much too busy with her creation of a white lily pomade to ward off wrinkles and with concocting Roman Balsam to prevent my developing freckles like Izzie's, not to mention making up effervescing draughts and aromatic tinctures for Izzie's biliousness, to take the lead in any social issue. She was only too happy to hand me over to my older sister Izzie, now a married woman and eligible to take over chaperoning me once the discomforts of her early pregnancy were eased. For the most part I too was happy with this decision, as when she wasn't criticizing my manners and my taste in clothing Izzie took her duties as chaperone quite as lightly as any girl could wish.

I must admit that I had not been entirely sanguine about the arrangement when I was first informed that Izzie, after less than a year of what seemed to be a very happy marriage, planned to close her husband's town house and to move in with us for the Season. Naturally I expressed all that was proper upon that occasion. I said that I was happy to learn that the move was not prompted by any differences between Izzie and her husband, and expressed sympathy at the news that Sir Joshua was to be sent on a diplomatic mission to Kievan Rus in search of an alliance against Lutéce. Thanks to Mama's quelling frowns, I stopped at that and did not ask precisely why, if the marriage was so happy, Izzie had chosen to remain in Din Eidyn and endure a year-long separation rather than accompanying Sir Joshua to Kievan Rus.

I was enlightened on this matter before my sister had been back with us a week. Mama might have been too prudish to explain to me that Izzie was increasing, but the fact could hardly be concealed when she was sick every morning. She had been feeling so ill during the early weeks of her pregnancy that she and Sir Joshua agreed it would be unwise for her to face the rigors of the long journey to Kievan Rus. And in deference to her obvious unhappiness, I did not express my entirely improper sentiment that I had put up with Izzie for a great many years already and had been looking forward to a Season without her constant critical attention.

I even did what I could to alleviate Izzie's morning sickness, and with some success, but unfortunately the good effects of my work did not become evident until after Sir Joshua had departed. If only they had told me sooner! But considering the prudery with which my darling Mama treated any discussion of Izzie's condition with an unmarried girl, I was lucky I did not have to puzzle it all out for myself while Izzie drifted around the house displaying a greenish complexion that made her freckles stand out most unbecomingly. And I was, after all, well repaid for my efforts. As soon as she felt quite well again, Izzie allowed Mama to push her into taking on the duties of chaperoning me through the Season. Izzie's relaxed chaperonage was a great improvement over being under Mama's watchful eye – not to mention that Mama expected me to spend precious days of the Season trapped in the house when she was disinclined to interrupt her stillroom experiments by taking me to a party.

Today, for instance, Izzie was interpreting the rules of society in a liberal manner by placing herself at the far end of the sitting-room, quietly plucking the strings of her great harp. Richert and I, conversing at the other end of the room, had all the privacy we required for a somewhat sensitive discussion. While he explained his dilemma I stitched on a lace insertion for one of Izzie's chemises. It would have been quite improper to have worked on the chemise itself in front of him, but the bit of whitework on net that I held in my hands could have been destined for any number of garments and was conveniently portable. The work was useful even now, when it was not quite complete. It gave me something to look at when I did not wish to meet his eyes, and an excuse for wincing when he disclosed his reason for wanting to court me. I pretended that I had pricked my finger with the needle.

Besides, Izzie had been complaining that she needed more chemises due to the laundress' dilatoriness in washing the soiled ones. I could have wished that Izzie were not quite so insistent on putting on fresh underlinen twice or thrice daily, but now that she had acquired what she considered a satisfactory supply of chemises I needed to finish the embroidery on all of them in order to prevent a return of her bilious indisposition – courtship or no courtship.

Not that I would have described this visit as *courtship*. It turned out to be more in the nature of *amateur theatricals*.

"I do not perfectly understand you, Richert," I said after his long and somewhat muddled introductory speech. "You wish to put it about that we are engaged to marry, but to have a private understanding that there is actually no engagement? What should I – or you, for that matter – stand to gain from such a peculiar arrangement?"

Richert ran one hand through his short reddish locks, ensuring that even those that had not before been disheveled stood on end. His hair was so springy that he needed no pomatum to maintain the *Coup au Vent* style; I could all too easily imagine running my own fingers through those resilient short curls. The Hob would doubtless complain that a proper young lady would not even think of such things. Well, I was not so far gone into impropriety as to actually do such a thing, but one cannot be hopelessly in love for ten years without having the occasional improper thought!

I had some uncharitable thoughts as well, such as that the *Frightened Owl* might have been a more appropriate style for my non-suitor suitor, my non-courting courtier. When not contemplating his features as those of the man I loved and must surely be destined to wed, I did occasionally notice that his nose and chin were rather sharp, his face narrow, and his mien upon certain occasions reminiscent of a fox who hears the hounds baying.

This was one of those occasions. "I *told* you, Pet," he said, and my heart beat faster when he used my old nickname. "That ghastly Turvoll female has seized upon me as her *beau idéal* of a romantic hero, and has taken to languishing over me in public in a most unsuitable way."

"Why?"

"Because she's an idiot!"

"Well, you must have done something to attract her attention. Did you stand up with her too many times at the Assembly Rooms, or what?"

"Don't be an idiot, Pet. I may let Mama nag me into some of the so-called social events of the Season, but I draw the line at wasting an evening at Gilroy's Assembly Rooms. They're nothing but a marriage market, the suppers are cheese-paring, and one is trapped in the ballroom all evening with nothing to do but evade designing young ladies. Even Almack's in Londin has a card-room!"

"Oh, right." I had forgotten Richert's aversion to Gilroy's – and his ability to miss the point. Not to mention his tiresome insistence that Anglia's social Season, in Londin, eclipsed Din Eidyn's Season in every possible way. "Well, where *did* you pay too much attention to her, then?"

"Nowhere!" he snapped. "It was quite a fortuitous encounter. And it seemed like the only thing to do at the time, but I can tell you, Pet, I wish to God I had not done it."

"Done what?" I stabbed the needle through the net and pulled the white thread too tight, then pushed and tugged gently to smooth out the unsightly bump while I waited for Richert to get to the point.

"Lamed Jenneret's wheeler when I shot."

"You *shot one of the Baron's horses?*" Why had I heard nothing of this? Granted, our social life had been somewhat curtailed since Izzie acquired all these new chemises. She was again suffering from bilious attacks, and would do so until I finished embroidering all of her new garments. Still, I should have thought the very stones of the city would have rung with reports of such a scandal as this promised to be.

"No, Pet, you should know me better than that! I merely shot through the traces; it was that fool of a coachman who failed to react in time and caused the horse to stumble."

"I think," I said, "you should tell me the whole story. Was it a bet?" To shoot one of the traces on a moving carriage sounded very like some of my brother Tam's tales; specifically, the kind of foolish challenge that got recorded in the betting-book at a gentlemen's club.

Grumbling, Richert gave me a very brief synopsis of the affair. On a moonlit night last week he and his friend Iveroth had been returning from a candlelit contest at Mackay's shooting gallery. They were passing the Hultstrom house just as guests departed from Eugenia Hultstrom's rout-party, and had happened to see Dorothea Turvoll being handed into a carriage which was definitely not her family's usual conveyance. Slightly perturbed, they had followed the departing carriage a short way; then they became very perturbed indeed as it turned away from the fashionable streets where the Turvoll mansion was to be found and onto the north-bound road out of the city. They were unmounted; the coachman ignored their calls to stop and whipped up his horses as if to get away; at the time, Richert said, it seemed the only thing to do was to part one of the traces on the harness. Crippling the wheeler had, he reiterated, been an unexpected consequence of an incompetent coachman. "My shot stopped the coach," he said, grinning, "and who should pop out, all fizzing in a froth of righteous rage, but Baron Jenneret himself? At first he threatened to call out whoever was responsible for laming his horse, but then he recognized me."

"After which, I take it, he lost his enthusiasm for a duel?"

"Yes," said Richert. "It is quite a bore, but the fact is that nobody ever does call me out." Deprived of such natural gentlemanly entertainments as gambling to excess, and dreaming of the military career which his father refused to countenance, Richert had for years put much of his energy and concentration into becoming the best marksman, the most deadly pistol shot, in all of Din Eidyn – possibly, in all our country of Dalriada. And he enjoyed the éclat of that reputation far more than he ever admitted in so many words.

"Let me guess," I said after he fell silent. "He was abducting Dorothea Turvoll, and you and Iveroth took her home and left Jenneret to deal with his stranded carriage and his lamed horse. And now you are more afraid of *Dorothea* than of *Jenneret?*"

"Jenneret's too much a coward to seek revenge, especially since he would be ruined socially if the story came out; if anything, he was more eager than we were to hush it up and pretend it never happened. But that idiot girl has persuaded herself that I am in love with her and that I followed Jenneret's coach on purpose to rescue her and that I am only awaiting a sign that she returns my affection – and she is sprinkling those signs all over Din Eidyn for the entertainment of the *ton*! I don't see," he grumbled, "why she couldn't fall in love with Iveroth rather than me, if she had to invent a romance over the situation! *He* is the very type of the dark, brooding hero so popular in those silly novels you girls love so much!"

Richert might not understand it, but it seemed obvious to me why Richert, rather than Iveroth, had become the target of Dorothea's fantasies. Not only was Iveroth's manner far too brusque to appeal to a romantically inclined young lady; worse than that, he was recently, and very happily, married to my dear friend Sabira. It would have required an even greater talent for self-delusion than that demonstrated by Dorothea Turvoll for a maiden to imagine that Iveroth could even notice her when he was so newly wed to an acknowledged Incomparable like Sabira, with her sea-green eyes and her crown of silver-gilt hair.

Sabira did not love Din Eidyn society quite so well as I did. In fact, she was in the habit of retiring to their country house by the sea each month around the time of the full moon, which might explain why Iveroth had been wandering around at loose ends with Richert on that bright night last week.

"If Miss Turvoll does fancy herself in love with you," I said, "I am sorry for her, but I do not quite understand why it is *your* problem." And in truth, I had little sympathy for Dorothea Turvoll. If I, who had loved Richert these ten years, could refrain not only from languishing after him but from giving him any suspicion of my feelings, could not this little chit of an heiress show a similar self-command over a man she could not have met more than two or three times?

"Because m'lady mother is on her side!" Richert snapped. "She is bent on seeing me married, and she thinks the Turvoll girl would be a most suitable match!"

"Then you will scarcely make your mother happy by pretending to be engaged to me."

"Oh, you'll do as well if not better," Richert said casually. "Our families' lands march together; your birth is incomparably better than hers; and the Dalkey heir has no need to hang out for an heiress – at least, I wouldn't if m'father would make me a proper allowance! Trust me, Mama will be happy to escape the connection with trade that Dorothea Turvoll would inflict upon the family."

All of these considerations had, of course, already occurred to me, but it would have been improper for me to mention them. And in any case, it was not a *sham* engagement that I desired.

"Mama thinks she'll be able to persuade me to offer for Dorothea because the girl's fortune would free me from dependence on my father."

I felt chilled. "That is...not entirely unreasonable, is it?" Richert was in the habit of talking to me as freely and as casually as though I were in fact the little sister he pretended to think me. I had heard quite enough of his financial problems – indeed, all of Din Eidyn knew of them. His older brother had been a wastrel and a gamester whose untimely death had been a relief to their father, even though their mother had taken it as a reason to go into permanent mourning and to add paroxysms of grief to the palpitations and other ailments with which she controlled her family. Sir William Dalkey's fear that Richert would go the same way had led him to keep his remaining heir on an exceedingly tight rein. Richert could live in the family town house at his parents' expense, his father maintained accounts for him with Din Eidyn's finest tailor and with Deverill the boot maker, he had only to admire a fine horse to see the steed added to the family stable – but he was perennially short of cash.

"But if I were engaged to you, m'father would take that as evidence of my maturity and stability, and would finally settle enough of an allowance on me to enable me to live as a gentleman should!"

I really did almost drive the needle into my hand upon hearing this statement. Did Richert *never* think one step beyond the obvious? Clearly he was in sore need of loving guidance from a sensible female such as myself. "But, Richert, when we broke the engagement your father would hardly continue to think you stable and mature!"

"Yes, but—"

"Oh, do hush for a moment!" I implored him. "I need to think."

"You mean you'll do it?"

"I mean no such thing," I said with all the firmness I did not feel. To become engaged to Richert was a temptation, a soap-bubble happiness that would only break me when the bubble burst. Or… was it possible that during the course of a sham engagement we would be so thrown together that he would finally recognize that we were always meant to be together?

"Izzie," I called across the room, "what a lovely piece of music that is. Do, pray, sing the lyrics for us." I could think while she sang, and perhaps the romantic mood of the music would work upon Richert at the same time.

"Elspet, I do not know the words to *Duighal's Gathering and March*, and if I did they would be in the barbarous Highland tongue and neither of us would understand them!" Izzie snapped.

Oh.

Perhaps that was not, after all, the best choice for romantic background music. I must confess that I am not particularly musical. "Well, then, would you please sing us that ballad you were playing the other day, the one about the two sisters?"

"All right, though that is better on the small Irish harp, but I have no idea where that can have got to. My stupid abigail must have misplaced it when she unpacked for me. Doubtless it will turn up eventually in some place like the linen press. But I can adapt it to the great harp.

"*There were two sisters sat in a bower,*" Izzie began without preamble.

"*Binnorie, O Binnorie,*
There came a knight to be their wooer,
By the bonnie mill-dams of Binnorie."

As Izzie's fingers twinkled over the harp strings and she lifted her voice in the plaintive strains of the ballad, I recognized that this selection was not exactly ideal for getting a man into the right mood; in the song, one sister pushes the other into the river and lets her drown so that she can get the man they both love. I would not, of course, ever consider pushing poor little Dorothea Turvoll into the river. If I couldn't attract a man without recourse to such crimes, I might better drown myself!

But the ballad did have the virtue of giving me a little time to think over this misguided proposition. And a solution of sorts did come to me. There was just one little matter to clear up first.

"Richert," I said, very low under the sound of Izzie's singing, "I do not understand why you would wish to pretend an involvement with me. Would it not be simpler to explain to Dorothea Turvoll about your special relationship with Vivienne de Larue?"

Richert actually looked shocked. "Pet! It ain't right for a gently bred young lady to talk about these things!"

"Which gently bred young lady did you have in mind? Me, or Dorothea?"

"Both of you," Richert said stiffly. "She shouldn't know anything about it, and for that matter, neither should you."

"Oh, Richert. All of Din Eidyn has seen you dangling after Vivienne this age. And you needn't try to gammon me that you visit her house for the sake of the card-parties, because I know your allowance won't support the deep play that goes on there."

"Young ladies," Richert said, if possible even more stiffly than before, "should not use vulgar slang like 'gammon.' Doesn't your governess have any influence on you?"

"Darling Richert, poor dear Kirsty gave up attempting to gentrify my speech when I was eighteen," I informed him, "and you are evading the point. What *about* you and Vivienne de Larue?"

"Whatever you may think you know about that matter," Richert said, now sounding exactly as if he had swallowed a poker, "it don't signify as far as this problem is concerned. A Dalkey don't marry a nobody from nowhere. She was only Vivi Fauchet, an impoverished refugee from the revolution in Lutéce, before she seized the opportunity to better herself by wedding Edouard de Larue. I know that – you know it – even Dorothea Turvoll knows that much!"

"How did that marriage better her condition?" I was distracted into asking. "Were not the de Larues also Lutécian refugees?" I had been a child when the revolution in Lutéce sent so many members of their aristocracy across the sea to seek refuge in Dalriada and Anglia, but even the most self-absorbed schoolgirl could not have failed to notice the impact that the sudden influx of noble Lutécians had on our society.

"Yes, yes, but the de Larues were a notable family," Richert said impatiently, "whereas no one who was anyone had ever heard of the Fauchets. Anyway, that's neither here nor there. The point is, marriage was never on the cards, and even Dorothea ain't so missish as to object to a gentleman's previous attachments of *that* sort. Even if someone were so ill-bred as to gossip to her about Vivienne and me, she wouldn't be put off. She'd know that a gentleman terminates these little involvements upon his marriage."

I decided not to argue further with Richert on a topic which he was so uncomfortable discussing with me. I did wonder, though, whether Vivienne de Larue understood as clearly as Richert thought that she was no eligible bride for him. I had overheard Izzie and her gossiping friends making far too many references, for my taste, to Richert's visits to her house. They giggled in a most improper fashion over the tales that he was admitted at all hours. No, the Widow Larue might well think that Richert was hers for the taking, and that the ancient Dalkey name and the towering Dalkey respectability would be quite enough to render her fully acceptable to those elements of Din Eidyn society that currently looked askance at her. But I had more important matters to discuss with Richert just now.

"Whatever Mrs. de Larue may think," I told him now, "*I* would not receive the attentions of a gentleman who is so openly involved with her."

Richert's face brightened. "Then you'll agree to pretend that we're engaged?"

"By no means," I said, suppressing some regret and reminding myself that a sham engagement was hardly what I'd dreamed of, superficially attractive though it might be. "As usual, Richert, you have leapt at the first plan that presented without thinking it through! If we were formally engaged, you would be expected to start dealing with settlements."

"Oh, our lawyers can do all that – and anyway, all they have to do is waste time."

"You mean, you hope they would be so slow that you would not be required to sign anything before your problem with Dorothea Turvoll is resolved."

"Well, you would hope that too, wouldn't you?"

Not necessarily. But every proper feeling revolted against the notion of allowing Richert to trap himself in marriage to me via a pretense of engagement that both our families would treat as the real thing.

Too bad that my proper feelings were so weak. No, I told myself. I would *not* give in to this temptation – at least, not while I still believed that I could get what I wanted much more honestly.

"There would be innumerable other problems," I went on. "If your mother believed in this engagement, she'd have to host some *ton* parties to celebrate it—"

"Not Mama!" Richert chuckled. "Trust her 'palpitations' to excuse her from any such effort. And your mother will hardly be eager to abandon her stillroom hobbies to throw tonnish parties."

I abandoned that argument and went on to a point he could scarcely dismiss so easily. "You have not considered the cost to *me* of entering into such a fraud, Richert. I am not getting any younger, you know; if I do not find an eligible suitor this Season, I risk being left on the shelf."

Richert scoffed at that. "As if I didn't know that last year you turned down Hultstrom!"

I wrinkled my nose. "He's *old*, Richert. Why, he must be over forty!"

"Ormsgil's daughter didn't think so."

"And Eugenia is quite welcome to him. And as for Lieutenant Cairdie –"

"What, never tell me he offered for you too!"

My goodness. However had that detail escaped the town gossips? "It does not signify," I said firmly. "He is too young for me."

"The exact same age as you, Pet. I think you insist on finding something wrong with every man who takes an interest in you!"

Since not one of my suitors had been Richert, he was right about that. But I was not about to explain that to him. "Well, *that* does not signify either, Richert. After I turned down three men last Season—"

"What, *another* secret lover? Who's the third, then?"

"None of your business," I said tartly, "and hardly a lover, just an idiot who thought I could be had at the price of a few languishing looks and some limping verses that barely rhymed. The point is, Richert, that if I appear to jilt you, who are so perfectly eligible, after having refused three offers last Season, I shall deserve the reputation of being too hard to please by half – which is very nearly as bad as being thought unable to attract any offers at all. And if I don't jilt you, how shall I find a husband when everybody thinks that you have volunteered for the position?" *Unless you finally understand how perfectly matched you and I are...* but I could hardly say that, could I? I needed him to realize it for himself, without my prodding.

"Oh! I didn't think..."

He never did, did he?

"But you're hardly more than a child, Pet!"

"I was twenty-two last birthday, Richert." He *knew* that, if he would but think! I had been six years younger than him all our lives; did he imagine that had changed? I had, sadly, continued to have birthdays while Mama put off and put off my Season to concentrate on getting Izzie married off. Only after Sir Joshua offered for Izzie had I been allowed, shamefully late in my opinion, to make my formal entry to Society.

"Oh! Well... I suppose... To me you'll always be that charming hoyden of a little sister, Pet."

As I knew to my cost.

"You must see that it would scarcely do my reputation any good were I to jilt you," I insisted. "People would say I didn't know my own mind, and that I was too old to behave so harum-scarum. No, a pretended engagement will not solve your problem, Richert. But I know what will."

He waited and listened to Izzie's song while I set a few more stitches and finished the nine-times-circle around the embroidered rowan leaves. This closing bit of work really did require all my attention; try to do it while I talked to Richert, and who knew what inappropriate influences might creep into the charm?

Izzie's voice rose at the dramatic conclusion to the song.

"Oh, sister, reach but me your glove,

Binnorie, Binnorie,

And Sweet Edward shall be your love,

By the bonny mill-dams of Binnorie." But of course the elder sister refuses, and the younger is swept away and drowned in the next and final verse.

"What a strange song," Richert commented. "It ends so abruptly – Does the wicked sister get away with it, then?"

"I suppose so," I said, "it ends there, where they find the other one drowned. It doesn't even say whether Sweet Edward saw through the wicked sister... But never mind that, it doesn't signify. We need not worry about a sad old story that never happened save in some poet's imagination; we need to solve your problem with Dorothea Turvoll. And I think I know how to do it." But there were two more stitches required, and then I had to close the stitching by drawing the needle through a split thread.

"We must make it appear that you have fallen desperately in love with me," I said when at last I set the needlework aside. "You will have to go riding in the Park with me, accompany me to galleries and exhibitions, and stand up with me at balls – not more than twice in one evening, mind you; that would be improper in you to ask, or in me to allow. But it will serve as well if you sit out with me, and take me to supper, and spend the rest of the time – in between dancing with other young ladies, of course – looking daggers at my other partners."

"It sounds like a dashed bloody bore to me," Richert said. "You're sure we couldn't just be 'engaged' for a while?"

"Positive," I told him. "Besides, nobody would believe in the engagement unless you behaved as if you had suddenly fallen in love with me. There's no way you can get out of it; you are going to have to *court* me, Richert." I suppressed a grin of triumph. At least I should get that much of my heart's desire, seeing Richert at my feet, and only he and I would know it was all a sham!

"Will anybody believe this? Your dowry…"

"Is no more than respectable," I agreed. "But as you pointed out, that is not important considering your family's wealth. For the rest, you'll just have to pretend you're madly in love with me," I said through clenched teeth. "Will it be that difficult?"

"I'm no great hand at acting."

"Yes, well, it would require considerably more acting to make Din Eidyn believe in an engagement on the spur of the moment!"

"True. Very well. This may work. And I couldn't ask it of anyone but you, Pet."

So he finally appreciated me! "Because…?" I could stand to hear a few encomiums on my many virtues, such as loyalty and the willingness to help an old friend.

"Oh, because at least I know *you* will not be hurt by the pretense that I am in love with you!" he said blithely. "After all, we grew up practically like brother and sister; I can count on you not to get any silly ideas from this play-acting."

Chapter 2

The Park was bright with green leaves and flowers in the cool, damp morning air. Far too many people, in my opinion, had been lured outdoors by the soft grey summer day that bade fair to show us the sun before midday. But the problem of threading our way through the throng was not mine; we were in Sabira's new curricle, and she held the reins. "Explain to me again," Sabira said thoughtfully, "exactly how this charade furthers your interests, Elspet?"

It was the day after Richert and I had come to an agreement that he might pretend to be courting me and I might pretend to welcome his suit – a "charade" that would require no great skill at play-acting on my side, at least. He was already engaged to escort Izzie and me to the theater tonight, but that left me with an entire day to fill. Mama and Kirsty were busy in the still room and Izzie pleaded her condition for desiring a nap almost as soon as breakfast was over. This left me nobody at home except the Hob to whom I could talk about this exciting turn of events – and the Hob was seldom a really satisfactory interlocutor.

A note to Sabira had brought her to my doorstep and to my rescue. She was driving her very stylish new curricle and invited me to take a drive through the Park with her, where we could talk freely. I should have preferred a brisk walk to work off my nervous excitement, but one cannot expect a creature of the seas to enjoy walking rather than gliding through the water. Sitting a horse was also not pleasurable for her; accustomed as she was to riding kelpies, she had once explained, she found it difficult to establish a sympathetic bond with the stupid, unaware horses of the land. Most people in Din Eidyn were unaware that Sabira was a finwife, and simply considered her eccentric; I was one of the few people who had the honor of her confidence. And as such, I would have felt churlish in complaining of this sedentary ride. At least we were getting some fresh air into the bargain.

"Why, he will be forced to pay some attention to me at last, and in the most romantic possible circumstances!" I explained. "Riding here in the Park, dancing the night away, murmuring sweet nothings in the back of our theater box… the possibilities are endless! And once he has got in the habit of treating me like a personable female whom he might plausibly marry, rather than as an annoying little sister, he might at any moment recognize that I am in fact a charming person and reasonably well-looking and… and better adapted than anyone else to a life with him, because I already understand him so well! Good day, Eugenia! How well that bonnet becomes you! I vow, you must have had it from Mignonette; no one else has quite her way with velvet ribands."

"You are a hypocrite," Sabira teased me under her breath after Eugenia Hultstrom's high-perch phaeton was safely past.

"Am not! That scuttle-shaped bonnet conceals quite two-thirds of her face, and what style could do the poor girl more good than that? Besides, she is not like to live for very long, and it's a kindness to let folk on the brink of death hear some cheering words."

"Is she ill?" Sabira gasped.

I restrained a giggle. "No, Sabira, so far as I know Eugenia is in the best of health. But she does not understand horses – you need only have seen the lumpish way she sits that pretty little bay mare Sir Flodin bought her – and I wager she will overturn that new perch-phaeton of hers tomorrow, if not today. No matter how much money one's husband has, it is always a mistake to show off horseflesh that is beyond one's ability to control."

"I shudder to imagine your strictures on my driving," Sabira said, "for you know perfectly well, Elspet, that I am no expert on horses – not those of the land, at any rate."

"Oh, but the pair you are driving are the sweetest, smoothest, most docile steppers in Din Eidyn! Iveroth selected them for you, did he not?"

"You know he did. And perhaps you are minded to be more charitable towards me than towards poor Eugenia Hultstrom!"

"Well," I drawled, "you *are* my dearest friend in Din Eidyn. Also, you have not, so far as I know, expressed the opinion that I am close to being left on the shelf because I frighten gentlemen away with my daredevil riding!"

"Did Eugenia say *that*?"

"She did indeed, the pudding-faced wretch! I suppose she will never forgive me for the fact that I refused Sir Flodin Hultstrom before he offered for her… though it was she, not I, who was so tactless as to make the *ton* aware of that! I should only be taking a just revenge if I encouraged her to spring those lively horses that she cannot hope to control. And you are my witness, Sabira, that I did no such thing!"

"Indeed," Sabira allowed, "I must commend your self-restraint – oh, Mr. Farquhar, do you bow to me again now? I had thought myself quite forgot by the Beau!"

The dapper gentleman on the high-stepping chestnut executed a second and even deeper bow; no mean feat while bestriding his spirited mount. No one had ever said much for Beau Farquhar's intelligence; but by the same token, no one had ever faulted his style either in riding or in dress. As well as having great personal charm, he was an acknowledged leader of fashion whose attentions could only add to a lady's consequence. "Alas, my lady, it is you who have forgotten us by remarrying – and of all people, to choose that stiff-necked Iveroth!"

"Yes, I see that you and the other gallants are all in mourning over my marriage!" Sabira teased.

Gavin Farquhar looked pained. "*Mourning*? During the Season? Such a solecism, unless one were positively forced into it by the death of a very near relation!"

She laughed. He was courteous enough to exchange a few more words with us and to wait for Sabira's hint, by gathering the reins, that she was ready to drive on, before bowing again in farewell.

"The problem with your expectations for Mr. Dalkey," Sabira said when we were private again, "is that you are overlooking his current infatuation. While his eyes and mind are filled with Vivienne de Larue, I fear he will hardly open them to see you."

"Is he so deeply enmeshed with the lady?" I knew the answer, but hardly liked to admit it.

"My dear, it has been the talk of the town this age. You must know that. Indeed, I am surprised that Dorothea Turvoll thought she had any chance with him while he is dangling at the Widow Larue's petticoat-strings."

"Presumably she knows, as does everyone else, that a Dalkey would never marry a Lutécian refugee of no family."

"Some people think that she improved her social position by marrying Edouard de Larue. To be sure he was also a Lutécian refugee, but at least his family name is impeccable."

"That has hardly raised her high enough to allow her to set her sights on the oldest family in Dalriada!"

"Perhaps not," Sabira mused, "especially considering the rumors about her first marriage… But, Elspet, I am not at all sure that Vivienne de Larue sees the matter in such a light. I think both you and Dalkey should be very careful if you start on this charade."

"What, to make folk believe in it? Don't tell me you too think it impossible that I should really attract Richert Dalkey!"

"By no means," Sabira assured me. "That is not at all what I meant! *Good* day, Lady Ormsgill. We have just passed Eugenia, looking quite charmingly in her new perch-phaeton. You are a brave woman, allowing your daughter to drive such a vehicle behind such spirited horses."

Lady Ormsgil simpered and said that it was no decision of hers, that Eugenia's husband was so enamored he could deny her nothing.

"What did you mean, then?" I demanded after Lady Ormsgil drove on.

"When I first came to Din Eidyn," said Sabira, "after the death of my first husband, I was so foolish as to attend a masque at the house of Vivienne de Larue. I wonder you had not heard the story; I suppose Iveroth, who brought me away, was more successful in hushing it up than I'd dared hope." She drew up the horses for a moment so that she could fix her entire attention on me.

"Elspet, Edouard de Larue's widow is *not* at all a nice person, and she has dangerous friends. I have reason to believe that she learned herb-witchery of the blackest sort from her bosom-bow Ailsa of Quoy."

"The Duchess of Quoy is no longer seen in Society," I pointed out. "They say that she is incapacitated by an incurable illness and has retired to her country estates."

Sabira's lips twitched as though she found something amusing in this sad fact. "That may be so – but Vivienne has access to the gardens at Quoy House, and enough knowledge to make evil use of the evil herbs that Ailsa of Quoy planted there. If she has not yet used her herb-witchery to complete Dalkey's conquest, she will surely do so if she believes him to be deserting her for you."

This was a problem that had not previously occurred to me, and I realized now that I needed to go home again, for it would be necessary to consult with our Hob about how to protect Richert.

***

The Hob had followed us to Din Eidyn for the first time last Season. He said that he had grown bored at our country estate, where we had three pairs of hands for every task and the servants needed neither help nor encouragement. Furthermore, my attitude and the tales brought back by the servants from Izzie's previous Season in the city made him think that I would be sorely in need of his help, if not precisely for domestic matters, then surely to navigate the social pitfalls awaiting me.

He was entirely right about that.

My mother has always preferred not to recognize the Hob. His attachment to our family is not consistent with the high place which she likes to think has always belonged to the Rattrays. Why could we not have a more dignified tutelary spirit, or at least an impressive ghost like those boasted by our neighbors? The Graemes of Kinross had a banqueting hall in which fairy music played at midnight. The Dalkeys could boast of a weeping lady in green who foretold the death of one of the family. Even the MacLeans, those coarse folk who were little better than farmers, were haunted by a headless horseman. But no. The Rattrays had only a little, brown, naked Hob – or so he was reputed to appear by those few who had seen him - who bounced invisibly about the house playing tricks on lazy servants and doing chores for deserving ones, who must have his saucer of milk like a farmhouse cat and who added not one whit to the dignity of the family.

"But, Mama," I said once when she was bemoaning our lack of connections in the society of the otherworld, "would it not be vastly uncomfortable to have a lady in green perpetually weeping around the house, and vanishing into a cold cloud when one walked through her? Consider how many Rattrays there are in the country, and most of them claiming connections with us. And remember how long it took Great-Uncle Percy to die after he took to his bed saying he would never leave it again? We should seldom enjoy any peace in the house."

I thought my point a reasonable one, but it earned me only a slap and an injunction not to show off my cleverness by meddling in the affairs of my elders. I took my burning cheek and my sense of grievance off to the Hob, who had ever stood my friend even though he did not permit me to see him. It was then he announced his intention of coming with us to Din Eidyn to see me through the social season.

"You will have little to do there," said I, still petulant about my mother's rejection, "for I shall not take part in the Season, not unless Izzie finds someone to marry this time. Mama says that it is entirely too much to expect her to shepherd two little, round, redheaded girls to balls and masques and midnight suppers in the search for husbands."

"Would it not be more efficient to sell off the two of you at once? Perhaps to the same man?"

"That may do in the land of the heathen Turk," I said, "but here in Dalriada, for a man to have two wives at once is considered quite ineligible. Besides, I have been a younger sister for over twenty years. Even were it possible, I have no wish to continue in my inferior position by becoming a second wife. If you are really my friend, Hob, you will help me get a husband for Izzie. 'Twould vastly improve Mama's temper. Until then there is no help for me."

The Hob left me then, saying that even a brownie could have too much of whining and complaining and that there was clearly no time to lose if I was to be turned into a lady fit for Din Eidyn society by the time my older sister was wed. But he got over his miff in time to accompany us to the capital, and had been a material help in getting Izzie well married – though, of course, she had no notion that she owed anything to the thread magic the Hob had taught me.

Now I required his aid more urgently than before. Izzie was safely married, so it did not signify that she seldom wore the gauze shawl I had given her with its embroidered charms to make her less sharp-tongued; and I had just completed the task of inserting charmed lace into each of her chemises to counteract the biliousness that had made her so ill when she was first increasing. I was entirely free to turn my needle and my slight talent for thread magic to the task of protecting Richert; the only problem was the shortage of rowan trees in the neighborhood of our town house. I had brought a few twigs from our country home with me, but they would have to be shaved fine and deployed with great care if I was to construct a tangle of red thread and rowan that would guard Richert against Vivienne de Larue's machinations.

Just figuring out how to make him wear the protective threadwork was a puzzle in itself! I could scarcely give him lacework insertions for all his shirts; men consider their linen complete if it is clean and white, and even a dandy like Beau Farquhar would never have needlework adorning his shirts. Besides, it would take me forever to embroider all Richert's linen, even if he allowed me to do so. I finally settled on an embroidered fob to hold his watch and his modest collection of seals, and found a sturdy ribbon to serve as the base of the work.

"That," said the Hob in his normal censorious style, "is hardly your most serious problem."

I agreed. "I may not have enough shavings of rowan twigs to work them into all the protective charms you have shown me. Also, at least one thread of each pattern must be red, and Richert is as finicky as Izzie about wearing colors that quarrel with his hair color."

"You yourself—"

"Yes, yes, I know," I said hurriedly, before he could revisit the matter of the Blush Rose Disaster. That gown had been ordered for Izzie by our mother, doubtless in a fit of abstraction when she was too busy considering a new decoction of lilies to recognize that Madame Olympe's length of warm pink sarsenet in the latest color from Lutéce, so attractive when held up by the slender, dark-haired dressmaker, would clash vilely with Izzie's carroty hair. Izzie managed not to wear the gown in public until Sir Joshua had offered for her hand, and at the beginning of this Season she had passed it on to me. That sarsenet made my darker auburn locks look as atrociously red as my sister's carrot top, and even an overdress of blonde did not tone it down sufficiently to make it wearable; I had been forced to put my foot through the scalloped hem in two different places before Mama would allow me to hand it off to my maid.

"You are quite clever enough with your needle to have repaired that pink ballgown," the Hob went on despite my attempt to quash that subject.

"But not to make it passable for a red-headed female to wear! I do not know what Mama was thinking of; she might as well have decked me out in a wreath of pink roses."

"Yet you expect young Dalkey to wear a red-embroidered watch fob!"

"There will not be very much red showing when it is completed," I said, laying down a neat row of crimson stitches over one of the rowan slivers, "and it will be nowhere near his face, and anyway gentlemen do not care about colors so much –"

"You just said that young Dalkey does care about colors."

"Well then, I will overlay all the red thread with gold work until no red shows anywhere! So if *that* is what you consider my most serious problem—"

"It is not. You are overlooking an obvious solution, one that would save you all this nonsense about a false courtship."

"And that is?"

As usual, I could not see the Hob, but from the tone of his voice I felt sure he was smirking. "Are you usually so slow? If you can persuade Dalkey to wear thread magic of your working, Elspet, why waste your time trying to make him immune to charms? You know well enough how to influence a man in your favor; lace this silly watch fob with charms to make him desperately in love with you, and once he puts it on, the courtship will no longer be a pretense."

I set my work down for fear that my suddenly shaking hands would take a stitch in the wrong direction. "It would still be false."

"Who would know it? Certainly not Dalkey."

"*I* would know."

"I'll wager you could forget it. Imagine the pleasure of having him truly at your feet, believing utterly in his protestations of love!"

I could imagine it, and the vision was so intoxicating that it made my hands shake even worse. The part I couldn't imagine was that where I believed in the love-words I had forced my swain to sigh out.

"I do not want to get him in that way," I said. "Besides—"

"Well?" the Hob prompted after I fell silent for a time. "What missish megrim deters you from going after your heart's desire, silly child?"

I straightened the half-finished embroidery on my knee and contemplated the interlocking chains of stitchery that would lock out any magical attacks on Richert. Eventually I found enough calmness within me to say, "My heart's desire is that Richert Dalkey would see me as I am, not as the playmate of his childhood, and would truly love me. I have no desire at all for a 'love' that he would put off with his garments on his way to the marriage bed."

The Hob huffed annoyance. "Then charm his nightshirts as well!"

He took himself off then, leaving me to complete the threadwork in privacy. I stitched quickly and had the basic charms all laid down before my maid came to help me dress for dinner and the theater. Indeed, I had more time to spare than I really wanted; after I put the watch fob away to be finished after I acquired more gold thread, I sat looking out of the window, my hands twitching with nervous tension. Finally I took up a length of fine amber silk, knotted it into a circle, looped the threads over and around my fingers and wove the pattern the Hob thought I should use. *Love me love me love me do*, the amber loops and tangles sang. Irritably, I pulled my thumbs free of the pattern and let it collapse back upon itself. Even Izzie had not required such help to bring Sir Joshua up to scratch, and I did not need it to make Richert notice me!

Besides, even if the Hob were so devoid of morals as to recommend such a trick, *I* knew that it was wrong. Terribly wrong. Terribly, unforgivably wrong.

My busy hands created the long, slender pattern twice more before Orrock came in. Twice more I let it collapse into a single long circle of silk.

Mama had told Orrock to lay out the opera dress Izzie had passed on to me from last season, but then she did not know that Richert was supposed to be stricken by a *coup de foudre* at the sight of me tonight, and to begin pursuing me *a la folie*. To help him remember his lines, I told Orrock to lay out my new dress from Olympe, the jonquil lustring with an overdress of Pomona green. Even Richert, with his annoying habit of not really looking at me and of seeing only the plump hoyden who had pestered him and my brother's other friends in childhood, ought to be startled into a momentary awareness of the new me when he saw me in that dress – especially with the bit of Pomona-green embroidery I had added around the jonquil hem! I might not cheat to the extent of trying to make Richert believe himself in love with me, but surely there could be no harm in the little touch of "Look at me!" that I had added to complement Olympe's skilled dressmaking.

Richert's eyes widened in a most gratifying manner when, after making his bows to Mama and Izzie, he turned to me and took in the full magnificence of my attire. Sadly, his first murmured words to me destroyed the gratification I had so briefly felt. "Very colorful for a young lady in her second Season, Pet!"

"But surely, at my age, I may be allowed more liberty than a girl just out of the schoolroom?"

He nodded politely, but his eyes repeated the stricture and I could tell he would have been better pleased to see me in the insipidly pale hues affected by most young ladies. Still, I consoled myself, at least he had *noticed* me. And he played his part well enough at the theater, leaning over my chair in our box and murmuring things that *could* have been lover-like compliments. In any case, he had the sense to make his comments inaudible to anyone else, so even Izzie could not know that he was really reminiscing about the day when I had both disgraced myself and earned the right to accompany my brother

Tam and his older friends on their adventures in the countryside.

"You always were a headstrong brat," he said under his breath while Izzie was still looking around the theater in the hope of espying some acquaintances. "I suppose I should have expected that the girl who stole Tam's new horse would insist on appearing in society in a gown more suited to a matron!"

"If you recall," I said in even lower tones, "I could ride Wildfire better than Tam ever could – and I can carry off this dress too!" I laughed merrily and tapped his wrist with my fan as though I were merely responding to the flattery he should have been lavishing on me.

"To be sure," he agreed promptly, "that gown does look better on you than it would on Tammas."

My brother joined us then, not quite late enough to be rude, and the conversation became general until the rising of the curtain prompted at least a third of the audience to lower their voices.

Dorothea Turvoll occupied her family's box that night, accompanied by the superannuated maiden aunt who had been dragged into service to chaperone her for the Season. While I was not precisely pleased to observe the languishing looks she cast towards our box whenever Richert stood near the front, the effect on him was most salutary. He redoubled his apparent attentions to me, and nobody but the two of us could tell that he was favoring me with more of his opinions on suitable dress for an unwed girl.

"A young lady's dress," he murmured, "if not white, should display only the most tender shades of green, yellow, pink, blue or lilac. Such restraint arrays the graceful wearer like another Iris, breathing youth and liveliness."

"You sound like my old governess Kirsty," I said through clenched teeth, forgetting to keep my reply inaudible. Izzie caught the last words, though not the subject and had to put her oar in.

"Indeed, Elspet dear, 'twould do you no harm to heed Kirsty's recommendations as to your behavior!"

"Were I still in the schoolroom," I snapped, "I might do so. But if you have some strictures on my behavior tonight, even Kirsty would recommend that you keep them until we are speaking in private!"

When Orrock was putting off my opera dress and combing my hair that night, Izzie came to my room. To my surprise, she had not come to criticize some imagined solecism, but rather to tease me about having acquired a new admirer!

"But surely," I said, pretending great interest in my reflection in the light of the wax tapers, "surely when you were so tactful a chaperone to us yesterday, you must have guessed at Richert's intentions?"

Izzie vowed that *then* she had had no thought but to comply with our old neighbor's expressed desire to have semi-private speech with me, but *now* she was fully convinced that he was courting me in all seriousness and that we would be married before the Season was over.

I hoped Dorothea Turvoll had been equally convinced.

It was a great pity that I could not believe in this courtship as easily as Izzie seemed to do.

Chapter 3

Vivienne de Larue glanced around the large drawing-room and endeavored to take her usual satisfaction in the crowded tables, the candelabra full of wax tapers setting the room ablaze, the chairs new-covered in straw-colored satin, the gentlemen absorbed in the fall of the cards and the onlookers jostling for a better view of the play. For some reason, these evidences of success and luxury failed to soothe her soul on this evening. True, her card party was as well attended as ever. The twin attractions of deep play and an excellent cellar brought the gentlemen of Din Eidyn to her house in such numbers that for several Seasons she had not worried over the few high sticklers who stayed away. Nor had she lost sleep over the fact that so few of the gentlemen brought their wives with them. If the silly society women chose to let their men venture out unguarded, it was no concern of hers! And if she turned her own bright eyes and sparkling conversation onto those men, it was only her duty as their hostess, was it not?

Only, of late, she had become unpleasantly aware that the success of her card parties, routs, and other entertainments had not, after all, led to a corresponding increase in the invitations she herself received to the homes of Din Eidyn notables. Young Ranald Westlin's family might look with complaisance on his losses at Vivienne's gaming tables, but they had not sent Vivienne a card of invitation to the ball at which the Westlins introduced Ranald's sister Sophie to Din Eidyn society. Sir Flodin Hultstrom might be seen enjoying a glass of the excellent port which Vivienne's butler opened, but

Vivienne had not been invited to the social spectacle of his wedding to that pudding-faced little Ormsgil chit. It was all most disappointing. Why did life always thwart her?

Marriage to Edouard de Larue should have significantly improved her standing in Din Eidyn; they might both be Lutécian emigrés, but her family had been scarcely better than commoners, whereas the de Larues were of the *ancien régime*. When her transformation from little Vivi Fauchet into the elegant Vivienne de Larue had not brought the social success she longed for, she had scraped acquaintance with the Duchess of Quoy. That friendship had resulted in some promising developments concerning the Duchess's magical techniques, but she had scarcely had the chance to profit from it socially before the dear Duchess's mysterious disappearance. And although the young Duke was polite about allowing her to visit Quoy House to take cuttings from Ailsa's garden, he had not so much as offered her a glass of ratafia on any of those visits. Well, it would all be different when she married Richert Dalkey. As the lady of the Dalkey heir, she would not follow fashion – she would lead it. And then those stiff-necked females who had sought to deny her acceptance by the *ton* would rue their snobbishness!

Only, where was Richert tonight? It was not like him to absent himself from any party of hers. Distracted by his absence, she glanced over her own cards and, not exactly by design, lost heavily to Sir Flodin Hultstrom after everyone except the two of them had dropped out of the bidding. She concealed her growing sense of dismay behind bright chatter and repeated assurances that she did not mind her losses in the least; it was, she said, only the price one must expect to pay for the honor of learning from so talented a player as dear Sir Flodin. And when might she hope for the even higher honor of entertaining dear Lady Hultstrom?

Sir Flodin had the grace to look embarrassed as he begged off for Eugenia, claiming that she had no interest in playing cards.

"Oh," Vivienne purred, "then it must have been a lie that I heard, something about an unconventional stake in the card-room at the Westlin ball… I wonder you will allow such vicious gossip about Lady Hultstrom to pass unchallenged, Sir Flodin!"

Hultstrom excused himself somewhat abruptly from the game, and Vivienne had to ask her neighbor at the loo table to deal the next hand while she counted out the guineas she owed him. "Now that was ill-considered, my dear," purred an unwelcome voice behind her as Sir Flodin withdrew with his winnings.

"I shall win it all back with the next hand," Vivienne said, "or the next… A true gamester never grieves over a temporary setback, Jenneret! But then, you might not know that; you are always looking for a guaranteed win with no risk, are you not? Marriage to a wealthy innocent is a *much* surer path to riches than exercising your brains at the gaming table, is it not?"

That would serve Jenneret out for startling her. The girls' families might have hushed it up, but she knew all about his two attempts to run away with heiresses – first the young widow Steinnland, now wed to Viscount Iveroth, and more recently the Turvoll girl. Her lips pursed in a moue of distaste. Jenneret must be growing desperate; at least Sabira Iveroth had been a beauty, but the Turvoll heiress was barely passable.

He chuckled and, to her fury not sounding in the least discommoded, seated himself beside her while the other players jested about the last hand and debated who would win the next one. "Westlin is certain to be looed," jibed an older man who had been badly dipped already, "for he has no notion of counting the cards!"

"Counting is for pettifogging advocats," young Ranald Westlin shot back, "a gentleman relies on his sense of how the luck is running!"

The man who had laughed at him colored. Normally Vivienne would have rejoiced over Westlin's proposition; her bills were paid by just such rich young sprouts with their belief in their luck. But it was no part of her plans, either for profit or for social success, to allow the scandal of a duel arising from some careless jests at her party. "Pray, Mr. Petrie," she addressed the ruffled advocat, "would you be so good as to procure me a glass of the champagne cup? I vow, the room is so stuffy I grow quite faint! I do not know how you gentlemen bear it, but I do see that you at least are not troubled by the heat!"

Norval Petrie, who had not practiced as an advocat since a large inheritance made him free to abandon his profession and enjoy society, was all smiles at this favorable attention from his hostess. Vivienne relaxed slightly, signaled that she would not join the next hand, and turned back to Jenneret.

"Do you join the play?"

"No, no. You must know that lookers-on see the most of the game, my dear lady. And my pockets are not deep enough to play loo at the stakes you enjoy – though I will accept a glass of that excellent port. No," he said under cover of the others' conversation, "I meant your reference to that bit of gossip about Hultstrom's young wife staking one of her brooches at the card-table. It was obviously malicious, and he took it in ill part. You might have had a chance to recoup your losses had you remembered what I tried to teach you: never show malice."

Vivienne turned away from him and feigned absorption in the play. When young Ranald Westlin made a nearly disastrous error in leading with his ace, she reminded him that he must protect himself by repeating the catch-phrase"Pam, be civil." The other gentlemen cried out indignantly that she was showing undue favoritism to a pretty boy. While they bantered, she surreptitiously scanned the room once again. Richert Dalkey was still not there.

"If you are looking for your cicisbeo," Jenneret said in her ear, his breath warm against her neck, "I fear your search is doomed to failure. You thought to make young Dalkey your next step towards acceptance by the *ton*, but that plan is an overreach that can only end in disaster."

Vivienne leaned back and laughed as carelessly as she could. "He is at my feet five nights out of seven, Jenneret; it makes no difference if he has another engagement for this night!"

"Ah, but he has not been 'at your feet' at all these last few nights, has he?" Jenneret sounded quite odiously self-satisfied. "Shall I tell you where he has been?"

Vivienne shrugged. "Dancing attendance on his doting mama, no doubt, and squiring her to those deadly dull family gatherings—"

"—to which you have not been, nor shall you be, invited," Jenneret broke in. "You are out in your reckoning, my dear, and shall be badly dipped yourself if you do not reconsider your bets. You might not consider a party in the Rattray theater box an enlivening occasion, far less a concert at Thurvaston House or a *conversazione* hosted by young Lady Herriot at her parents' townhouse, but Dalkey has found his own entertainment at these events."

"All the better for him," Vivienne said with another careless shrug, "I do not wish him to become quite *ennuyé* before it suits me to allow him another audience." But she felt a prickle of cold chills, despite the heat engendered by so many warm bodies and burning tapers. Jenneret was even better informed about Richert's recent engagements than she was herself. Was it possible he knew something more – something that she had not heard? She recollected that Izzie Herriot had been a Rattray before her marriage, and was said to have returned to her parents' house while her husband was on a lengthy diplomatic journey to that barbarous empire far in the East. The Rattray family seemed to be unduly prominent in this catalogue of Richert's activities.

"The entertainment he is said to have discovered," Jenneret said, "is young, and female, and—"

Vivienne's tinkling laugh interrupted him. "And increasing, and by all reports sadly bilious with it! If you think to persuade me Richert has abandoned *me* for that plump little Lady Herriot—"

"She has a younger sister," Jenneret said.

Vivienne could barely conjure up a picture of the younger Rattray girl. Was she not just a duplicate of her married sister? A round little squab of a thing, and with that unfortunate coloring – nobody Vivienne had ever thought of as the slightest competition.

"You are grasping at straws," she said contemptuously. "Richert Dalkey is madly in love with me, and he will forget these dull family affairs the instant I raise my finger to him."

"Elspet Rattray is young," said Jenneret, "her family is near as old and well established as the Dalkeys, and their lands march together. I speak not to discompose you, Vivienne, but to save you a punishing letdown. I did try to tell you that the Dalkeys do not marry beneath them."

And he made his farewells, leaving Vivienne with a blinding headache and a room full of guests whom she no longer had the slightest desire to entertain.

Chapter 4

Richert had proposed that we ride in the Park that morning, but he was unconscionably late; I had been waiting in my riding habit for over half an hour, while a groom walked Caramella up and down before the house, when at last a visitor was announced. Even as I flew up out of my chair, though, I was disappointed; the caller was not Mr. Dalkey, but Baron Kinross.

The title was momentarily disconcerting; for a moment I expected to see old Lord Kinross, with his outmoded wig and his disapproving stare, stalking into the room like a molting heron. Instead I saw the friend of my childhood, taller and with a better complexion than the young Alastair Graeme with whom I'd raided birds' nests on the cliffs of Kinbrae.

"Alastair – Mr. Graeme," I corrected myself, for we were children no longer. Then I recalled that the old Baron had died the previous winter, and how he had just been announced, and corrected myself again. "Lord Kinross, I should have said!"

"The title still sounds odd to my ears," he said with the smile that transformed his dark face.

Izzie swept forward and between us, to act the chaperone before I could take his outstretched hands. "Pray forgive my baby sister's awkwardness, Lord Kinross. What a pleasant surprise to see you here! We had last heard that you were in Galicia with the United Armies of Dalriada and Anglia."

"As well united as a cat and a dog," Kinross smiled, "and about as effective, until Wellesley took command. No, I had to sell out and come home to manage the estate after my father's untimely death. Had Wellesley not required all his staff members to join in the monumental organizational task of putting the Anglian and Dalriadan armies under joint leadership, I should have been home this winter. As it is—" he laughed deprecatingly, "I find that our old steward has matters well in hand, and wishes nothing more than that I should get out from underfoot. So I have been freed to come to Din Eidyn—"

"Just in time for the last, and best, two months of the Season!" Izzie interrupted brightly. "What better place to renew old acquaintance and make new friends? Once your presence is widely known, you will be quite swamped with cards of invitation and I shall expect to see you at every ball!"

"As to that—" Kinross began. He stopped himself and started over. "Nothing would give me greater pleasure, Lady Herriot. I had scarcely dared hope that you would grace the parties of the *ton* this season; I hear that I have to congratulate you." I admired the way he did not glance at Izzie's waistline.

"Oh, I do not dance, but I have been pressed into service to chaperone little Elspet," Izzie said. "It is a tiresome duty, keeping tabs on an inexperienced girl, but I felt I might as well make myself useful while my dear husband is unavoidably absent. You had heard that he has been sent abroad?"

"Yes, to Kievan Rus, in search of a treaty against the Lutécian threat," Kinross said warmly. "And I am heartily glad to hear that Sir Joshua is of the same mind as myself regarding the urgency of that matter. My first interest in Din Eidyn—"

Izzie interrupted him with a titter. "Oh, you must not talk to us of politics, my lord! Such matters are far beyond the understanding of ladies. Do be seated, and tell me rather if you intend to attend Lady Dalkey's ball. I hear 'twill not be such a sad crush as Eugenia Hultstrom's rout-party was said to be, for the Dalkeys invite only the best people. We shall see no jumped-up merchant's daughters there!"

I assumed this was a dig at Dorothea Turvoll, whose attendance at that party had been the beginning of Richert's current problem. Naturally, it went right by Alastair – I mean, Lord Kinross, as I must now become accustomed to think of him.

"I do not believe I have received an invitation," Kinross said. "Possibly my breeding does not meet Lady Dalkey's standards."

I could barely repress a giggle at that, for the Graemes of Kinbrae were a family nearly as old as the Dalkeys, not to mention boasting that famous hall where fairy music played at midnight. Alastair's mother had been heard to express the opinion that the Dalkeys' Green Lady, who wept over future deaths in the family, was rather a *common* sort of apparition in comparison.

I remembered the conversation because Mama had stepped on my foot just before I could ask Lady Kinross how a Hob ranked in the hierarchy of family spirits. My toes ached for *days* after that.

When Alastair, I mean Lord Kinross, could get a word in edgewise between Izzie's assurance that he would surely be invited as soon as Lady Dalkey was aware of his presence and her sprightly gossip about the doings of everybody else in the *ton*, he bowed to me as if desirous of drawing me into the conversation. "Let us allow balls and routs and drums to take their proper places as evening entertainments; my purpose in calling today was to inquire if you ladies would care to ride in the Park. It is a remarkably fine day," he said.

Izzie fluttered and demurred and referred to her condition so delicately that if Kinross had not already been aware that she was increasing, he might never have guessed it. "And I fear my sister has another engagement."

"I see Miss Rattray is already dressed for riding," he said, giving an approving glance to my riding dress of slate-colored cloth, the jacket ornamented down the front with military-styled frogs of silver braid.

"Yes, but she is engaged to ride with Mr. Dalkey," said Izzie.

I glanced at the clock. Richert was already forty-five minutes late; it was indeed a fine day; and even if he were really courting me, I would be a remarkably poor-spirited female were I to spend the day frowsting within doors and languishing for a man who might have forgotten our engagement altogether. Richert was backsliding; at our next meeting I should have to warn him that he was forgetting to act like a man so desperately in love that he had no eyes for any other female.

And if he did remember me, it would be a salutary reminder of his negligence should he call here only to find out that I had gone out with another man. It was too bad that the 'other man' was only somebody who was like an indulgent older brother to me, but one cannot have everything. I jumped to my feet. "Yes, but Mr. Dalkey is so late that I fear he has forgotten his promise. By all means let us take a tour of the park, Alast —Lord Kinross. Perchance we shall meet him there."

Izzie pursed her lips and shook her head slightly. I suspected that on my return I should receive a lecture about showing myself too eager to accept a gentleman's invitation. In general I might have agreed with her, but it didn't matter in this instance; it was only Alastair. Lord Kinross, I mean.

And it was pure joy to sit my favorite mare and ride with – *Kinross*, for heaven's sake I must remember that or he would think me hopelessly rag-mannered – someone who could be counted on to match my pace and better yet, someone I need not flirt with or try to impress. Sixteen when my brother Tammas was fifteen and I twelve, Alast – *Kinross* – had been considerably kinder than Tammas. He never complained when I evaded my governess and insisted on joining their excursions. In fact, for some years I had been used to pray that God would let Tammas and Alastair change places. Not that I intended admitting to having cherished such childish fancies.

"You are very thoughtful today, Miss Rattray," Kinross commented shortly after we passed the gates to the Park. "Or are you bemoaning the crowd that makes it impossible for you to gallop as if we were on the high downs of Kinbrae?"

The Park was indeed crowded today, and I had every intention of keeping my mare to a quiet pace, but I could not let this pass.

"Don't challenge me, Lord Kinross," I said with a grin. "Do you remember what happened last time you said that some feat of riding was impossible for me?"

"Do I not!" he laughed. "Dalkey and I enjoined you strictly not to risk your neck on your brother's new horse, and Tammas said not to worry, for he had told the stable hands not to saddle Wildfire for you under any circumstances and that at only twelve you were too short to lift the saddle onto him yourself. And what should happen, but the first time we went out without Tammas we were joined by a red-headed little hellion riding Wildfire bareback, *ventre a terre!*"

"And you will admit that I could ride him."

"Yes. After causing us to die a thousand deaths when you jumped the chalk pit, you pulled him up and circled back to join us, looking as douce and quiet as a little maid still under her governess' tutelage ought to be. Although Wildfire was not nearly so well behaved – do you remember?"

I felt a blush rising. "Yes. He snapped at your horse and very nearly caused him to run away with you."

"He did no such thing!" Kinross protested. "The snapping I remember, but you should remember that I held my mount back with no difficulty."

I giggled. "Oh dear, here we are once again squabbling like brother and sister! What I remember best is the look of astonished admiration in Richert's eyes and the compliments he paid to my riding. *You* were not so effusive, Lord Kinross."

"It was not my style," Kinross said drily.

"And I recall the strapping my father administered when I came home with Tammas' new horse all tired and muddy. He said that if I wished to act the boy, I could take a boy's punishment. But I never cried, do you know?"

"I could have guessed as much. You never were a watering-pot."

"Anyway, it was worth it, for you two never again objected to my tagging along with you. And where two great grown lads of sixteen and eighteen accepted my presence, Tammas could hardly send me away." My eyes grew misty, remembering the beginnings of that long-ago summer of freedom and adventure, the wind in my face as I galloped Wildfire, Alastair's set face and Richert's laughing one. "I believe – no, I know it was then I fell in love with Richert Dalkey."

Kinross' mount shied at something I could not see, and he was some moments controlling the spirited horse. When he looked at me again, his face was unwontedly serious.

"I suppose," I said defensively, "you will say that I am romancing, that one cannot fall permanently in love at such an age, or at least that an attachment in youth cannot survive ten years."

"No," said Kinross gravely, "I do not think I should say any of those things."

"Then perhaps you feel it is unbecoming in a young lady to open her budget so! Indeed, Lord Kinross, I should not be so frank with anyone else. But who more fitted for me to confide in? You are like an elder brother to me, only far kinder than Tammas ever was. In fact, I used to pray that you and he might change places!" I had not meant to let that out, but somehow with Kinross I found it exceedingly hard to remember that he might not be interested in all my thoughts.

"Did you now!" He sounded amused, but not particularly gratified.

"You think I was a silly child."

"No – I –"

We rode on in silence for a few moments. I greeted several acquaintances, guessing that Kinross needed time to collect his thoughts. I hoped that when he did speak, he would not pronounce too harsh a judgment on my childhood dreams, or worse, mock them. He had been too kind to speak roughly to me when I was a child. But of course, he was a man now, and doubtless his spirit had been tempered and hardened in the war. It had been foolish of me to assume he was exactly the same person that I had gone riding and birds-nesting with so long ago.

"I might say," he said at last, with a laugh that sounded slightly forced, "that it was hardly kind in you to wish my estates might go to Tammas."

"Oh, piffle! One does not think of inheritances at that age. I just wanted you to be in truth the dear, kind, understanding brother you acted towards me." I glanced at his face; it was still set in lines that troubled me. "I've always thought of you that way, you know."

"What, even now?"

"Certainly. Have you changed so much?"

"Of one thing I can assure you," he said, sounding much too serious for my liking, "my sentiments towards you have not changed since I was sixteen and praying that you would not break your neck on that damned horse."

"Nor mine towards you," I said, "so now we can be comfortable again, can we not, Lord Kinross?"

"I should be a deal more comfortable," he said, "if you could bring yourself to call me simply Kinross. Every time you say 'Lord Kinross' I have the feeling my father is standing just behind me."

"Then I must be Elspet to you."

"That you have always been," he said, "only… not in company, do you think? People who do not know us might think I meant to offer you an impertinence."

At that moment I espied Richert, walking towards us and leading his horse.

This was easily explained, as was his lateness. He was walking beside Vivienne de Larue's phaeton.

Doubts assailed me, and I drew in my breath involuntarily. Kinross glanced at me with concern written on his face.

But as soon as Richert saw me, he abandoned Vivienne de Larue with a quick word of apology and hurried forward to meet us. "I apologize for my lateness, Pet. I encountered Mrs. de Larue on my way through the Park to meet you. Common courtesy required me to dismount and walk a few steps with her." He swung himself into the saddle as he spoke.

For three-quarters of an hour? And pray tell, what 'courtesy' required you to walk publicly with that lightskirt widow on the way to meet the girl you are supposed to be courting?

"She… had something in particular she wished to discuss with me," he added in further excuse.

Oh yes, I'll wager she had something in particular to say to you. And judging from her expression when she saw us – cat in the cream jug – she was not discussing your promise to end your liaison with her now that you were contemplating honorable marriage.

I stole another quick look at the Widow Larue through my eyelashes; I had no wish to make eye contact with her and be forced to speak in greeting. Her face reassured me slightly. She no longer looked like a cat in the cream; rather, she looked like a cat just after someone had snatched the jug and placed it out of her reach.

Excellent.

And there was no danger of meeting her eyes, for she was looking down and rummaging for something in the pocket of her dashing scarlet carriage dress. I found it unreasonably irritating to see the woman decked out in a color that I could never wear, even were I a married woman and allowed greater freedom in my choice of costumes. Her carriage passed us, driving too closely by half to the mare I rode, and I felt a distinct itch between my shoulder blades. Was it my imagination? No, for I could see fragments of dried plants on my lap.

Herb-witchery! Sabira had tried to warn me.

I could not even twitch my shoulders to dislodge the bits of herbs; they felt frozen in place.

Nor could I move my legs.

A moment later my mare reared and took off at a gallop, first threading her way among passers-by and then veering off the track to the greater freedom of the grassy Park. Ahead I could see the spreading branches of trees – too low – I should have to bend almost flat over my horse's neck to save myself from being scraped off.

And I could not bend.

I discovered that I could still shift my whole body, though, and I shifted my weight to the back of my saddle. It was, of course, much harder to keep my balance this way. But I had trained Caramella well during our winter in the country, and she slowed at once in obedience to my signal.

A moment later another horse was behind us, and Richert seized my bridle and yanked on it, to the detriment of Caramella's soft, sensitive mouth.

"That was hardly necessary, Mr. Dalkey," I exclaimed, too annoyed to remember our supposed courtship. "I had the mare under control again; there was no need to hurt her and embarrass me by theatrics."

"Pet, you may be proud of your riding skill, but it certainly did not appear that you were in control! And in any case, please remember that I am supposed to be madly in love with you. That I rescued you is bound to make an impression on the onlookers."

"Lord Kinross did not offer me such an insult. *He*, at least, trusts my ability to control my horse."

I was so angry that I had not noticed that after we turned our horses to join the path, Kinross had joined us.

"Pose as you like for my benefit, Pet, but any true lady would be shaken by such an experience. Can you not drop the pose and admit your debt to me before we face the horrified onlookers?"

"I'll have you know that I am perfectly in control of Caramella, and have no need to pretend to a distress I do not feel in the slightest!" Most of my body was still numb and unresponsive, but at least I could talk again – obviously – and enough flexibility had returned to my fingers to allow me to twitch my reins. To my relief, Caramella responded to the slightest of touches. Evidently Richert's wild grab at the reins had not destroyed the sensitivity of her mouth. He had always been better with mechanical devices like his beloved pistols than with living beings.

"If you claim that you were always in control," Richert said waspishly, "you shall have some pretty apologizing to do to the groundskeeper, not to mention buying his forgiveness!"

"That will not be necessary," Kinross said. "He has already been paid to forget the incident."

As we returned, I looked ruefully at the gouges Caramella had left on the greensward. A large tip would have been required to buy forgiveness for such damage. "How much did it cost you, Kinross? I hope my pin-money will suffice to reimburse you." I might have to forgo any new hats or dresses for the remainder of the Season – unless, that is, I could materially improve the private arrangement that I had with Madame Olympe.

"I cannot—" Kinross began.

"In any case," Richert interrupted whatever Kinross had been about to say, "a true lady *would* have been shaken by the experience, and would have been properly grateful to me—thus improving on our..."

He stopped, evidently having remembered just in time that Kinross was not privy to the agreement between Richert and me.

"I cannot accept a young lady's pin-money as recompense for what any gentleman would have done," said Kinross stiffly.

I ought to have argued, but I was preoccupied with my own thoughts. Could Richert have planned the entire incident to bring attention to his "courtship?" No, he could scarcely have paralyzed my whole body like that. It must have been the doing of the herb-witch. Thank goodness Richert was protected by the watch fob. It was fortunate that I had convinced him he must wear it always to support his pretense of being desperately in love with me.

I, however, had been wearing no such protection.

But how had Vivienne caused my horse to bolt? Did I need to stitch protective charms into Caramella's saddle as well?

I recollected, now, seeing a flash of white to my right just before Caramella bolted. Perhaps the mare had been startled by a sudden movement of Vivienne's. I had not thought to train her against such a surprise; there had been no careless riders to startle her on the purple hills where my family's lands merged with those of Kinbrae.

"You might at least *pretend* gratitude when we rejoin the others promenading on the proper path," Richert said peevishly.

He was right about that, in any event. To quarrel over the insult to my horsemanship would hardly enhance the fraud of our courtship.

But I had best consult Madame Olympe in any case. Not to mention the Hob.

Chapter 5

Vivienne de Larue was home an hour before the groom and stable hands expected her. After her first failure, she had seen no point in continuing to drive until she encountered Dalkey and that little red-headed chit again.

The child's survival was clearly due to a slight miscalculation on her part; who would have guessed she rode so well that she could slow a runaway horse while all but paralyzed by the herb-charm Vivienne had learned from the Duchess of Quoy? Perhaps the herbs had been so old that their power was attenuated. It was only by good fortune that she had that little packet in her pocket from a previous outing, for she certainly had not anticipated wanting that charm for a simple drive in the Park.

Or, more likely, she had not been able to shower the girl with enough herbs to make the charm operate at full strength.

The failure of her charm on Richert Dalkey was more puzzling. That one she had been prepared to use, and she had applied it as soon as she saw him riding through the Park – probably on his way to the Rattray town house. It had certainly seemed to be successful, for he had dismounted and walked beside her, leading his horse, as soon as he was cognizant of her presence. Could the red-headed chit have worked magic of her own to neutralize her love-charm? Impossible! She could not have known that anything other than Dalkey's well-known liaison with Vivienne had impelled him to give her all his attention. And in any case, it was scarcely credible that a girl fresh from the country, who had not even been invited to meetings of the Mythic

Society, would have such powerful magic at her disposal.

It was a mystery.

Perhaps she had best visit Quoy House to take new cuttings of the herbs she used for casting a glamour over the recipient. And this time she would distill them into a strong potion to add to his wine on his next visit to her house. He would surely visit again; in the worst case, someone as punctilious as Dalkey would come to break off with her and to give her a handsome parting present. He would hardly be so ill mannered as to refuse to take a farewell glass of wine with her, and the potion therein would cause him to forget that he had ever meant to abandon her.

As for the girl… there were other, and more aggressive charms. Nor was herb-magic Vivienne's only weapon against annoying little girls. Any social contact could be turned to her advantage.

The problem would be engineering that social contact in a society whose females still did not invite her to the best gatherings.

***

As usual, I found no difficulty in securing Mama's permission to visit Madame Olympe's mantua-making shop. It was clear that I should require more gowns for the parties of the Season if I was not to commit the solecism of wearing the same ball gown to so many affairs that it became familiar to the *ton*. Mama suggested that our dear old governess Kirsty should accompany me, but I avoided that by promising faithfully to take my abigail with me. Mama did not know that Orrock was accustomed to wait in the antechamber while I penetrated Olympe's private workroom. Kirsty would likely not be so obliging.

Gentlemen were never permitted to enter this holy of holies, whereas some dashing blades frequently lounged in the antechamber to offer opinions on their ladies' costumes. So, to my mind, I was behaving with the greatest propriety in seeking the seclusion of Olympe's private rooms. The only possible difficulty was Kirsty's objection to allowing an unmarried girl to go anywhere where she might be unaccompanied and out of sight, and I was well versed in evading that issue. My companion today, my abigail Orrock, knew better than to mention our arrangement to anyone at home. Though I believed in treating servants decently, Izzie turned off her abigails on any whim. Somewhat unfairly, I benefited from Izzie's reputation without having to burden my conscience with her methods.

I was fortunate today; when she saw me, Madame Olympe dismissed all her assistants to the common room. I surmised that she had some private task for me.

Once alone with me, she dared drop her assumed accent of the French tongue. She had explained to me that unlike the slight prejudice against Lutécian emigrés in society, the reverse was true for ladies who wished to succeed as mantua-makers or milliners. In her walk of life, a Lutécian origin was all but *de rigueur* as a guarantee of stylishness and superior taste in dressmaking. The same was true for my hairdresser, Patrice-Henri, who had begun life as plain Patrick. Olympe, however, had never quite relaxed enough to trust me with her birth name. She probably believed that I did not know it.

"If you are waiting for your new walking dress, it is almost ready, Miss Rattray! And you need not fear but that I shall send it to your house in good time for you to add your special embroidery to it! Pray, what do you plan this time? A simple drawing of attention? Something to show the onlooker the grace of your figure, though that is hardly required now that you are so much slimmer than last year? Or are stronger charms required, requiring more time in the preparation?"

I reassured her that there was no particular hurry about the walking dress, for which I had chosen a French cambric in Prussian blue. I understood that the upper sleeve, being slashed with satin of a slightly lighter color, would require extra time for her seamstresses to prepare. Olympe sighed that she wished her other customers would display a similar understanding of the exigencies of fancy needlework.

"Few of them, I suspect, have had my experience in cutting out a dress pattern or setting in a sleeve." Until I was out, Mama had kept my dress allowance so small that I had been obliged to such shifts as these. Fortunately I have always been skilled at needlework, nor is my ability restricted to the fine embroidery which Kirsty taught and the Hob, in his own way, elaborated upon.

"Then – if you have time – it would be most helpful if you could add a border of Attention and another of Beauty to the flounce of Lady Cecelia Lauder's new evening dress," she said, bringing out that costume and offering me needle and pale blue silk thread with a hopeful look.

"I would, of course, remunerate you at the usual rates."

When I did not immediately accept the sewing materials, and instead mentioned that a double charm was more difficult than a single one, she gave a sigh of acceptance. "Very well, one and one/half the usual."

"Double payment would be appropriate for a double charm, would it not?"

A deeper sigh. "Miss Rattray, you will drive me to the poorhouse yet!"

I seriously doubted that. Mama's dress bills for me were far more than what I earned by my occasional surreptitious work of enhancing the dresses Olympe created with pleasing bits of thread magic. That paid only enough to be a significant addition to my pin-money, although even that I could well use. At an agreement of double rates, I set to work with a will. I would have to stitch quickly indeed to insert both charms in the time available. Perhaps I should suggest to Olympe that in future she send me advance notice of the charms she desired. That would have allowed me to do the basic construction in my room, using a secondary magic to keep the twisted threads in the necessary shape so that they need only be tacked to the dress when I visited the dressmaker's establishment. But I saw no need to tell Olympe about *all* I had learned from the Hob. She did not even know the source of my abilities, and that too was something she had no need to know.

"My teaching would be to no avail," the Hob had told me once in one of his rare good moods, "if you had not the talent. Your great-grandmother had it too; a pity it has not descended to the rest of your family."

My great-grandmother Elspet, for whom I was named, was said to have been a society beauty, in fact, an Incomparable in her time. Mama was given to repining over the fact I had not inherited her looks; I was absurdly gratified to hear that I owed at least one thing to her.

I wondered how much thread magic had contributed to Great-Grandmother Elspet's success in society. But having seen both her portrait and my own reflection in the mirror, I dared not hope that my own thread magic would make me an Incomparable like my ancestress. A modest social success, and Richert Dalkey's love, were all I aimed at.

"Did you never try to teach Izzie thread magic?" I had inquired when the Hob so far unbent as to grant that I had my distinguished ancestress' talent.

The Hob snorted and I jumped. A snort apparently originating in mid-air, when you cannot even see the expression of the relevant party, can be rather startling.

"It is not possible to teach Isolde anything beyond the accomplishments befitting a young lady. Her drawing-master and music-master and your governess have those matters well in hand."

It was fortunate that Kirsty had once served with a wealthy emigré family and had acquired fluency in several languages, or we should have had a French tutor cluttering up the household as well. Izzie had at least learned sufficient French to pass in polite society. She had paid less attention to her German and Italian lessons, deeming them unnecessary and not to be considered proper accomplishments.

But that conversation was in the past, and I didn't need to be dreaming over it when I wanted to get some useful gossip out of Olympe.

"I encountered Vivienne de Larue in the Park yesterday," I said, keeping my eyes fixed on the needle I was threading.

"I understand she drives there frequently," said Madame Olympe, her voice carefully neutral. I pushed the end of blue silk through the eye of the needle and looked up through my lashes. The dressmaker was staring over my head, as though there was something extremely interesting on the far wall of her personal workroom. I did not recall anything of particular interest there – no pictures, no hats to be added to make the perfect costume, not even some prints from *La Belle Assemblée.*

I ran the silk through the pale lilac muslin of Lady Cecelia's walking dress and took a minute backstitch to secure my work by passing the needle through the end of the thread. "A very strange thing happened just afterwards."

Madame Olympe remained silent, so I went into more detail. "Richert Dalkey was walking beside her phaeton, leading his horse. But when he saw Kinross and me riding, he mounted his horse and joined us."

"You could scarcely expect Mrs. de Larue to be pleased by that! Mr. Dalkey—"

"I know all about Mr. Dalkey's liaison with her."

"Well, you should not! And if you do, you ought not to take any cognizance of it."

"He assured me that he meant to break off with her. Or did you not know that he is courting me?"

That, at least, got the reaction of an indrawn breath.

"And he had engaged himself to ride out in the park with me that morning, so it was hardly strange that he excused himself to join Lord Kinross and me."

"I collect," said Madame Olympe slowly, "that the strange thing to which you refer was finding that Mr. Dalkey had forgotten his engagement, or that he preferred walking with Mrs. Larue to riding with you?"

"By no means." The delicate tracery of the first charm, a simple pattern of interlaced curves, was going quickly; the real work would be when I crossed over it to add the outlined leaves and flowers that added the power of Beauty to the curves that would impel Attention. "I *am* aware that young men can be fickle and indecisive, Madame Olympe. It would not surprise me to hear that Mr. Dalkey has not yet brought himself to break off his liaison with Mrs. de Larue."

"Then…"

I closed the interlacing curves and began on the first leaf outline.

"The strange thing occurred as her phaeton passed us. A shower of dried herbs fell over me. She was driving a perch-phaeton," I added, "so to throw something over me was not difficult. A moment later I felt a strange paralysis come over my limbs."

"She must have been furious that Mr. Dalkey abandoned her for you – prior engagement or not. And an angry stare from such a woman might well make you feel almost paralyzed for a moment."

"It lasted longer than a moment," I said, stitching a shape of flower petals above the outlined leaves. "It lasted long enough for my mare Caramella to run away with me. And just before she took fright, there was a flash of something white from the other side of the path. Almost," I said, "as if Mrs. de Larue had waved something to startle Caramella."

"Well, a skittish horse can take offense at the slightest thing."

"Olympe," I said firmly, dropping the "Madame," you know everything there is to know about the *ton*, and so you must know that horses do not run away with me. Ever."

"I have heard that you are an accomplished rider and that your seat on a horse is held up as an example to other ladies," Olympe acknowledged grudgingly, "but even the most skilled rider can suffer an accident in a moment of inattention. And it sounds to me as though your attention was more on Mr. Dalkey and Mrs. de Larue than on your mare."

"You are forgetting the shower of dried herbs," I said, "and the fact that my paralysis lasted almost long enough for Caramella to scrape me off on a low-hanging tree branch."

"But she did not do so, or you would hardly be here, quite uninjured, today."

"Although I could not move my limbs, I *could* shift my weight backwards, and Caramella is trained to halt on that signal. Moments later I regained the use of my fingers, and that was quite enough for me to move the reins and guide Caramella into circling around and walking back to the path. By the time we reached the path I had enough power over my limbs that no one noticed anything."

"That is not what I heard," said Olympe, thus betraying her prior knowledge of the incident. As I'd thought, nothing happened in Din Eidyn society that did not make its way to the dressmaker's ears. "The *on-dit* is that Mr. Dalkey, with admirable presence of mind, galloped after you and seized the bridle of your horse just in time to save you from a fall."

"He had no need to do that," I said sharply, "for I had everything under control before he reached me. And in any case, that particular bit of gossip does not explain my paralysis or the shying of a calm, very well-trained mare."

I left my needle in the fabric and leaned forward, meeting Olympe's eyes. "*Osla Clugston*," I said, deliberately using the undistinguished Scottish name with which she had begun life, "I need to know what I have to deal with here. Just how black is Vivienne de Larue's witchery?"

Olympe's eyes dropped. "Pray do not call me by that name," she whispered. "Were any of the *ton* to question my origins…"

"It shall go unsaid… so long as you answer my questions!"

"I wish I had never let the name slip to you!"

The fact was that she had not, exactly, done so. I owed my knowledge of her true name to my hairdresser, Patrice-Henri, whose chattering tongue must have been hinged at both ends. When he slipped up and revealed that he had been born plain Patrick Henryson, he hastened to minimize his lie by claiming that many of those who ministered to Din Eidyn's fashionable set found it useful to transform their plain Scottish names into something that implied Lutécian origins and the famous Lutécian flair for fashion and style.

"I need to know," I repeated, "so that I can protect myself and Mr. Dalkey."

"If Vivienne de Larue were… as evil as you think her," said Olympe slowly, "would she not have cast a glamour upon Mr. Dalkey to make him violently in love with her?"

I would like to believe that had been true from the beginning, but his casual promise to end the liaison had hardly been the words of a man beglamoured. I explained as much to Olympe, and then added: "Furthermore, he has just begun to court me, and she may not have heard the rumors immediately. In any case he has not visited her since his courtship began, so she would have had no chance to bespell him since then."

"He has not visited her? Not even to make his farewells?"

"Mr. Dalkey avoids unpleasant scenes and puts them off as long as he can. Like many gentlemen," I added as an afterthought, not wishing Olympe to think him a weakling.

"She might have bespelled him in the Park?"

"No, that she could not do, for he was wearing the watch fob I had given him."

Olympe raised her eyebrows. "I gather this courtship is progressing with unusual speed!"

"There are slivers of rowan concealed in the embroidery," I explained, "and protective spells worked in red thread – all, of course, covered by gold work, because Richert – Mr. Dalkey – hates and fears all magic. He thinks all practitioners of magic are black witches who have sold their souls to the devil." And in Vivienne de Larue's case, I feared he might be entirely correct.

"I see. I suggest you disabuse him of this mistake well before your marriage."

"We are not even engaged," I said quickly. *Nor like to be, unless I can find some way of making him understand that I am a woman grown and not the child he remembers.* But there was no need to make the most fashionable dressmaker in Din Eidyn privy to a piece of information that would be such a delicious morsel of gossip. And speaking of gossip, it was time I returned to my original question.

But Olympe forestalled me. "The *on-dit* is that Vivienne de Larue hopes to improve her social status by wedding Mr. Dalkey. So it is understandable that she would react poorly to being thrown over by him."

"He told me himself that a Dalkey does not wed a woman like that!"

"Ah. But it is also said that she is dissatisfied with being a woman 'like that,' a woman whose parties attract many more gentlemen than ladies, a woman who is not invited to most *ton* parties."

"Surely she has other means of establishing herself socially!"

"She has a history of attempting to do so through other people," Olympe said drily. "Her marriage to Edouard de Larue was a step up the social ladder, but not as high as she thought to go. Nor did her friendship with the Duchess of Quoy serve her purpose. It will be very difficult for her to surmount the rumors that follow her like black clouds."

"What rumors? More witchcraft? Black Masses?"

But Olympe had gone as far as she meant to go. "Nothing of that sort. In any case, they concern only her past, and are hardly relevant to your question."

"If they have caused her to become my enemy, I should think they may be quite relevant!"

"I dare not risk passing on tales which may well have no foundation. If you insist on hearing them, I suggest you apply to your sister or to one of your *ton* friends who has been on the town somewhat longer than you. Have you completed the embellishment of Lady Cecelia's dress? Let me pay you what is owing."

I left the dressmaking establishment with my reticule stuffed with royals and my head even more stuffed with questions. The rumors about Vivienne de Larue must be black indeed if even Madame Olympe feared to retail them. And Izzie was frequently less than helpful about my questions; the more ardently I desired to know something, the more she liked to make me work for an answer. I should have to find some way of introducing the subject very casually.

Chapter 6

In any case, I had no chance to speak privately with Izzie before the Dalkeys' ball that night. She had gone out to purchase a new shawl which she claimed that she positively had to possess in order to help conceal her condition at the ball. Evidently the Norwich shawl, the silver-embroidered gauze shawl at fifty guineas, and the rest of the shawls with which Sir Joshua had gifted her were all inappropriate to the occasion, or were of the wrong color to go with her new dress, or something of that sort. In any case, since she planned to sit among the chaperones and plead her condition as an excuse for not dancing, it was a mystery to me why she desired to conceal it.

"It is one thing to hint that I may be unable to dance," Izzie snapped when she came home, "and quite another to have everybody whispering that I am already showing it!" And she vanished upstairs, where she and her abigail were entirely occupied with dressing her for the dinner and ball until moments before our departure.

For that matter, I was somewhat preoccupied myself. Not only did I need to stitch an inconspicuous line of interlocking squares around the hem of my beautiful bronze-green ball dress, but Patrice-Henri arrived halfway through the work to dress Izzie's head and mine. Our usual styles with the back hair pulled up and a few curls allowed loose to frame the face were hardly adequate for a formal engagement such as this. He dressed Izzie's hair in the Grecian style, with smooth bandeaux coming down from the forehead that obviated the need for a curling iron, and mine was piled high on my head with clusters of ringlets over the ears.

After his departure I finished my embroidery and put on the ball dress with due care not to disarrange Patrice-Henri's work, while Orrock fussed that I should have dressed before he styled my hair and that she saw no need for me to add a line of stitching that nobody would even notice to a dress that was already sufficiently ornamented.

Well, she could hardly be expected to understand my reasons, could she? I had not taken the abigail into my confidence for fear the entire servant's hall would be discussing my thread magic. Who could tell how many of them were superstitious enough to share Richert's prejudices on that subject? Mama would be most displeased if half the servants gave notice and cited my actions as their reason.

Orrock was right, though, in saying that the dress was already striking. With a trimming of gold-embroidered velvet around the low neckline and down the front of the gown, complemented by a green lace medici round the back and shoulders and bronze satin shoes with full bows, I felt it was an ensemble worthy of capturing any man's attention. Richert would be obliged to dance with me twice in order to maintain his façade of courtship, and during the other dances I meant him to observe that I did not lack for partners; the pattern stitched round the hem of my dress should be sufficient to ensure that. It would, of course, help our pretense of courtship if he were to lean against the wall and scowl while I danced with other gentlemen, but I could scarcely expect that tonight; as the son of the hostess, it would be his duty to dance with the other guests, paying particular attention to those who had been sitting out too long. Richert was far too correct to commit the solecism of neglecting his mama's guests in favor of play-acting the enamoured suitor.

Izzie was just completing the final touches to her toilette when the carriage was brought round, for we were among the favored group who had been invited to dine at the Dalkey house before the ball. For an event of this magnitude even my parents joined us, so I had no chance to question Izzie, and upon our slightly late arrival (my mother had been unable at first to find the case containing her diamond earrings, so long had it been since she had worn them) we proceeded with the other guests to the dining room, where we were – for the most part - seated in order of precedence. Not being of a titled family, none of us were near the head of the table, but the guests were so many that we were separated anyway. In any case it was hardly the setting in which I might coax or bribe Izzie to divulge rumors so spicy that Madame Olympe had refused to communicate them.

To my chagrin, Richert did not seem to notice my dress when we were announced; to my delight and in defiance of precedence, he was seated next to me at dinner, where at least he could be impressed by my conversation and by the gold trimming that emphasized the neckline of my ball dress. I believe in displaying one's best assets at these affairs. Propriety, sadly, forbade a dress short enough to give him a good look at my shapely ankles, but more ladies than I sported dresses cut very low – in one case so low that I was distracted for some part of the dinner wondering why the lady's bodice did not fall off.

Indeed he did notice my dress, but not in such a manner as to provide me any particular gratification. His first words to me, in an undertone, were, "I wonder your Mama permitted you to show yourself in such a rig."

As a matter of fact, she had not had the chance to comment on it. I had kept a silk shawl shot through with gold close about me until we left the house, and the carriage, of course, was dark. "Other ladies wear dresses of a similar cut," I murmured, indicating with a slight nod Sophie Westlin's young stepmother, the one whose dress so strongly hinted at an imminent disaster.

"Those other ladies," said Richert, "are married women, not young girls whom it behooves to show a becoming modesty."

I turned my shoulder to him and conversed with my partner on the other side, whom I knew very slightly from an introduction at the Assembly Rooms. His name was Coates, and he was a hunting enthusiast and a bruising rider. Even had he not told me so on our previous meeting, I should have known this almost as soon as he opened his mouth. Throughout the first remove, while doing justice to the turtle soup, the ham, the fowl with oyster sauce and the *haricots á la mode de Lutéce*, he discoursed to me of the unparalleled virtues of Leicestershire for hunting, the fences and bullfinches he had jumped, and the superb hunter he had just bought for a song.

During the second remove, while he was occupied with a baron of beef, there was a general shift in conversation and I turned with some relief to Richert. He was looking quite black, as befitted a man deprived of converse with the woman he loved, and I complimented him – so quietly as not to be overheard by anyone else, of course – on playing his part so well.

"Oh, it's not on your account," he said with deplorable lack of tact, "just look at who is seated on my other side!"

I could hardly do that without craning my neck, so he told me. "It is *Dorothea Turvoll.*"

"Well," I said pacifically, "it is difficult to determine precedence among untitled, unmarried ladies. Though I am rather surprised to find that the daughter of a mercantile family should follow immediately after a Rattray."

"It is all Mama's doing," he said gloomily, "sandwiching me between the two young ladies she thinks me most likely to marry. And on top of that, to hear that skirter Coates boasting of his hunting prowess! Miss Turvoll has no conversation beyond *Indeed, Mr. Dalkey* and *I am sure you are right, Mr. Dalkey,* and so I could not help but hear him preening himself on hunting and claiming to be a neck-or-nothing rider."

Mr. Coates was rather young, and his high voice very carrying, so much so that I felt sure all his neighbors were now aware of his accomplishments upon the hunting field.

"I take it you disagree with his self-assessment?"

Richert laughed. "He has been out with the Quorn precisely once, and I never saw such a fellow for riding out of his way in search of a gate to open! As for that 'superb' hunter, I saw it at Tattersall's; one of Jenneret's breakdowns. Long-backed and short of wind; I wish it may not die under him the first time he takes it out."

It was not until we rose to leave the men to their port that I was able to take in the full glory of Dorothea Turvoll's dress. To think that Richert had uttered animadversions on my simple gown of bronze-green silk! Miss Turvoll was decked out in a rose-pink slip of stiff, heavy lustring under a three-quarters frock of transparent silver-striped gauze, the frock ornamented by a profusion of knotted ribbons in cloth of silver. To this ensemble she had added matching silver slippers with diamond rosettes, ruby earrings and necklace, and a wreath of roses twined with a chain of diamonds to confine her headdress *a la Chinoise.* Not only was her costume excessively ornamented for any young girl, but the weight and variety of her jewels made it seem that they were wearing her rather than the other way round. And the long dangles of the necklace somehow made her face look longer, and her nose more prominent, that was strictly compatible with even passably good features.

She caught my eye and, doubtless mistaking my amazement for admiration, took my arm on our way to the drawing-room and seated herself beside me on our arrival.

"It is so comfortable," she said, "to converse with one whose station is like my own, for all those titled dames quite intimidate me! As for the gentlemen, they stare so as to put me quite out of countenance. Still, we ladies must confess to dressing to attract the gentlemen, must we not?" She giggled. "Your necklet of pearls is quite lovely, and it will hardly draw too much attention from your ball gown." She stroked the dangling floral pendants of her ruby necklace in such a way as to leave no doubt as to her satisfaction with her own appearance.

It would have been rude to tell her that we were not precisely of the same station, for a Rattray must always take precedence over a Turvoll.

During the interminable half-hour before the gentlemen joined us, I learned several things. Apart from her appalling dress sense, Dorothea Turvoll seemed to have a sweet, uncritical nature. Lady Dalkey had received her so kindly! It was so exciting to be going to a real society ball! For some reason she had not been invited to such a grand affair before now!

I doubted she would have received an invitation to this one, had Lady Dalkey not still considered her a likely bride for Richert. Her father's connection with the textile industry rendered her ineligible to much of the *ton.* During a pause in Richert's castigation of my perfectly unexceptionable dress, I had overheard him explaining the details of some new type of loom to his neighbor. He had a very loud voice and, evidently, not enough sense to confine his conversation to fashionable topics. Even talking about the war in

Galicia – a delicate subject when half the guests were of the anti-war party – would have been preferable to thus emphasizing that trade was the source of his fortune.

Dorothea did have the politeness to admire the cut of my own dress, and I ventured to give her a hint. "We have always patronized Madame Olympe, who is a most talented designer. Rather than merely copying the fashions depicted in *La Belle Assemblée*, she adapts their features to design what will best show off the best features of a lady's form." I was almost certain that I had seen Dorothea's ball gown in a recent issue of the fashion magazine, only with less excessive ornamentation and on a particularly tall and slender model.

"Oh!" This appeared to be quite a new idea to Dorothea. "But Lisette makes for some of the greatest ladies in the realm. Lady Cecelia's mother, the Countess of Rosleith, patronizes her, and so does Viscountess Auchinmor."

I mentioned that both these ladies were somewhat advanced in age and had figures that only benefited from the concealment afforded by such a stiff fabric as the heavy lustring of Dorothea's dress.

"Oh!" she said again, and after a moment's silence, "What was the name of your dressmaker again?"

"Madame Olympe," I said, "on Finlay Street." And if Dorothea patronized her, I might have a chance to do her a small favor regarding the effect of her dress. Or a small disservice, depending on what would best suit my cause… although I did feel guilty at the idea of luring this bird-witted innocent into Olympe's establishment only to do her harm.

"Perhaps," said Dorothea, "I may ask Papa to set up an account for me there. I am not entirely pleased with Lisette's suggestions for my Assembly dress – it will be my first appearance at the Assembly Rooms, you understand, and I do greatly wish to create a sensation."

Well, if she did change dressmakers, it would be Madame Olympe's task, and not mine, to guide Dorothea's mind away from 'creating a sensation,' and towards 'giving the impression of a sweet young girl who is not really horse-faced.'

"It must be exciting to look forward to your debut at Gilroy's," I said. "Few girls have the confidence to put it off until the middle of the Season." I was, in fact, curious as to how a girl with neither breeding nor extraordinary charm had obtained vouchers from the stiff-necked Society ladies who guarded the entrance to Gilroy's. Oh, but of course; Lady Dalkey was one of the sponsors, and after conceiving the notion of marrying Dorothea to her son she would have done everything possible to smooth the girl's path.

"I do like dancing," Dorothea said, without confirming my guess about the vouchers, "although I have not yet had many opportunities to enjoy the practice. But now that I am being invited to dances I can be sure of many partners, for Papa hired a dancing-master to teach me everything – not just country dances, but the minuet, the quadrille, the cotillion, and Scotch reels." She giggled. "To be sure, he had time enough for teaching, for the music master left us, saying that he could teach me nothing about using the pianoforte. Was that not a prettily turned compliment?"

I was not so sure of that.

"And the French master gave me up as incapable of learning the language. To be sure, I do not see the point of learning French or, or…" She paused, wrinkling her brow in thought. "Or any other foreign languages," she finished, evidently having failed to think of any. "Dear Papa always says that plain English is good enough for him, and I am sure I ought not wish to be better than him!"

"What is your mother's opinion?" I asked.

"Oh, she is dead, you know. But you need not feel sorry for me, because it was so long ago that I have no memory of her!"

"I suppose, then, your father entrusted your upbringing to a governess?"

"Several of them," she said, surprising me. "Oh, not all at once, you understand, but one after another. They kept leaving, you know. Most of them said that they were unable to teach me any more. It was wise of them, do you not think, to be so aware of their own limitations?"

That was not precisely how I would have interpreted the statement, but Dorothea seemed happy enough, and I had no wish to argue with her.

The gentlemen did not join us until the musicians were already tuning their instruments in the ballroom.

Lady Dalkey, for all her swoonings and palpitations, must have found an unexpected store of energy, for someone had seen to the decoration of the room in a style appropriate for *the* dance of the Season. The wax tapers burning along each wall were, of course, necessary at any dance, but the number of them here was so great that the room was already warm when we entered it. I suspected it would be far worse after a quantity of people had been dancing in it for a while, and I hoped that Izzie, seated with the chaperones, would not be overcome by the heat. The scent of flowers was almost equally overwhelming; Lady Dalkey had taken full advantage of the warm season's bounty. Between the clusters of tapers, garlands of real flowers interspersed with silk ones draped the walls. Still more flowers were festooned in graceful curves on either side of the two sets of French doors, the one leading to the terrace on one side of the room and the other, on the opposite side, to the rose garden.

Richert, naturally, had to open the ball with a lady distinguished for her title and breeding, if not for youth and beauty, while I suffered the attentions of young Mr. Coates. He appeared to be under the illusion that our conversation during dinner had rendered us friends for life, and I, of course, was far too well-bred to quash his pretensions. Fortunately the opening minuet separated the two of us for most of the dance. The moments when we were actually face to face were too brief for him to resume his stories of the hunting field. I did begin to suspect that he had no other interests, but I was proved wrong at the conclusion of the dance, when he urged me to sit out the next dance on the terrace.

"You were better to solicit some other lady, Coates," Richert interrupted my demurrals, "for Miss Rattray is promised to me for this dance." And his face was as black as that of any young man who caught someone else making up to his lady-love.

"Oh, but I wished to finish the story I was telling Miss Rattray over dinner," Mr. Coates protested, "for the conclusion throws a most interesting light upon my character!"

"Allow me to suggest, sir, that you might enjoy more success with a young lady who is more careless of her own character!" And he led me away to head the first set of a galliard.

We had no chance of conversing during the first measures, in which we parted to make four changes of a circular hey with the second couple. "You are doing quite well at this," I complimented him when we rejoined to lead down the middle of the set and back. "You really appeared quite angry at Mr. Coates' attentions to me!"

"For heaven's sake, Pet, did you expect me to *like* seeing that skirter attempting to look down my little sister's bodice?"

"You should not talk to me like that," I said.

"Oh, you must be used to a bit of slang after all the years you tagged along after Tammas and me!"

The figures of the dance parted us before I had time to explain that my objection was not to the impropriety of his language but to his calling me his little sister. As long as he insisted of speaking to me like that, what hope had I that he would come to realize that I had grown up? I could not, of course, make this particular point explicitly to him, but it ought not to be necessary; it was in his interest, too, to learn to speak of me as a beautiful and desirable young lady. Carelessly equating me with a sister would hardly further his hope of discouraging Dorothea Turvoll by his attentions to me.

By the time we joined hands again, I had cooled down enough to realize the riskiness of attempting to school him on the techniques of courtship during a country dance where the others might hear us. In truth, a dance in which we were always meeting and parting was no place for any sort of conversation, and during the succeeding figures I made no more attempts to converse.

Besides, I could not think of anything I really wanted to say to him – at least, nothing that would have been quite *convenable*. I might wish that he devoted half the energy to sneaking glances at my neckline that poor Mr. Coates had displayed, but that sort of interest would have to come unprompted from him for me to derive any pleasure from it.

The dance lasted long enough for me to catch a glimpse of Dorothea Turvoll's face. She was sitting with the disconsolate attitude of one who has failed to secure a partner and doesn't mind who knows it. And when she raised her eyes and looked directly at me, two spots of red burned in her cheeks and she looked as though she quite hated me.

Good. It's working. Now she needs to give up on Richert and set her cap at somebody else.

At least, Richert's plan seemed to be working. My own was not progressing well at all.

The next figure of the dance set me almost directly facing Lady Dalkey. She did not look overly pleased. Well, she would just have to stop dreaming of the Turvoll heiress for her son's bride and start thinking of me in that role. The size of my dowry was irrelevant beside the Dalkey fortune, and my birth was far better than Dorothea's; Lady Dalkey would be happy enough to see me married to her son, once she got the idea.

Neither she nor her son appeared to be particularly ready to think of me in that role. Well, I would just have to persevere. I was still possessed of the persistence and daring that had inspired me, at twelve, to take off on Tammas's spirited new horse. And I was quite confident that, given time, I could gentle Richert and accustom him to loving me just as I had once gentled Wildfire. It was just that men are slower than horses to accept a new idea, and not quite as intelligent. He had made up a party to visit the Water Gardens two days hence. We could easily slip away from the others for a quiet stroll in the shady paths behind the principal fountains, and that would be an excellent setting in which to make him see me as I really was. Some dashing maidens even boasted of having exchanged covert kisses behind the shelter of the shrubberies there. I wondered if I would be so daring. I wondered if there was any way to make Richert consider the possibility. If he would kiss me just once…

At the conclusion of the dance, Richert moved very slowly to return me to my seat. I wondered if he longed, as I did, to go on dancing without a change of partners? That would, sadly, be quite ineligible. Richert would never even contemplate such a faux pas. And a surreptitious glance towards Dorothea Turvoll disabused me of any lingering fragments of that fantasy. A potential partner was finally moving towards her! It seemed probable that Richert wanted to make absolutely sure that Norval Petrie engaged Dorothea's hand before he could be expected to do so.

Poor Dorothea looked distressed by this timing, as who would not?

Standing up with an aging roué like Mr. Petrie was quite a come-down from being solicited to dance by the man of her dreams. Still, she regained her good cheer as Mr. Petrie led her out onto the floor. At least she was no longer a wallflower!

Richert handed me into my chair with his customary grace and offered to bring me a glass of ratafia, but was spared the trouble by Kinross, who asked me to stand up with him in the next set. We wound up being the very next couple to Dorothea Turvoll and Norval Petrie, and I had ample opportunity to observe his manner towards her. It was finely calculated to be just barely within the line of proper behavior, or so near that an inexperienced girl would not quite be able to make up her mind to give him a public rebuke. He clasped her hands a little too long during the turns, stood just a little too close when they set to one another, whispered something that raised her blushes as they passed down the middle of the set.

"Odious man!" I exclaimed under my breath.

Kinross looked quite startled. "How have I offended you?"

We parted, passed our opposite numbers, and rejoined. "Not you," I murmured, "Mr. Petrie. He is putting poor Miss Turvoll to the blush."

He shrugged. "At least she has got a partner."

Men! By the conclusion of the dance I was quite out of patience with them all – Kinross, Richert, and Mr. Petrie. And Dorothea had but a thin time of it for the rest of the evening; evidently merely procuring an invitation to Lady Dalkey's ball was not sufficient to make our family-proud Dalriadan gentlemen eager to further their acquaintance with the girl. I felt more and more temptation to add a little something to Dorothea's new dress for the Assembly Rooms. When we chanced to exchange a few words later in the evening I urged her again to consult Madame Olympe.

This was not really particularly kind in me, for Richert had often said that no power on earth would compel him to put up with the boredom of an insipid evening at Gilroy's Assembly Rooms – and in any case he was now well warded against magic, even my own. But I think I do deserve some credit for disinterestedness, for I could count on Richert's courtship only until he felt safe from Dorothea's languishing looks. Under the circumstances it was somewhat risky to encourage other gentlemen to take notice of her. But what harm could a few dances at Gilroy's do? It wasn't as if I meant to lace her dress with charms to provoke violent love, or even languishing devotion.

Chapter 7

Kinross was mildly surprised to hear raised voices inside his club. It almost sounded as though somebody was spoiling for a duel – a most unlikely occurrence there. Most of his fellow members were, like himself, military officers or ex-officers who had too much respect for bullets to invite them while peacefully at home. And more than half, like old General Dalkey, were long past the age of quarrels about nothing.

His brow cleared as the shouting began to be interspersed with laughter. He strolled into the common room to find Major Maddox seated before the betting book, quill in hand, while Beau Farquhar laughed at his friend Richert. "Say no more, Dalkey," the Beau said, "I've no wish to drag a young lady's name into this. But the *ton* is abuzz with exaggerated tales of your prodigious feat of marksmanship, and I wish you will tell me the truth of the matter. You cannot really have parted the traces between moving horses and a moving carriage! And by moonlight to boot!"

The friendship between Dalkey and Kinross dated from their earliest days. They had few secrets from one another. Dalkey had already told Kinross, in strictest confidence, of the episode which had inspired Dorothea Turvoll to fix her maiden fancy upon him. The tale had gone no further from Kinross' lips.

It appeared that others had not been quite so discreet.

"Only one of the traces," Dalkey smiled.

"Still! *Incroyable*, even for a man of your skill!"

"I could call you out for giving me the lie!" Dalkey threatened.

"But you would hardly do that," interposed Major Maddox, ever the peacemaker. "It would be plain murder, man! The Beau's no hand at all with a pistol."

Beau Farquhar flipped open the enameled snuffbox in his hand. "None at all," he said equably. "Why, I might get powder burns on this waistcoat, and that would be tragic indeed!"

"And you don't ride to hounds because your boots might get mud-splashed, and you don't box because a nose-bleed might ruin your shirt," said a young man whose starched collar rose high enough to leave room for a fancifully knotted cravat. "'Pon rep, Beau, I can't think why we all admire and imitate you!"

The Beau raised his quizzing-glass and inspected the young sprig's neckwear. "And I, my dear Innes, can't think why you imagine that you are imitating me! *Do* you call that thing a cravat?"

Innes flushed. "It's a new style – the Horsecollar. Perhaps you are not familiar with it."

"Ah, I see. That accounts for its resemblance to stable tack. But not, Innes, positively *not* a spotted cravat – not if you insist on claiming to imitate me!"

A burst of laughter drowned out any reply the young man might have attempted.

"There is no need for any such unpleasantness as a duel," said Major Maddox over Dalkey's disconsolate mutterings. "Surely a simple wager will suffice to settle the issue."

"I am under no obligation to prove my skill!"

"None at all," said the Beau equably, "particularly if you do not object to more gossip bringing notoriety on the young lady."

"Farquhar has the right of it," said Maddox. "Leave the matter as it stands, and there will only be more curiosity about the original event. Commit to repeating the feat under the next full moon, and interest will shift to that wager."

"I'll lay a monkey to a pony, Dalkey," said the Beau, "that you cannot repeat it – *if* you ever did such a thing in the first place!"

"Farquhar, money is one thing, but will you risk your horses on such a venture?" a bystander asked.

"He need not," Dalkey said quickly. "I'll wager to part the traces on a carriage of your choosing, Farquhar, drawn by my own grays!"

"That does make the bet more equal," observed a bystander. "The Beau risks his blunt, the young hothead his own horses."

"There is no risk to the horses," Dalkey asserted with confidence, "and my own coachman shall drive the carriage, for he knows he will be perfectly safe!"

Major Maddox dipped his quill into the inkstand and began recording the bet. "To be performed on the night of the next full moon...",

"If cloudless," the Beau interposed quickly. "I'll not risk Dalkey claiming that his eye was off because of uncertain light. Should the night of the next full moon not be fine, I am perfectly willing to wait until the subsequent one."

"On the night of the next *cloudless* full moon," Major Maddox recorded, "Mr. Dalkey to use a pistol of his choice, at a distance of..."

"Call it twenty-five yards," said Dalkey carelessly.

Another bystander whistled. "Put me down against Dalkey, as well!"

When the terms of the bet were settled and recorded, Dalkey nodded to Kinross. "Good to see you here, Kinross! Do you want to make some easy money? Bet on me while the odds are all the other way! By tomorrow some of these rich young sprigs will have recalled that I never miss my shot!"

"And I," said Kinross, "never wager among friends."

"Why then, you miss half the pleasures of life! Will you take a glass of wine with me?"

Kinross paused. "In truth, I had hoped to come up with your father here."

"And so I'm sure you will, if you stay half an hour. The poor old buffer all but lives here these days, since Lady Askerton left the Iveroth household and returned to hang upon Mama's sleeve. But what's your business with him?"

"Political," Kinross said repressively.

Dalkey shook his head. "You are in danger of becoming a damned dull dog, Alastair, d'you know that? I assume you mean to take your seat when the Council of Lords meets next month. There'll be politics enough to bore any man then; why bother with them now?"

"Well, I shan't bother you with them, at any rate!" Kinross laughed, clapping Dalkey on the shoulder. "I see you are like Major Maddox; you wish only to do the fighting, and let us dull dogs of the Council decide where you are to fight."

"If only I could!" Dalkey sighed, slumping into a chair. "The *Register* is full of accounts of how that new mixed regiment performed against the Lutécians at Castelo Rubro last month. An entire regiment of sharpshooters, Alastair! If I could but have been among them—Do you know, I've a good mind to enlist as a common soldier!"

"I really do not recommend it," Kinross said gravely. "I had the chance, you know, of observing army life at all levels during my years as an aide-de-camp to Wellesley, and I do not think that you would care for life in the ranks." He forbore to add that he suspected comments like that threat to enlist contributed to General Dalkey's opinion that his son, though two years older than Kinross, was too volatile to be trusted with a commission.

"Yes." Dalkey looked like a hungry man staring at someone else's dinner. "I cannot think how you could bear to sell out and come back to Dalriada! Do you not find civilian life confoundedly flat?"

"It has its compensations," said Kinross. "I find myself quite able to accept the hardships of sleeping in a dry bed and eating a dinner that is not principally composed of oil and garlic. In any case, it was time I settled down." Wellesley himself, while sorry to lose one of his aides, had said that Kinross could be more help to the war effort as a member of the Council of Lords, bolstering Dalriada's support of the joint Dalriadan-Anglian expeditionary force, than as a member of his staff.

"Sometimes, Kinross, you are so sober that I think you are the elder of us, and by a good ten years at that! Next you will be telling me that you plan to marry and set up your nursery."

Kinross stiffened. "I have... no immediate plans in that direction," he said in a tone that quelled any further jesting on that topic.

Ah, well," Dalkey subsided, "If I could only find a few more idiots like Farquhar to bet so extravagantly against my marksmanship, I should have enough to buy myself a lieutenancy in the 95th Regiment of Foot."

"You do not hold out for a cavalry regiment?" Kinross was surprised.

"Riflemen," Dalkey said, "are the army of the future! Only crack shots need even apply to the 95th, and God knows they are finding few enough of them among the musket wielders."

"In that case, the ranks of your favorite regiment are doubtless being filled with poachers," Kinross suggested.

"That's as may be. D'you think I care where the men under my command come from, so long as they can shoot straight? I tell you, Kinross, the very fact that Anglians and Dalriadans serve together proves the future of the regiment!" He shook his head and lost some of his animation. "Not that *I* shall have much opportunity to join that future. Between Mama's palpitations and m'father's objections, I've precious little chance. And even after I win Farquhar's money, I've another need for it."

"Been gaming on tick?"

"Never! No, I'm planning to wind up my association with a certain lady, and I need to end with the usual parting gift."

"Then you're serious about courting Miss Rattray!"

"Don't matter if I am or not," Dalkey said, "nobody will believe it as long as I'm visiting the other lady."

"And is it of so much matter to you that the *ton* should take your courtship seriously? Surely when the young lady accepts you—"

"If I were going to pop the question, I'd have no hope of winning her as long as the Larue woman was in the background. Anyway, I've other reasons for wishing to be rid of that entanglement. Kinross, I suspect that Vivienne de Larue is a witch."

Kinross was hard put to it not to laugh at Dalkey's serious tone, if not at the suspicion he voiced. What, was Dalkey only now suspecting that a woman who had been friendly with the Duchess of Quoy, a woman who had hosted a Black Masque, a woman on entirely too good terms with the head of the Mythic Society, might herself be a practitioner of witchcraft?

"If so," he said when he had recovered his gravity, "you are undoubtedly right to cut the connection as soon as possible."

"Yes," said Dalkey glumly. "It makes my skin crawl to think that she may have gained my attention by black arts. It would be the worst sort of imprisonment!"

"If she had," Kinross pointed out, "you would not be worrying about it. You would not be able even to suspect it."

Dalkey brightened. "Well, there's something in that! Still, 'tis time to put paid to that entanglement. M'father will never believe I'm serious about settling down as long as she remains in my life!"

General Dalkey came into the club then, and Kinross abandoned the son in favor of a long, quiet discussion with the father. There was no question but that the General supported the war with Lutéce and would be a valuable counterweight to the voices of those he contemptuously called the "Peace at any Price" party; but if his time in the military had taught Kinross anything, it had been the value of reconnaissance and planning before action.

But he did wonder, even while discussing probable alliances with General Dalkey, why Richert Dalkey seemed more concerned about other people taking his courtship of Elspet Rattray seriously than about her own opinion of him. Elspet was not one to wear her heart on her sleeve, and Kinross felt sure that Dalkey was not privy to her confession of having nourished a childish infatuation for him all these years. So why was Dalkey so casual about the lady he meant to make his wife? He hoped that, however the courtship played out, it would not end in heartbreak for little Elspet. A loveless alliance of convenience with the man she loved – No, it would not come to that; if he came to believe that Dalkey meant to offer his hand without his heart, Kinross vowed, he would find some way to put a spoke in his wheel.

Chapter 8

There had been some disagreement about the time at which our party should set out for the Water Gardens. Music and dancing there would be from the time of opening, but the fabled illuminations could be enjoyed only after dark. Mama and Kirsty stated, rather than suggested, that we would naturally wish to avoid the sort of vulgar behavior that was rumored to occur there at night, and that a late-afternoon excursion, to return at twilight, would be most *convenable*. My father, as usual, had no interest in so trivial a matter. Izzie and I felt confident that Richert Dalkey and the two friends whom he had invited to join him would protect us from any vulgar encroachments, and that her status as a married lady was sufficient to make an excursion at any hour perfectly respectable. So, once my mother and governess had been distracted by a discussion of the virtues of Olympian Dew for the complexion as compared to a home-brewed mix of strawberries and cucumber pounded to a paste, we agreed with Richert that he, Mr. Westlin and Lord Kinross should not call for us until early evening and that we should plan to dine at the Gardens on their famous sliced ham and arrack-punch.

On the day of the excursion, Mama was so occupied with compounding a new receipt for a lip salve composed of alkanet and attar of roses, promised to brighten any lady's smile without suggesting a vulgar addiction to *paint*, that she had no idea when we actually departed. I had to admit that Izzie, though sometimes snappish, was a far more satisfactory chaperone than our mother. She was almost entirely free of that petty preoccupation with maidenly behavior that could so sadly limit my opportunities to be alone – or almost alone – with my dear Richert.

I had hardly troubled my head with Kirsty's warnings that a young lady could not be too careful when visiting a public place that was open to any commoner with a few skillengs in his purse. Richert and his friends would see that we were not annoyed by such folk, and I saw no need to worry about it. I meant to enjoy myself with the dancing, the fairy-like illuminations, the pretense that Richert's attentions were heart-felt and not merely an elaborate disguise to protect him against the languishing Dorothea Turvoll – and the possibility of turning those attentions from charade to reality if we took a turn down one of those shady paths that Mama so disapproved of.

The last thing on my mind was the threat of having my pleasure spoiled by the sort of person whom I would never encounter at our home or Richert's.

Our first sight of the Water Gardens quite surpassed my most vivid imaginings, for I had not before managed to visit them after dark when they were at their best. Never had I seen so many lamps, brilliantly colored and arranged in tasteful patterns. Here they illuminated the spreading branches of a tree that overhung a quiet pool; there, the wires that suspended them were so subtle as to create the illusion that they floated in mid-air; most wonderful of all, lights burned positively underneath a great triple fountain, so that the jets of water rising from the surface appeared to have their own color and light. I did wonder if my friend Sabira had volunteered her services to the proprietors to achieve this last effect, so magical did it seem. But later in the evening I was able to catch and taste a drop of water from the Illuminated Fountain, and it was not salty at all, so the mysterious lights were likely only a feat of engineering.

Richert had reserved for us a supper-box at the front of the open pavilion and above the lowest level of boxes. Here we could observe the passing throng without being troubled by any impertinence from the young bucks who strolled between pavilion and orchestra, putting young ladies to the blush by deploying their quizzing-glasses and, in many cases, seeking to engage them in badinage that went quite beyond the line of being pleasing. Izzie took her seat with an eagerness that suggested she would be in no great hurry to rise again; for the last week she had been complaining to Kirsty and me that as her condition advanced her feet and ankles had begun to swell painfully. I had had it in mind to embroider some special slippers to alleviate her discomfort, but after that ride in the Park I had allowed myself to be distracted by the need of creating special protections for myself against the herb-witch. I had purchased a small cross of rowan wood in the Langmarket and, following the Hob's instructions, had wrapped it with an intricate criss-cross of red silk thread, so fine that it blended unnoticeably into the warm wood tones of the cross. It was not at all a convenient ornament for someone of my coloring, and I regretted the string of pearls which it replaced, but until I could get more slivers of rowan with which to stitch protection into all my dresses I would have to put up with that slight inconvenience.

Izzie might waste the evening sitting in our box with my good will, but I indicated to Richert that *my* feet did not hurt in the slightest and that the music being struck up by the band gave me the liveliest desire to join in the dancing. He led me out with a good will; he was an excellent dancer, and the only thing I regretted was that as his partner I had my work cut out to keep up with the steps and could not simply relax and admire the grace of his movements.

After that first dance, Kinross solicited a turn with me, and Richert ceded his place at my side without the slightest sign of displeasure. I consoled myself with the reflection that his manners in company were far too good to allow him to act the romantic lover. I might have recommended such a course of action in the interest of our charade, but I knew that even if he had really craved to spend every minute of the evening with me, he would hardly have committed the solecism of surrendering my hand with a bad grace.

Maybe he *did* long to be with me, at that. After Kinross and I had dropped into third place in the set and had nothing to do but wait while the first and second couples completed their star, I stole a glance in Richert's direction and saw him looking distinctly unhappy.

Or perhaps he was looking embarrassed.

In any case, as I realized a moment later, he was not looking at *me*.

"But will you not introduce me to your friends, dear Richert?" Vivienne de Larue's voice, high and sweet, floated over the last bars of the music.

Kinross offered me his arm and urged me to follow him down a path leading away from my embarrassed suitor, but I leaned back on my heels so that he could not well force me to move. I had never been one to run away from a confrontation; I stepped off the dancing floor, all but dragging Kinross with me, and joined Richert.

He had flushed unbecomingly, but had no way out of the introduction. I took the opportunity for a lengthy survey of the "lady" whom I already knew by sight and, to some extent, by reputation.

In the character of a rival for Richert's affections, she was like the reverse of Dorothea Turvoll: petite rather than lanky, with a piquant little face under a cloud of dark hair *en Camille*, and rather under- than over-dressed. Her pink muslin gown was so nearly transparent that the spangles on her slip twinkled merrily in the lamplight, and the slip itself was not all that solid; it clung in a way that displayed more of her form than I thought quite proper. It was distinctly possible, nay, almost a certainty, that she damped her petticoats to achieve that effect.

I hoped she would contract an inflammation of the lungs from walking through the cool park in such an unseemly and inadequate costume.

Even dear Richert's address was barely adequate to the complications of introducing the not-quite-a-lady who had been his inamorata to the young lady who was supposed to have captured his heart. A few muttered words, a stiff bow, and a pleading glance to me comprised all the introduction.

I would have been happy enough to leave it at that, but Vivienne de Larue had no intention of allowing Richert – or me – to escape the awkwardness inherent in the encounter. Before he had quite finished speaking she began to praise me for my freedom from stifling convention in visiting the Water Gardens by night.

"Surely no lady need fear a venue which has already been countenanced by no less a leader of society than the widow of Edouard de Larue!" I was goaded into replying.

This earned me a curtsey so sweeping as to verge on theatrical mockery, and sugary thanks for my generous approbation of her conduct... for, she said, not many young ladies so inexperienced as I would have dared the disgrace of meeting her socially.

"If you thought your presence would disgrace me," I burst out in the middle of this hypocritical speech, "I wonder you solicited Mr. Dalkey to introduce us, Mrs. de Larue!"

She laughed, made play with her fan and her bright dark eyes – emphasized, I noticed, with a lining of kohl in the Egyptian fashion – and vowed she had hardly thought Mr. Dalkey would take her little jest seriously, and that she would quite understand if I feared to risk my reputation by spending more time in public with her.

"You are most considerate," I assured her with an irony quite equaling her own, "but perhaps you do not quite understand the matter. A Rattray can hardly suffer social injury from speaking with a de Larue."

I meant, of course, that she was too far beneath me to be any sort of a threat to my position. Vivienne de Larue, wisely, chose to interpret my meaning otherwise. She chattered on about my sweet virginal innocence and the danger that what I might not know how to go on when not under my Mama's eye, until I could think of nothing but the desire to show her I was no child to be discounted at her whim.

"On the contrary," I said coldly, "I can assure you that I should offer you the same greeting in any circumstances."

"Oh, your Mama would hardly permit that!" she laughed merrily. "Do you go to the opening of the new play at the Theater Royal on Thursday next? I vow and declare, I should think shame to embarrass you by visiting your box there! Indeed I do feel sorry for you, Miss Rattray. It seems hardly fair that as an unmarried lady you will be confined to a stuffy family party in your own box, while an unmarried gentleman like Mr. Dalkey has the freedom to visit where he will!"

"On the contrary," I said, wishing I could hold my head several inches higher, "I – and any member of my family – shall be pleased to meet you there, Mrs. de Larue!"

She begged Richert, then, to procure her a glass of punch, and led him away with a mocking, triumphant backward glance at me.

"An unfortunate encounter," Kinross said as they left.

I was already regretting my hasty words. "Oh, do not you begin to criticize me as Richert is always doing, holding up some exaggerated mirror of what he imagines to be proper conduct for a young lady! I thought you were my friend, Kinross!"

"I am," he said, "and well you know it. But Vivienne de Larue is not your friend, Elspet, and I think it a pity that you were goaded into issuing what she will certainly take as an invitation."

As the heat of the encounter passed, I began to have similar sentiments myself. "Well, what's done is done," I said impatiently. "Will you dance again, or shall we rejoin Izzie and Mr. Westlin in the supper-box?"

"I never refuse the opportunity to dance with a lady who skims the floor as lightly as a feather," he said, and surprised me by putting one arm about my waist as the music began. It was a waltz.

"Oh," he said in apology when I stiffened in surprise, "do you not waltz yet? My apologies; I have been from home so long that I made certain you would have been approved long since." And he would have released me, but now that I realized what was happening I stepped forward into his arms.

"Lady Dalkey herself, the first time I visited the Assembly Rooms, introduced Mr. Coates to me as an acceptable partner for the waltz," I said, to reassure him that his absence from Town had not led him into a social solecism. And the memory of that awkward first waltz led me into a most unladylike giggle, for no matter how stiff he might be, Kinross must always be a far more acceptable partner than Mr. Coates. At the very least, he would not bore me with tall tales about his horsemanship while we danced!

It turned out, too, that he was not stiff in the least. Indeed, in his arms I felt as light as the feather he had compared me to, and found the music more intoxicating than any arrack-punch could have been. Only two things prevented me from quite floating away in the delight of waltzing with someone whose steps matched mine so perfectly – and from the giddy pleasure of seeing Richert, tardily returned to the side of the dancing floor, scowling at this demonstration that I was hardly dependent on him for a partner.

I had to admit, now that I was no longer out of temper, that Vivienne de Larue had quite deftly maneuvered me into granting her a degree of social acceptance that I might soon regret most dearly.

And the cross of rowan wood had been no protection, for she had not even used herb-magic to do it.

Chapter 9

When I confessed my error to Izzie, she flew into such a temper that I dared not discuss the matter further before we returned home and could have it out in privacy. And when we did get home, she stormed into her bedroom, called for her abigail and refused to allow me any private discussion with her.

I dismissed my own abigail as soon as she had unbuttoned my dress, and then said into the air, "I wish I could have the benefit of the Hob's advice, for I fear I have made a grievous error."

"There is naught surprising in that." An admission of error was catnip to the Hob. His voice came from the vicinity of my dressing-table, but from some distance above it, as though he had suddenly become tall enough to look me in the eye. At the same time the pivoted mirror above the table began to swing back and forth; I deduced that he had seated himself on it and was enjoying the pleasure of rocking himself on the furniture.

"That moving mirror will startle Orrock if she returns to this room," I commented.

"You have dismissed her for the night."

"Even so."

"I have every reliance on your ability to explain so small a matter. Though perhaps I have over-rated you. What is this grievous error?"

I explained, with some reluctance, what had passed at the Water Gardens. With the retelling I sounded even more naïve and awkward than I had felt at the time.

The Hob gave a long, low whistle when I had finished. "Error indeed! Do you know nothing of Din Eidyn?"

"I thought," I said, now feeling sulky as well as naïve, "*you* had joined us specifically to instruct me in those ways. Anyway, I do know that Vivienne de Larue has so far failed to gain the acceptance she craves from *ton* society; that for her to be seen visiting our family box at the theater will be a marked step towards her goal; and that I ought on no account to have issued the invitation. But why should Izzie fly into hysterics at the news? Surely she must realize that our best strategy now is to make as little of the event as possible. In any case," I said, growing indignant in my own defense, "if she desired to control my social interactions, ought she not to have been with me rather than nursing her swollen ankles in the supper-box?"

"Do you wish me," the Hob asked, "to join in condemning your sister's careless chaperonage, or to tell you exactly why she is so unhappy with you now?"

Both would have been good, though I would have enjoyed the first more.

After waiting for me to stick my neck into the rhetorical noose, the Hob spoke again, in his deepest, most serious voice. "Isolde had already invited her friend Celeste Jamison to dine here and accompany you to the theater on Thursday."

"I do not quarrel with her right to issue invitations," I grumbled. "It is *my* right to do so that is being questioned." Even if the invitation in question had been a terrible idea which I regretted almost immediately, what call had Izzie to fly into a rage about it?

The Hob sighed deeply. "Celeste Jamison was Celeste Epinet before she married Jamison."

"Another Lutécian refugee? If Izzie wants to invite a refugee friend, that makes her opposition to my doing the same quite hypocritical, do you not think?"

The mirror vibrated fiercely back and forth, and a series of thumps made me think that the Hob must be drumming his bare brown heels on its surface. "I do think, and deeply. It is you who are not thinking. The Epinets were close to the Fauchet girls, Vivienne and Marguerite, before any of them married."

78

I frowned, more confused than ever. "Marguerite?"

"Vivienne's younger sister."

I had never so much as heard her name. "And whom did she marry?"

"No one," the Hob said. "She is dead."

One last angry kick sent the mirror swinging madly, but not another word of explanation did I get out of the Hob that night. He had evidently been annoyed enough by my slowness to leave me to my own devices.

***

As happened more and more frequently these days, Izzie made no appearance at the breakfast table the next morning. One of the housemaids brought her a tray of chocolate and croissants. Bearing a new pattern and my measuring and marking tools, I slipped into Izzie's bedroom behind the maid.

"Elspet, what are you doing here?"

"I thought I would make you some new slippers to alleviate the discomfort you have been complaining of," I said. That much was perfectly true, and I didn't want to come out with my other reason until the maid had left us alone. "I need to measure your feet, to make sure the fit is perfect."

Izzie favored me with a watery smile and slid one bare foot out from under the covers for my inspection. "You are a kind child, Elspet, but I do not think that my problem is caused by ill-fitting shoes."

"Nor do I," I agreed, "but these slippers will be something special. I shall embroider them myself, you see, and I promise that they will be most soothing to your feet."

Izzie smiled again. "Are you not a little old for these games, Pet?"

"What games?"

"Oh, come now! I remember when you tried to make us all believe that the family Hob had taught you how to work charms with tangles of thread. When you were a child, it was no harm to indulge you by pretending to take the game seriously. But you are a young lady now, Pet. You need to curb your fantasies – and to heed the advice of your elders and betters with regard to your choice of friends!"

No wonder the Hob had given up on teaching Izzie any of his thread magic. But I had no wish to quarrel with her on that subject, and now Izzie had given me an opening for what I did need to discuss. "It is a little late to mend matters now," I said, bending my head in a show of contrition. "I wish I had known more about Mrs. de Larue before we encountered her at the Water Gardens."

"What needed you to know, beyond the fact that she is not received in the best society?" Izzie queried sharply.

I traced around the sole of her foot. "How slender your feet are! You should insist that your bootmaker design new half-boots from your measurements; it's small wonder that such tiny, elegant feet hurt when you force them into ordinary shoes in the common design."

"Sir Joshua does admire my feet," Izzie said in a pleasanter tone. "He says that delicate feet and shapely ankles are the sign of a true aristocrat." She stared at the exposed ankle, frowning. "Perhaps it is for the best that he is not here to see how sadly they are swollen now. I wish this child may not destroy all my beauty!"

"Your feet are still elegant compared with mine," I said truthfully. "But tell me, why is it such a disaster that your friend Celeste Jamison might encounter Mrs. de Larue in our box? I had thought they were childhood friends." At least, I had thought so since last night, when the Hob enlightened me as to the connection.

"They were," said Izzie. As if unconsciously, she drew her foot back under the covers and pulled up a shawl over her arms and neck. "At least – Celeste Epinet and Marguerite Fauchet were friends. Vivienne was a little older, but it did not seem to matter – then. But everything changed when Edouard de Larue came courting Marguerite."

"You mean Vivienne," I corrected her. Even I knew which Fauchet sister Edouard had married!

"I mean Marguerite," Izzie said sharply. "Yes, he met Vivienne first, but from the moment he saw Marguerite... They say he was like a man possessed."

"What, was she an herb-witch too?"

Izzie frowned. "What do you mean, 'too'? Oh, never mind. No, Marguerite wasn't a witch, silly girl! She was young and very, very lovely. Together, the sisters made a striking pair, for Marguerite was as fair as Vivienne is dark. The two of them were called the Matchless Incomparables by some foolish people, because they set off one another's styles of beauty so well. No, Edouard was truly in love with Marguerite, or so they say…" She fell silent, examining her fingernails. "I am very fond of Sir Joshua," she said at last.

"I never questioned that!" But now I wondered. Could Izzie have been in love with this Edouard de Larue? The room seemed darker and closer than it had a moment earlier; probably a cloud had passed over the sun.

"*Very* fond," Izzie said again, raising her chin. "He is – is a most estimable gentleman, and I am proud to be his wife! Only, only… our marriage was all a matter of suitability and settlements… Sir Joshua is not a man to fall in love *a la folie*, as Edouard did with Marguerite. And I am sure I am quite happy, for a husband given to fits of desperate emotion would hardly be a comfortable companion! But Edouard and Marguerite… There was a sort of golden glow about them. I was not out yet, but even I could tell, on the rare occasions when I did see them together…"

She paused again, but now her eyes were fixed on some distant image that only she could see.

"But Marguerite died," I prompted eventually.

"Yes. The sisters went together to visit Edouard's parents – they were elderly, and lived very much retired in the country; it would not have been *convenable* for Marguerite to have made such a visit alone, and the Fauchet girls had no parents – at least none that anyone in Dalriada ever met. And Vivienne said, afterwards, that she and Marguerite had always vowed that marriage should not separate them."

Another silence fell. "Afterwards?" I asked.

"There was an accident. There in Braemuirie, where Edouard's old parents lived. Marguerite fell into the river and drowned. It was a nine days' wonder; nothing could be proved, but there was enough gossip to kill his parents too, or so they say. Certainly they died very soon afterwards. And after Edouard buried his true love and then his parents, he came back to Din Eidyn… but by then he was married to Vivienne."

I drew in my breath. The rumors swirling about Vivienne de Larue were blacker than I had imagined. No wonder she found acceptance by the *ton* so elusive!

"I wish I had known all this before – before we went to the Water Gardens," I said at last. "I see now that it was very wrong indeed in me to countenance the lady's encroaching ways."

"I wish you had too," said Izzie bleakly, "but it is not considered proper to speak of these things to an unmarried girl." She stared through me, tapping her fingers on the counterpane. "It is not unheard of," she said finally, "for a man who has lost a girl he truly loved, to turn to her sister for some faint echo of the magic that first entranced him. It may have been no more than that in Edouard de Larue's case. We will never know, will we, now that he too is dead."

"But," I hazarded, remembering the point that had first enraged her, "your friend Celeste does not think so."

"No," said Izzie. "She has always believed that Vivienne murdered Marguerite to get Edouard, and then poisoned Edouard when he began to grow suspicious of her. And she has said as much, too, in and out of Din Eidyn, until Vivienne hates her and believes her failure to win acceptance by the *ton* to be all Celeste's doing." Her eyes focused on my face once again. "Now do you see why Thursday night is like to be an extremely difficult occasion for all of us?"

I did indeed.

Chapter 10

Vivienne de Larue was not receiving visitors; she was in the stillroom, creating a decoction of the herbs that would, when dripped into a glass of wine with the proper words, compel Richert Dalkey's love. The creation of the potion was a complex task, and she was not pleased when the servant who had been strictly ordered not to interrupt her scratched on the door.

"Yes, what is it?" she demanded, opening the door a crack. She wished no curious footman to observe her work.

When the man passed Baron Jenneret's card through the crack, though, she sighed. "Tell the Baron I shall be with him directly." She and Jenneret shared too many secrets for her to risk offending him. A pity she had not already permanently silenced the man, but she had been preoccupied with the Dalkey project. And he *was* sometimes a source of useful gossip from his Mythic Society, not to mention the gentlemen's clubs and other places that her sex prevented her from entering. She closed the door, moved her little pots of herbs away from the fire, and made other preparations to protect the secrecy of her work.

When she entered the drawing room, Jenneret rose and made a leg. The unaccustomed courtesy roused her suspicions; where witnesses were absent, he usually made a point of treating her more casually, as if to underline their partnership in various secret enterprises. It was not to favor her with interesting news that he had called, then.

"You... come with a request," she said. It was second nature to announce her deductions in a faraway, almost singing tone that suggested her information came from sources unavailable to ordinary folk. But Jenneret was not fooled; he favored her with a knowing smile.

"A request, my lady, and an opportunity which you would be foolish to disdain – and all the world knows that the lady Vivienne is no fool!"

The flattery, as well as the hint of the title which would be hers once she married Dalkey and disposed of his father, softened her response.

"Very well," she said, sitting down, "let me hear about this opportunity."

It was no less than an overture from the Duke of Balcladich, leader of the Peace Party, suggesting in the most delicate terms that he would be grateful for any help that the lady Vivienne, with her many connections, could give in persuading certain gentlemen of the War Party to his side – or else, Jenneret added, rendering them unlikely to sit in the Council of Lords when next that body deliberated.

An opportunity – or a dangerous temptation to reveal powers not generally known?

"In what way does he think a mere woman can meddle in political affairs?" she asked to gain time as well as information.

"Oh, he knows that all the world comes to your parties," Jenneret said with an air of assumed carelessness.

"But not, I fear, to talk politics – particularly with a female!"

"No. But if one of the gentlemen in question – say, Lord Kinross, or the Earl of Torquhan, or the young Duke of Quoy – were to lose heavily at the tables, he might be... amenable to persuasion, if you returned his losses. Torquhan I know to be sitting on the fence. Both Kinross and young Quoy will be taking their seats in Council for the first time. And then," Jenneret added, "General Dalkey, though firmly of the war party, might be distracted on the day of the vote by some accident to his heir."

"You expect me to harm Richert Dalkey?"

"Well... he is hardly a good prospect for marriage, is he, now that he's dangling after the younger Rattray girl? Granted, should you bring him up to scratch, *that* would distract the General. But on the whole, I think you will do better to give up that project and concentrate on other ways of pleasing

Balcladich. I have it on good authority – in fact, from the lips of the Duke himself – that should your work in this matter prove satisfactory, he will countenance you in the best society. He could even see to it that you were given vouchers to Gilroy's Assembly Rooms. Would it not please you to see such birth-proud ladies as Lady Dalkey forced to receive you there?"

The prospect was tempting indeed, but still Vivienne hesitated. "What if my poor efforts were not enough to give the Peace Party the victory?"

"Only neutralize the gentlemen I have named, and the Duke will show his gratitude."

"I stand to lose financially by the means you suggest."

"Ah, but you have other means at your disposal."

"I do?"

"You forget, dear Vivienne, that I was in the confidence of the Duchess of Quoy before her unexpected disappearance. Naturally I have done nothing to encourage the rumors around your name, but…"

The threat was unmistakable. And as the head of the Mythic Society, Jenneret was well placed to substantiate rumors of Vivienne's covert activities.

She bit her lip. "I should require proof in writing of the Duke's promise."

"That," said Jenneret, "you will not get, nor should you expect it. The Duke is known as a man of honor; his word must suffice."

"A man of honor who stoops to these means to conquer his enemies!"

"All's fair in love and politics," Jenneret said easily, "and he has not specified the means; he only solicits your interest in this matter." He jingled a heavy purse. "On your acceptance, I am to advance you this sum against whatever gaming losses you may suffer through this project – I mean, of course, as an earnest of the Duke's commitment; the means, as I have said, are up to you."

"I must have a moment to consider!"

"The offer," said Jenneret, "is contingent on your acceptance today. There is not so much time to lose before the first meeting of the Council, and the Duke has it on good authority that the War Party means to bring the matter to a vote immediately."

She thought quickly. Richert Dalkey she meant to have under her sway in any case, and she could then easily manipulate him to distract his father on the day. Kinross did not visit her salon, but with the imprimatur of the Rattrays at the coming theater party, she thought she could maneuver to meet him socially and to use her herb-magic to sway his mind. As to the other two, Torquhan visited frequently and liked deep play. Quoy was young enough to be persuadable by a beautiful woman, and she could – *would*, now that the stakes were high enough – gain access to him via her visits to the Duchess' gardens. And the purse Jenneret dangled before her would at least recoup her recent losses to Sir Flodin Hultstrom.

"Very well," she said. "I accept the Duke's proposition."

***

I'd asked Madame Olympe to let me know if Dorothea Turvoll commissioned a dress for the Assembly Rooms, and to tell me when she was near to finishing the work. The first message, if indeed she sent one, never reached me; the second came just before a deadly dull dinner with my parents, Izzie, and some ancient friends and political allies of my father's. As soon as I could politely excuse myself from the endless arguments balancing increased taxes, unrest in the back country, and the need for defence against the Lutécian threat, I hurried upstairs and pestered Orrock to unbutton me in record time; demanded more candles; and dismissed her to her bed. Madame Olympe's note was tactfully phrased as if she thought me interested only in the creation of my own dresses, but she mentioned as an aside that Dorothea Turvoll expected to be fitted for her new ball gown within the week. I had little enough time to spare, then, if I wished to enhance that gown as well as my own.

In a nightgown that was not really warm enough for the chilly, damp summer nights of Din Eidyn I sat cross-legged on my bed and worked the necessary patterns in the air, holding loops of fine silver thread – the dress, Olympe had said, was to be trimmed in silver lace – until a word taught me by the Hob stabilized the completed shape and allowed me to slip it free of my hands. My fingers grew cold and stiff and clumsy as I worked; each repetition of the pattern was more difficult than the last. I ought to have told

Orrock to build up a fire in the bedroom – but Mama believed that no one ought to need a fire in summer, and such an unusual request might have drawn her attention. She might even have decided that I was sickening for something and needed to stay abed for the day before our projected theater party. That would have been fatal; I needed to get these tangles to Olympe tomorrow.

The mirror of my dressing table began to sway. "You are sadly fumble-fingered tonight," the Hob observed.

Of course the working of thread magic had drawn his attention; I ought to have expected it.

"I'm *cold*," I said pettishly. "My hands are freezing, and I've still to make three more copies of this pattern."

The mirror gave one last violent spring and I heard something very like the thump of bare feet landing on the floor. A moment later a warm glow suffused the air around me.

"That's better!" Even in the stress of the moment, I remembered not to thank the Hob directly for his services. The ways of the Fair Folk are not our ways, and Hobs in particular have their very own rules of etiquette. Thanks would imply that he had done me a service, and such a hint of his acting like a servant would offend him so much that I would not see... well, hear... him for weeks. So would any gift more than his nightly bowl of milk. And as for thanks commensurate with his services – everyone knew that the one sure way to get rid of a Hob was to make him a suit of clothes. He would equate such a gift as asking him to wear our livery, a deadly insult that would inspire him to vanish forever.

These, and other rules for dealing with the Fair Folk, had been taught me by Izzie's and my old nurse, in the long-ago days before she was pensioned off and replaced with a governess. Kirsty had no patience with what she deemed at best lies and at worse fairy tales. Izzie had immediately discarded all we had heard from Nurse Chanett, and even I had learned not to repeat old Chanett's wisdom where Kirsty could hear me. But I did not forget. I knew better than to enter a hollow hill or dance in a fairy ring, no matter how enticing the music; should I find myself lost in the countryside I would reverse my jacket to confuse the pixies; and under no circumstances would I mount an unknown, unbridled black horse.

And I would never commit the solecism of thanking a Hob for any service.

Now that my fingers were warm, I finished the last three patterns deftly enough. There was still a good length of silver thread left; absently, I knotted it into a circle and looped it over and under my fingers. Thumbs under the cross, free the loop over the little fingers, pick up the central thread and draw it under…

Love me love me love me do, the pattern sang wordlessly under my hands. I shook the clinging thread off my fingers and let it collapse again.

"For a moment," said the Hob's deep voice, "I enjoyed the illusion that you had decided to be sensible about your young man."

"It is wrong to compel another's feelings," I said, and snapped the leftover silver thread in two. I picked up my last three patterns, laid them atop the others and made a discreet bundle of the long, thin shapes inside a folded paper. Tomorrow Orrock might wonder why I was carrying a package to Madame Olympe, but she was far too well-trained a servant to ask. If Hobs turned their human hosts off for slight breaches of etiquette, the gentry were well known to turn off their servants for even less. I would never do that, but Izzie changed her personal abigail very nearly as often as she changed her dress, and that was sufficient to keep the household in a state of frightened obedience.

I did wonder, sometimes, how it would be to have servants who were not afraid all the time. When Richert and I were married, I intended to run my own household on very different lines.

On the next morning, far too early for polite callers to interfere with my plans, I made my way to Madame Olympe's establishment. The delicate patterns in silver thread were in a long basket carried by Orrock, covered by a length of fine gold-embroidered amber silk sent by Mama's brother in India. He wrote that the Indian women did not sew the stuff but simply wrapped it about their bodies; I had asked Mama whether I might not see if Olympe could contrive something more suitable from it in time for the next ball. That gave me both pretext for the visit and disguise for the threadwork intended for Dorothea's dress. And, with luck, it would also give me a new and excessively becoming ball dress for this Season.

As usual, I told Orrock to wait in the outer workroom while I carried the basket into Madame Olympe's sanctum. She greeted me with a distracted air and complained that Mr. Turvoll had given her far too little time to prepare this dress for his daughter; even now three seamstresses were working on it in the outer room.

"Can you dismiss them?" I asked, carefully removing the slippery folds of fine amber silk from my basket. "I have some… *private* work to do on that very dress."

As I held up the Indian silk, the embroidery in fine gold thread caught the light and the silk itself shimmered between golden yellow in the highlights darkening to deep bronze and amber in the shadowy folds. To be sure it would be a difficult color for a redhead, and one that Izzie had rejected out of hand, but I thought that I could carry it off. With some regret I put the length of silk aside so as to free my hands for embroidering. Perhaps we could discuss my dress while I was making my improvements to Dorothea's gown.

Olympe remarked that she had not engaged me to work for the Turvolls, however privately. But she had heard that Dorothea Turvoll was languishing over Richert Dalkey, and that he was presently courting me. With some suspicion, she enquired over the precise nature of the embellishments I meant to add to Miss Turvoll's Assembly gown.

We had to wait while the head seamstress brought in the gown and then, on a firm order from Madame Olympe, retreated and left the two of us alone with it.

It was reminiscent of the gown I had seen Dorothea wearing at the Dalkey ball, but only in its rose and silver coloring. Here the bright, assertive rose color was softened to the softest of blush pinks in a gauzy overdress. Beneath this, a white gown of softest silk sparkled round the hem with a fine border of silver lace. The fabrics were perfectly chosen to drape gently over a young girl's delicate figure, hinting without vulgar display, and the colors of the overdress would reflect desirable color onto Dorothea's complexion.

"She should have engaged you from the start," I exclaimed in admiration.

"You know to a shade how to please her tastes without allowing her to swathe herself in stiff, gaudy fabrics."

Madame Olympe preened very slightly. "We persuaded Miss Turvoll to allow us to supply the fabric as well as cutting out the dress," she said. "The very best cut would scarcely have redeemed the stiffened taffeta she wished to use, and as for the color—!"

"She will feel amply repaid for her confidence in you when she sees this dress," I said, "and even more when she wears it… with just a few discreet embellishments." I lifted the top pattern from the stack in the basket and held it up for Olympe's admiration.

She paled and retreated a few steps.

"What? It is nothing *evil*," I told her. "The girl is no threat to me – and in any case, I would not do such a mean thing. It's just a little pattern that will make men inclined to dance with her."

Olympe sank down on the one chair that was not covered with samples of fabric. "Yes. I can tell how it will draw them to dance. Do you not *hear* it, Elspet? Stop chattering for a moment, do, and listen!"

In the still dimness of the workroom, away from the windows, the fine silver threads seemed to dance with light from nowhere. And now that I listened closely, it seemed to me that I could catch the faint, high notes of a fairy reel; an infectious music that set toes tapping and heels clicking. The workroom seemed to darken as we listened, and the silver threads to glow even brighter.

I laid the interlaced threads carefully over the back of another chair and jerked the curtains open as far as they would go. "It is… just a little louder than usual because I made the pattern to stand by itself," I said, a bit uncertainly. "You should hear nothing after I release the threads and tack them to the dress. Now clear a space for me to work, please."

And indeed, after the white silk slip was laid out on the table and I released the stiffened pieces of loose embroidery so that I could stitch them into place, the fairy music was scarcely audible to human ears. Anyway, I talked over it until Olympe recovered her color.

"I had to work the patterns this way because I would scarcely have time, in one session, to create them directly on the fabric," I explained, taking tiny quick stitches to anchor the silver threads. "The working will be fragile, of course; we must hope that Miss Turvoll is not so clumsy as to catch the hem of her dress on anything, and that her partners have equal grace. There, you see?" I touched the tacked-on threads of the next pattern and reversed the Hob's command, and the glittering silver threads blended with the soft folds of the silk as though they had never been stiffened.

"I – can still hear – the other pieces," Olympe said.

So could I. "Best not to think on it," I said. I should just have to keep talking over that faint, subtle music until the work was finished, the circles closed, the faint bright tinkling notes again hidden from conscious hearing. "In any case, Olympe, it is only a very small magic, and nothing in the least harmful. It will only make people standing close to Miss Turvoll think what a pleasant thing it would be to dance, and they will naturally associate that feeling with her and beg her to accept them as partners."

"I wonder you dare risk giving her such an advantage," Olympe said, relaxing slightly on her chair. "Are you so sure of Mr. Dalkey, then?"

"Mr. Dalkey," I said, "never goes to the Assembly Rooms. And even if he did, I do not think this little charm will override his desire *not* to be languished over by Miss Turvoll." Especially if he was protected against all magic, even mine, by the rowan shreds and red thread patterns concealed beneath the glittering embroidery of his watch fob.

"Even so…"

"The child spent most of the Dalkeys' ball sitting on a chair against the wall and looking hopeful, except for the duty-dance Mr. Dalkey gave her… and standing up once with that Mr. Petrie, who ought to be enjoined by law against persecuting innocent little girls!" I said, remembering my annoyance at how Norval Petrie had embarrassed Dorothea. "Olympe, I couldn't *stand* it. She has enough against her already, with that vulgar father and his talk of mills and looms and factory hands, and that long drooping nose… and the display of jewels! Do you think you can possibly persuade her not to drape herself with rubies and diamonds for the Assembly Rooms?"

"It is not my place to advise a client on such personal matters," Olympe said.

"Well, at the very least you could discuss the jewels most likely to set off a young girl's beauty in a delicately colored dress like this one! If you can persuade her that pearls would be more flattering than a vulgar show of colored stones—"

"My part in this is almost over," said Olympe. "I have only to do the last fitting before I send her the dress, and her father the bill."

"Can you not discuss accessories while you do that fitting?"

"I suppose I *could* do that," Olympe said faintly. "But what if she too hears the music, and sees the fairy lights glimmering on the thread?"

"She will not," I promised, beginning on the fourth pattern, "and neither will you, once all these are released from the stiffening charm and well attached to the dress."

Olympe still looked nervous, and it would take me a few minutes yet to tack down the fifth and sixth patterns, so I cast about for something to distract her. "Izzie," I said as I snipped off my thread and squinted to thread the needle anew, "has told me *all about* Vivienne de Larue now, so you need not strain to avoid the subject. What do *you* think? Did she really murder her sister? And Edouard's parents? And Edouard himself?"

"If there were evidence of such crimes, she would have been found guilty of murder and hanged long since."

"Mmm. Maybe… and maybe not. She would not be the first beautiful and highborn lady to escape punishment for her crimes," I said, thinking of the fabled Lucretia of Borghese and other examples throughout the history Kirsty had crammed into my head.

Olympe laughed. "Highborn? Hardly that! The Fauchets were quite common in Lutéce, and everybody knew it, no matter what airs the girls put on after they fled the Revolution for the safer shores of Dalriada. And as for Edouard… Marriage to him was to have given Vivienne impeccable social standing. It hardly benefited her to lose him."

"Unless," I said, taking tiny stitches whose white thread blended with the glimmering white silk of the gown, "he began to suspect, after their marriage, that she had put Marguerite out of his way."

"After?" Olympe echoed.

"Well, he would hardly have wed her if he had entertained such suspicions beforehand," I pointed out. Three more invisible tacking stitches, and the fifth pattern was secure. I spread out the sixth pattern on the last breadth of white silk, spoke the word of release and began tacking it into place.

"Edouard was an only child," Olympe said. "His mother lived quite retired from the world of fashion, and he had no sisters or close female friends."

"What, not even a pretty bit of muslin?"

"You," said Olympe, "are not supposed to know that such women exist."

I sighed. "And in public, I play the ignorant maiden. But between us women, Olympe, did Edouard have no traffic whatsoever with the female sex?"

"That is my understanding. He was a remarkably staid young man, for all his Lutécian origins. That is why he would not have suspected anything."

I puzzled over the complex interlacing at the center of the last pattern. It must be tacked down too securely to fall loose during a vigorous dance, yet my stitches must not split the silver threads or tie them down so tightly that the flow of magical suggestion through the knotwork would be impeded. "Forgive me, Madame, but I do not quite grasp your point."

Olympe sighed. "He never spoke with Patrice-Henri, who dressed poor Marguerite's hair for her burial. *That* is the point."

"Why? Was there something about her hair that proved she was murdered? Had someone pulled great hanks of it away from her scalp?" I could think of nothing else one could learn from a dead girl's hair, and even what I had suggested could be taken as evidence that Vivienne had tried desperately to save her drowning sister.

"Nothing like that," Olympe said. "But Patrice-Henri was convinced that Marguerite was helped to her death, and he believed that the right person could prove it by studying her long golden hair. *I* had not the skill to help him. But a strong worker in thread magic, someone who was taught it by a magical being…"

Her voice trailed away and she appeared to be staring right through me, at something only she could see.

"Working with thread," I said after a long pause, "is not the same as working with hair. And in any case, Marguerite Fauchet is long buried now, is she not?" I drew the line at grave-robbing to work thread magic on a dead woman's hair.

"She is," agreed Olympe. "Have you completed your work on Dorothea's gown? Why do not you call your maid in now, to help us hold up the amber silk and decide what cut would be most flattering to you?"

"Cannot one of your seamstresses do that?"

"I am thinking of you," Olympe said. "Arrack – is that her name, how strange – oh, *Orrock* – can, at need, tell anybody who asks that you were excessively interested in having me design a ball gown from your uncle's Indian silk. It would be best if that were thought to be the only topic we discussed today."

Chapter 11

The theater in Auchinbeck Square set the night at defiance with a display of wax tapers in wall sconces and hanging chandeliers that banished shadows and shed a flattering golden light on the faces I saw around me in neighboring boxes. Ladies in shimmering silks and velvets made play with their fans or moved so as to make their jewels flash in the light. Equally finely dressed gentlemen bent over the ladies to murmur sweet nothings, or monopolized a box of their own where they could freely shout bawdy comments at any women of easy virtue they espied. This scene was already familiar to me; despite the fact that, like the Water Gardens, the theater was open to any commoner with a few skillengs for admittance, it was deemed respectable for young ladies – properly chaperoned, of course – to visit the place. We were, of course, expected to sit in a box rather than rubbing shoulders with the lesser sort who filled the pit. That was perfectly all right with me; the pit had the added disadvantage of being located directly beneath the massive chandeliers that turned the theater into a blaze of light, thus exposing occupants to the risk of occasional drips of hot wax that burned skin and ruined clothing.

Still, it seemed strange that Society did not frown upon young ladies' sitting in boxes from which they could see and be seen by anybody else rich enough to take a box for the night, including many a practicing courtesan and the Pinks of the Ton ogling her wares. And there was, of course, constant traffic between the boxes as theater-goers sauntered about, visiting one another's boxes and exchanging compliments and badinage.

For instance, there was nothing to stop Vivienne de Larue, already in her box and displaying a gown even more scandalously low-cut and diaphanous than her costume at the Water Gardens, from visiting our box. Fortunately, at the time of our arrival her attention was occupied by no fewer than three hovering gentlemen.

Izzie elbowed me. "See that man?" she hissed, indicating the middle-aged man standing at Vivienne's left elbow and frankly staring down the low neckline of her diamanté crimson gown. "That is Baron Jenneret, the founder of the Mythic Society! If your rash challenge to Mrs. de Larue results in her forcing *that* acquaintance upon us, Elspet, I shall never forgive you!"

Very likely I should never forgive myself.

I did not know whether to be glad or sorry that Mama had not chosen to make one of our theater party, saying that Izzie and Celeste Jamison together were quite adequate as chaperones, and that she trusted Mr. Dalkey and Lord Kinross to take good care of all the ladies. If our mother were present, she might have known just how to depress Vivienne's pretensions. I had signally failed in that task, Izzie did not sound any too confident in her own abilities, and her friend Celeste, only a few years older than Izzie, was an unknown quantity.

On the other hand, since Mama was not at the theater, whatever happened, she could not kill me until we returned home.

Was it possible that the herb-witch was having too much fun with her collected gallants to interrupt the flirtations just to annoy me? Possible, but hardly likely, I concluded as Vivienne de Larue intercepted my brooding stare with a laughing glance of her own and raised her fan in salute, as much as to say, "I shall deal with you later, foolish child!" She looked slightly less happy a moment later, as Richert Dalkey moved to my side where she could see him, but my confidence was not much improved. Especially when she favored him with a languishing look and shook her head slightly at her three cicisbeos. That look, too, I could interpret well enough: she would be happy to exchange Baron Jenneret and the other two gentlemen for Richert.

And who wouldn't?

"It's all your fault," I murmured to Richert, too low for the other occupants of the box to hear, "that your *inamorata* has scraped acquaintance with me. I depend upon you to see that she does not seek to ruin me by bringing Lord Jenneret to this box." This was quite unfair in at least two different directions. Richert had done his best to prevent me responding to Vivienne's provocation in the Water Gardens, and I could think of nothing short of positive violence by which he could keep Jenneret out of this box. But I was in desperate straits and in no mood to be fair.

"Mr. Dalkey and I will engage to prevent your being insulted by any overtures from the Baron," Kinross said from behind me.

Evidently my voice had not been quite so low as I had believed, or else Kinross's hearing was preternaturally sharp. Perhaps his experiences in the Galician war had trained him to pick out one person's voice in a chaos of sounds, though why he should have chosen mine to listen to escaped me.

I had no idea how Kinross could keep the Baron away from us, either, but something about the calm certainty of his tone soothed me. Moments later the curtain rose, and the level of conversation in the house sank to a low roar as fully half the audience lowered their voices and pretended attention to the play. I had not expected to need to pretend – the theater was not yet so commonplace an experience for me that I came only to see and be seen but on this night I found it impossible to lose myself in the passionate speeches of the lovers or the broad comedy of the deceived husband, the mere tradesman who existed only for his well-born wife to make a fool of. The interval would be upon us before I knew it; the interval, and Vivienne de Larue.

Possibly she and Izzie's friend Celeste would slay one another on sight, sparing me the necessity of negotiating this social quagmire.

I did not really think I could count on that.

If only Izzie were to suffer one of her bilious attacks and request the gentlemen to take us home! But since I had interlaced all her chemises with thread magic against just such attacks, she had enjoyed excellent health.

What if I were to be taken ill? Dizziness, a near-faint? I could always blame the hot, close atmosphere of the theater with its thousands of burning candles.

I could not.

A Rattray did not sham sickness to flee the field of battle.

Generations of starched-up, prickly, unsympathetic Rattray ancestors rose up before my inner eye, reproaching the very thought. Great-Grandmother Elspet would have been ashamed of her namesake.

The Hob, too, would scarcely sympathize with a silly chit who let herself be teased into an unwise invitation, and then ran away from the consequences.

Thinking of the Hob, I fingered the hem of my dress and pulled at a loose end of thread. The magical tangle I had tacked around the hem at the last minute came free, and I gathered the bright silken threads into a loose skein around my fingers. Did I know no thread magic that would help me to control this situation?

I could not think of anything, and I doubted the Hob would oblige me by joining our party and giving me instructions. Still, manipulating the thread gave me something to do and helped calm me somewhat. While Dalkey and Kinross laughed at comic allusions so broad I could not comprehend them, my hands in my lap smoothed and twined and twisted the silk thread. While Izzie and Celeste sighed over the tragic parting of the lovers, the threads curled about my fingers in a pattern so familiar, no thought was required.

The curtain came down over the stage, the low roar of a hundred conversations doubled and redoubled, and I looked down at the bright tangle in my lap where I had automatically made, once again, the pattern I had sworn never to use. The one that would coerce the love I wished to win from Richert.

The one that would poison our happiness, were I fool enough to use it.

And yet – and yet –

The pattern was long and narrow. The Hob's word, whispered under my breath, stiffened the silk threads and held the tangle without need of a base fabric, or of stitches to attach it to the fabric. And I slid it into one of my long gloves, where it seemed to burn against the skin of my arm.

I would not deprive myself of *any* weapon in the coming moments, not even that one.

Mere seconds after I had concealed the thread tangle I dared not use, Vivienne LaRue appeared at the entrance to our box, followed by two men whom I could not make out clearly; they did not enter with her, but lingered just outside, in the dimness of the hall. Both were very tall; not Jenneret, then. I breathed a small sigh of relief.

Possibly too soon.

"Lady Herriot, how good to see you again!" Vivienne said, as brightly as if she and Izzie had parted company only yesterday. "But I vow, I am so happy that I forget myself. Dear Miss Rattray, how good it was in you to invite me to visit during the interval!"

I had certainly not been quite so forthcoming, nor so specific, as all that.

"Mr. Dalkey, of course, I know quite well," she said with an arch smile that I supposed was intended to reel him back to her side. "Miss Rattray, will you not introduce me to your other friends?"

"Mrs. Larue," I said through stiff lips. "My sister, Lady Herriot, and Lord Kinross."

"What a fortunate chance to meet *you* here, my lord!" Vivienne exclaimed, favoring Kinross with another of her brilliant smiles, and – seemingly by chance – moving forward so that the candles at one side of the theater shone through her clinging, gauzy dress. The light made it clear that I had been wrong in thinking she had damped the chemise under her dress, the better to show off her figure. She was not even wearing a chemise.

"Mrs. Jamison I believe you know already," I completed the farce of introductions.

"But not by that name." She made a deep curtsey that afforded the gentlemen ample opportunity to look down what there was of her bodice – a mere two bands of crossed and pleated silk. "Dear, dear Celeste, what a joy to encounter you again!"

Celeste Jamison made a minimal curtsy, a scarcely perceptible dip of her knee that somehow managed to suggest the ice-rimmed shores of a winter sea.

"It seems but yesterday," Vivienne gushed, "that we were two bare-legged little girls playing outside your parents' humble cottage!"

A stiletto concealed amid the flowery greeting. I made mental note of the technique; I might have occasion to use it one day.

Preferably on the "lady" standing before me.

"Does it," said Mrs. Jamison in tones even more icy than her bow. "How

99

strange. To me, it seems a lifetime ago. Or have you forgotten that there were *three* girls?"

"Poor dear Marguerite!" Vivienne sighed. "Her memory is always with me." She raised a hand to her kohl-darkened eyes as if to dash away a nonexistent tear. "But let us speak of happier things! A theater party is no place for these sad reminiscences."

"*Two* lifetimes," said Mrs. Jamison inexorably. "You forget Mr. de Larue."

"Dear Edouard!" Another gesture towards her eyes. "Never, never do I forget him, endeavor though I may to drown that great sorrow in shallow gaiety. But speaking of gaiety – Mr. Dalkey, Mr. Kinross, you will take a glass of wine with me? And for the ladies, my footman has brought ratafia."

One of the tall men stepped just into the box, and now I could see that he was a liveried footman who bore a tray burdened with wine glasses. Vivienne made a pretty business of handing out the ratafia to Izzie, Mrs. Jamison and me, while she took wine like Kinross and Richert.

I wondered if she had been bold enough to lace the drinks with magical potions, but on reflection I could see that I had little to fear. Vivienne had certainly handed out the glasses herself in order to make sure that each of us received exactly the drink she meant us to have. Of the five of us, Richert and I were surely her only targets, and we were both protected by rowan, red thread, and the protective tangles taught me by the Hob. I supposed it was remotely possible that she meant to coerce her old friend and present enemy into a warmer attitude towards her, but if so, her plan failed at the beginning; Mrs. Jamison shook her head and placed her glass of ratafia back on the footman's tray. "Thank you," she said, "but I do not drink—"

Vivienne burst into sprightly speech, admiring the play, the actors, the very candles that blazed around the theater, and quite covering the rest of Mrs. Jamison's sentence, which sounded very like "in the present company." I made a note of this technique also; if one did not hear an insult, one could avoid responding to it.

After the footman withdrew with his single, rejected glass of ratafia, Vivienne continued bubbling on about, it seemed, any topic that came into her head. To be sure, none of us had anything to say to her, so I was almost grateful to her for filling the icy silence in the box. Izzie and Mrs. Jamison stared steadily at the drawn curtain as though the stage were still filled with lively action. Richert, of course, was too well-bred to ignore a lady with whom he had but recently had the most intimate of connections. He smiled and laughed at Vivienne's comments, and even bent his head to hear her when she dropped her voice to deliver some innuendo she would not have dared voice out loud in the presence of real ladies. I watched him closely and felt reassured that her potion, had there been one, had failed before the protections I had embroidered into his watch fob; there was courtesy in his words and gestures, but no warmth in his eyes. I thought.

As for Kinross, he followed Richert's lead, only with more apparent enthusiasm. His smile held the genuine warmth that Richert's lacked, and he seemed almost to encourage her when she strayed into the realm of little jokes that were improper to voice before other ladies. Doubtless his object was to protect us from more contact with her by engaging her attentions.

I thought.

I drew a breath of relief when she announced her intention of returning to her own box before the play should resume. "I've dismissed my footmen; you'll escort me, dear... Mr. Dalkey?" she purred, placing one hand on his arm in a most unseemly display of affection.

"Allow *me*," said Kinross, all but stepping between them. "I should be honored, Mrs. de Larue."

"In that case," said Richert, "I most certainly ought not to leave these ladies unattended." He withdrew his arm and stepped back to stand beside me. No potion had ensorcelled him, it was clear, and I took another relieved breath.

It had been, I thought, most generous of Kinross to make it possible for Richert to remain with me. So I thought as he escorted Vivienne out of her box, and so I thought until the curtain rose again and the roar of conversation dropped by half.

By now Kinross had had time to walk the entire length of the outer corridor and back several times over; why was he still away?

I moved to the front of the box, from which I could survey both sides of the theater, and found my worst fears confirmed. Kinross was leaning over the back of Vivienne's chair; I could not hear their voices over the general din and the shouting of the players, but the interchange of laughs and smiles told their own story. Vivienne's other cicisbeos had disappeared; had she sent them away to concentrate on Kinross?

And why, *why* had he not returned to us? Could Vivienne's undeniable beauty have caused him to forget all propriety of word and action?

Perhaps, I told myself, he feared Richert would not keep his promise to break off with Vivienne now that he was – supposedly – courting me. Perhaps Kinross thought to aid me by cutting Richert out with the lady.

Or perhaps – the suspicion uncoiled like an icy snake reaching up my spine – perhaps Vivienne had handed the wineglass with the potion to the wrong man. Perhaps it was not the Hob's expertise with thread tangles, or the use of rowan and red thread, that had protected Richert from the herb-witch's manipulations; perhaps he had only drunk an innocent glass of wine, while Kinross – who was *not* protected – imbibed the potion.

I had time enough to contemplate this dreadful possibility, which made me feel quite ill with worry, during the final acts of the play. In defiance of all polite custom, Kinross continued to flirt with Vivienne and to ignore the ladies he had supposedly escorted until the curtain came down upon the happy joining of the lovers as they successfully gulled the foolish husband into complaisance. Izzie joined me at the front of the box and beckoned imperiously to Kinross; he murmured a few words into Vivienne's ear and, at long last, withdrew from her box and returned to ours.

Izzie announced that I had the headache and that we did not desire to stay for the farce, and Kinross was at least too polite to abandon us again; he saw the three of us to our coach and, to my dismay, made an excuse to Richert that he would join him later rather than riding with him beside the coach to our house.

I had just time for one small gesture, probably futile, before I was forced by convention to follow Izzie and Mrs. Jamison into the coach. That gesture seemed to startle Kinross; he looked up, his eyes wide. Probably he was shocked that I would put my hand on his sleeve as that shameless Vivienne had done to Richert.

"I shall do myself the honor of calling tomorrow," he said after a momentary pause and a catching of breath, "to assure myself that Miss Rattray is quite recovered."

"There is no need," I assured him.

"*I* feel the need."

"Then ride with me in the Park before breakfast, if you need proof that I am not so easily overset by an evening's entertainment!"

"Elspet, do not keep the horses standing!" Izzie snapped.

I seated myself and we were off before I could even discover if Kinross meant to keep the engagement I had so forwardly proposed.

Chapter 12

To my relief, Kinross called the next morning in good time to spare me the nuisance of requiring a groom from the stables to escort me – for I could hardly ride out alone, for fear of being rated as careless of convention as my rival. I had planned to keep Orrock busy buttoning and rebuttoning the gray riding habit, dressing and re-dressing my hair, for as long as possible in order to give Kinross time to show up. Instead, I found myself flying through the fastening of the silver-frogged bodice with trembling fingers, while Orrock had just time to drag a comb through my hair and pile it in a casual knot on top of my head. Oh well, it was only my old friend Alastair, even if he did go by 'Lord Kinross' now. It wasn't as if I needed to fiddle with dangling ringlets and other aids to beauty for his benefit.

He probably wouldn't have noticed in any case. Like Richert, he probably still saw the hoyden of our childhood games when he looked at me, and not the young lady of Din Eidyn society.

On our way to the Park I apologized for keeping him waiting, and he assured me that I had been more prompt than any other young lady he had had the honor to escort.

Oh? And how many other young ladies would that be?

I was not, of course, so lost to propriety as to pose that question, nor did I understand the waspish feeling that led me to pose it. "I was really apologizing to your horse," I said, "for keeping it standing. I ought to have dressed immediately this morning, instead of taking time for a cup of chocolate and then scrambling into my clothes all in a hurry."

"I would hardly describe the result as having been achieved by any kind of scrambling hurry," Kinross said.

"No, you have better manners than to do so, but I know what you must be thinking!"

"I sincerely doubt that." And his eyes were very warm as he looked upon me.

It was not until we had turned into the Park that he broached the matter which had impelled him to make this appointment.

This promised to be a remarkably fine day. The early sun shone clear and turned the drops of morning dew on the grass to bright crystals, and there were, for once, no clouds hovering to promise the usual gray of a Din Eidyn summer's morning. As one might expect at this hour, the Park was remarkably thin of company; the ladies and beaux who would throng it later, riding and driving to see and be seen, were doubtless still lingering over their own chocolate and waiting until the morning chill should leave the air. I myself did not feel chilled; the blood thrummed in my veins at the sight of the all but empty path before me. "Kinross, let us have one good gallop before the crowds make it impossible!" I said, and, assuming his complaisance, clucked to Caramella and sat forward to urge her from her placid walk, first into a bouncing trot, then her much smoother canter, and finally into a flying gallop where my hat tugged on its strings, the cool fresh air bathed my face and the trees on either side of the path went by almost in a blur. I had to lay my rein on her neck just once, to encourage her to give a wide berth to some foolish nursemaid who had seen fit to shepherd her small charges right onto the bridle path; then we flew on until I drew her up right before the gates on the far side of the Park.

Kinross was some distance behind me, and when he reached the gates I teased him for being so slow.

"I paused to calm some hysterical woman who claimed you had tried to ride down the children in her care," he said with a friendly grin. "A few skillengs were remarkably effective in soothing her distress."

"I hope you also recommended her not to take the children on the principal riding path of the Park, when there are plenty of safe paths for pedestrians on either side!"

"Oh, I think she understands that now," said Kinross, turning his horse. "Let us walk the horses back now; they need to cool down slowly."

"Would not a trot suffice?" I was reluctant to give up entirely the pleasures of swift motion. Let us trot for a few moments, and I could get away with urging Caramella into a canter.

"I wish to talk with you," Kinross said, "and I do not wish to make the attempt while you are bumping up and down on that mare."

"She is as smooth-paced an animal as you could hope to see!" I defended my beloved horse.

"At walk or canter, I agree with you. Her trot, though, leaves much to be desired – but never mind that," Kinross pulled himself up short, "I do not wish to waste our morning in bickering over horseflesh!"

Neither did I; besides, if we continued this line of conversation honesty might force me to admit that Caramella's trotting pace did indeed leave something to be desired. This minor flaw seldom troubled me, for I never trotted her when we could canter. Kinross, though, who had the freedom to travel long miles on horseback rather than being immured in a stuffy carriage, would naturally consider a smooth trot a *sine qua non* in his mounts.

"Well," I said somewhat sharply, "you said you would call to make sure I was recovered from that headache, which, by the by, was an invention of Izzie's! I trust you are now reassured on that account, Kinross! So if you do not wish to discuss Caramella's paces…"

"Your supposed headache," Kinross said, "served double duty, in allowing our party to leave the theater and in giving me an excuse for calling. What I really wished to talk about was… a rather different matter."

We rode on in silence for a few paces while I fought the urge to prod him into speech. Eventually he sighed and said, "Something quite strange befell me last night. I would say that I wished to explain myself to you… but how can I explain the inexplicable? I daresay you noticed nothing odd in my manner…"

Another heavy silence ensued. Finally I broke it. "You did seem uncharacteristically eager for the company of Mrs. de Larue. Was that in order to get her out of our box and away from me? If so, I owe you my thanks."

Kinross shook his head. "I would that I deserved your gratitude, but no... if I had had the wit, I should have removed her from the box earlier, but the truth is that I could think of no way to do so. No, it was very strange, but for some minutes there I positively felt that my will was not my own! I loathe that woman, yet at the same time I felt desperately eager to remain in her company. It was that fit of madness which led me to escort her back to her own box, and to remain there until common courtesy required me to return to your party. I, I have never felt anything like it; it was as though the wine we shared intoxicated me beyond all mortal experience!"

"I think," I said slowly, "you know the explanation, Kinross. Vivienne de Larue is an herb-witch. Doubtless she had prepared a glass for Richert that was laced with charms of love and infatuation; her mistake was in giving it to you instead."

"I should like to believe any explanation that absolves me of blame," said Kinross, "but it seems most unlike the lady to make such a careless error. And if your analysis is correct, she was not only careless but incompetent; how else to account for the fact that the enchantment lasted less than half the duration of the play? Surely she would wish to entrap Dalkey for longer than that."

I bit my lip, but could see no way to avoid the confession. "Kinross... we have never spoken of this... do you know that our familiar spirit, our Hob, taught me some little magics to do with interlaced threads?"

"I had suspected as much," he said gravely, "but I know that you have too much integrity to try to ensnare a lover with such tangled magic. Dalkey is quite safe from you in that respect, is he not?"

"He is!" I was only too happy to agree. "But you see, I have been concerned that Mrs. de Larue might try something of this sort to win him back. I do not know if you have noticed his new watch fob?"

"It is difficult not to notice something so heavy with gold embroidery. Not exactly in his style, I should have thought."

It was much more comfortable to talk about the magics I had worked to protect dear Richert than to confess what I had done to Kinross last night.

"Well, you see," I explained, "the gold work is necessary to cover up the real charms. Beneath that stitching is another layer of protective charms worked in red thread, with slivers of rowan interlaced. I wanted to give him the strongest protection I might – but I dared not confess what I had done, for fear... you know... he hates and abominates all magic."

"I know," Kinross said, "but surely he would not have recognized it in your stitchery?"

"Perhaps not," I laughed, "but he would never wear anything covered in red embroidery! The red stitchery is for his protection, and the gold overlaying it is a sop to his vanity."

Kinross laughed too. "I had not thought of that aspect! Do you suppose that is why he is mad after this newly formed joint regiment of riflemen? The uniform, I understand, is dark green; far more flattering to one of his coloring than the red coats of the rest of the army!"

"Or even the lighter pink coats of the Anglians! But," I asked, suddenly worried, "is he truly serious about joining this regiment? And would that not mean his departure for Galicia?"

"Oh, his father, the old General, thinks it nothing but a boyish fancy," Kinross said, neatly evading the question of what he himself thought of the plan, "and he will certainly not give Richert the money to buy a commission on the strength of his desire to distinguish himself as a sharpshooter!"

That was reassuring, at all events.

"Though," Kinross added thoughtfully, "I wonder if such a commission might not be the making of the boy!"

"Kinross! He is no boy; he is two years older than you!"

"So he is," Kinross admitted with a surprised air. "And yet I have always felt that he was the younger of us. When we were both boys, it was his role to propose daredevil stunts and mine to persuade him out of breaking his neck."

"And now," I said, "you are both grown men who are fully capable of managing your own affairs. And I think Richert is more mature than you give him credit for. When he marries, the General will recognize that he is steadier than he had thought, and will naturally give him an allowance commensurate with his rank in society, and will entrust him with the management of the estates, and..."

"And I shall hardly recognize him in the sober married man you envision!" Kinross laughed, but he sounded rather shaken. "Well, well, it may be so. Dare I ask whether your prognostications for Dalkey's future are based on some event as yet unknown to me?"

It took me a moment to disentangle this excessively tactful inquiry. "If you mean to ask whether he has offered for me," I said bluntly when I figured it out, "the answer is no – not yet, in any event!"

"Not yet!" Kinross sounded relieved; I could not imagine why. Did he *want* Richert to be risking his life in the Galician war, rather than safe at home and happily married? What kind of friendship was that? Well, Kinross himself was a veteran of that war. Perhaps he esteemed the character-building nature of the experience more highly than I did. As a mere female, and hence ineligible to hold opinions in public affairs, I had never understood why men considered it so important to shoot and be shot at, whether on the field of honor or in a war.

"But his attentions to you recently have been so marked that he must surely, if he is a man of honor, be planning to make such an offer."

This was near the bone indeed, and to discuss the matter would be even more difficult than discussing my interference of last night.

"I fear my interest in Mr. Dalkey's affairs has led us astray," I said to turn the conversation. "I was about to confess to you, Kinross, that your sudden loss of interest in Mrs. de Larue was not exactly due to a failure of her magical attack."

"No? You surprise me."

"No." I swallowed before I could go on. "While you were in her box, it seemed to me that you might be under some compulsion. So I drew a loose thread from my dress... and wove... a tangle that would, I hoped, break that compulsion. It was... I had no time to think, much less to consult with the Hob... so I used, perforce, the only pattern I knew by heart that might overpower Mrs. de Larue's witchery."

"I am in your debt, then."

I swallowed again. "If it has had no lasting ill effects... Even so, I owe you an apology, Kinross, for working magic upon you without your permission."

"I do not see that you had any alternative," Kinross said. "As you see, I am very much unharmed by whatever little cantrip you performed... and I doubt whether I should have escaped so lightly if you had *not* offset the lady's magic with your own."

I would have been more than happy to leave it there, but Kinross and I had vowed in our youth always to be honest with each other. That he was a man full grown and a veteran of the war, and I a young lady out in Society, ought not to abrogate those vows. "It was not," I said, in so small a voice that he had to lean towards me to hear, "a small magic. It was a charm to compel your love."

"Impossible!"

"You might rather say, dishonorable! Kinross, I am sorry, I am indeed, but I could think of nothing else in the moment... and I *dared* not leave your mind enslaved to that witch's desires! Please believe that I would not otherwise have used the charm, any more than I would use it upon Richert!"

"I meant no criticism of *you*," Kinross said, "and clearly you have no need to bewitch Dalkey. I meant only that your charm can have had no effect upon me beyond that of counteracting Mrs. de Larue's witchery."

"You mean... it did not make you fall in love with me?" I felt oddly disappointed. And yet his manner this morning had hardly been that of a man enchanted.

"I can assure you, Elspet," Kinross said gravely, "that my sentiments towards you remain exactly what they were before last night's theater party."

That should have been vastly reassuring. Yet for the remainder of our ride together, and even after I returned and summoned Orrock to help me change my dress, I felt uncomfortably quiet and thoughtful. It seemed to me that I was missing some important factor in the tangle of our lives, mine and Richert's and Kinross'; something that would turn my understanding of everything quite upside-down and inside-out.

***

By Friday evening Vivienne de Larue was beginning to be seriously concerned. She had been certain that both Kinross and Richert Dalkey would call upon her as soon as possible; indeed, she had lulled herself to sleep after the theater with delicious visions of the two of them jostling in rivalry for her charms. Having some competition would surely spur Dalkey on to claim her for himself; while as for Kinross, he should be so desirous of her favorable attention that he would be easily swayed on the little matter of the war in Galicia. How much could the war matter to him, after all? His service under that Anglian, Wellesley, meant that no one could question his courage. And now that he had sold out to manage his inherited estates, it was only natural that he should disapprove of further spending on a war that only impoverished Dalriada without holding out any promise of future wealth.

Indeed, she thought that she might have accomplished her object with smiles and half-promises alone, with no need of the special wine with which she had dosed both gentlemen. But it was as well to be sure...

On Friday, as usual, there was no lack of gentlemen to pay her morning calls. Not only Lord Jenneret but also the Duke of Balcladich visited her, the latter hinting broadly that he expected to see some return on his investment. She dimpled, batted her eyelashes, and assured him that matters were well in hand.

Some hours later, after enduring the clumsy gallantry of two fashionable beaux, the loud jostling of three young sprigs of the nobility who fancied themselves Corinthians, and the platitudes of a clergyman who evidently thought her ripe for reformation, Vivienne began to feel concerned. Well, it was Friday, when the *ton* attended Gilroy's Assembly Rooms. She knew that Dalkey considered that fashionable meeting-place a dead bore filled with the husband-hunting young ladies who alarmed him; he, at least, would surely grace her rooms that night. But just to be sure, in a brief moment of leisure she dashed off a pretty little note to him, saying how much she had enjoyed the previous night and that she looked forward to his company tonight, when they could be quite alone without any of those tedious theater-goers interrupting them.

Well, 'quite alone' excepting the usual visitors to her usual card-party, but she did not count them. Unless one of the noblemen targeted by the Duke of Balcladich came, she felt free to leave the others to enjoy their gaming while she slipped away for one of those delightful tête-a-têtes with Richert Dalkey. To think she had been near to considering that young man a dead bore, with his chatter about shooting and military matters! She had even, briefly, wondered whether he was not too dull to marry. But then, he had been on the town long enough that he would hardly expect to live in her pocket once they were wed. She would be content to enjoy the social position his name brought her, while he might go about his sporting pursuits with her good will.

But that he should be snatched from her by a little, undistinguished, red-headed chit of a family that had neither great titles nor a great fortune to recommend it – *that* was not to be borne. Hence, the potion she had administered in his wine.

She received no reply to her charming note. Most likely he had been out all day and, returning only in time to dress, had decided to present himself rather than writing a billet-doux that could precede him by only a few minutes.

By midnight neither Dalkey nor Kinross had put in an appearance, and Vivienne was developing a headache as she attempted to combine gaming, light banter, and the constant undercurrent of concern about her evident failure of the previous night. The Earl of Torquhan came shortly thereafter to grace her salon, and he quickly began plunging deep as usual; unfortunately, he was not losing consistently enough to trouble him, for his pockets were as deep as the play. When her hand of loo was over, Vivienne excused herself to take a place beside Torquhan at the hazard table, where he played against her representative. She favored him with a brilliant smile and chatted brightly while he put down a rouleau of guineas on the number that had just brought him good fortune with a smaller stake. When that number failed him this time, he exploded with a curse. "The Devil's in the dice tonight! Oh… my apologies, Mrs. de Larue. But did you ever see anything more vexing than the behavior of these accursed dice?"

Since the winnings of the house financed her card parties, her fashionable dresses, and the rest of a fashionable life beyond anything Edouard de Larue's estate could support, Vivienne felt the fall of the dice was anything but vexing. But Torquhan knew this and, man-like, expected her to sympathize with him anyway.

"This is no sport for a man as clever as you," she said sympathetically, evading the question. "There is no skill involved, only blind luck – and as you say, the luck is not with you tonight. Perhaps you would prefer a game where you can exercise your brains. Would you care to try your luck at piquet?"

"Aye, if I could but find someone to play with," Torquhan grumbled.

It was no surprise that he had difficulty finding a partner for piquet, Vivienne reflected, for in truth his wits were as dull as his conversation. Yet he was a powerful man in Din Eidyn society, no naïve pigeon ripe for the plucking; few people wished to alienate the Earl by winning too much from him at a two-handed game where he could hardly blame anything but his own stupid play. So neither those who gamed for amusement nor those who sought an easy fortune were eager to play at cards with the Earl. Vivienne knew that, and felt sure that when she proposed herself as his opponent Torquhan would be only too happy to accept the challenge. Of course, she could make sure that he won just enough to make him happy, without winning so much as to cause her financial trouble… They withdrew to a little room opening off the main salon, "the better to concentrate in a battle of wits," she said with another flashing smile, and she called one of the footmen to bring a fresh pack of cards. The pack was wrapped and sealed with the name of the printers in bold type, and Torquhan made rather a business of breaking the seal; Vivienne had affixed it herself with great care. She was continually surprised that other gamesters never adopted her practice of having their own seals printed, to guarantee that the cards beneath the seal were untouched and unmarked. Perhaps they feared exposure by the printer. Vivienne had nothing to worry about there; after a sufficient quantity of seals had been made, she had offered the printer the honor of taking a glass of wine with her. She understood that his dull-witted nephew was currently running the business into the ground…

She had called the game a battle of wits, and so it could be between two equally matched players. With Torquhan, Vivienne found that the battle was to ensure that he won enough hands to keep him playing happily. She was not accustomed to using the subtly marked cards to tilt the play in *that* direction, and had to keep up a continuous line of chatter to distract him from the fact that he was losing every hand. Distraught and with an aching head, trying to monitor the fall of the cards in the Earl's favor, she had not her usual control. Against her best resolutions, Richert Dalkey's name came to her lips while she shuffled and dealt the cards.

"Dalkey? You'll not see that young sprig here tonight," Torquhan said as she dealt. And then, after taking a look at his hand. "I declare a *carte blanche*," and he spread out his cards face-up so that she could see he held no court cards.

Vivienne bit her lip. She had intended the Earl to receive a better hand than that. Were her fingertips losing their sensitivity to the invisible indentations on the backs of the cards? Or had she been distracted by his firm declaration that Dalkey would not visit her house that night?

"A poor hand for play, my lord," she said, "but you have the consolation of an immediate ten points, have you not?" She marked down the compensatory score to Torquhan's credit. "You were saying… about Mr. Dalkey?" She could not keep herself from returning to the painful subject.

"Ah, yes. I looked in at Gilroy's Assembly Rooms before coming here." The Earl snorted. "What a squeeze! And the young folk have all gone mad after that detestable romping dance imported from Allemania, this so-called *waltz*. I never in my life saw something so unbecoming as that bevy of maidens and matrons growing red-faced and short of breath as their thoughtless partners swing them hither and yon! I shall exchange three cards."

Vivienne was so eager to get Torquhan back to the subject of Dalkey that she positively dealt all three cards right off the top of the deck, without even checking to see if she could slip in a card from lower down that would improve his hand.

"I take it you saw Mr. Dalkey at the Assembly Rooms?"

"Oh, yes, the young fool was there, capering about as wildly as any of them! I do not know what ails these folk, that they cannot be satisfied with a minuet in a time slow enough to permit of the graceful positions which we learned in *my* younger days! Now it is nothing but quadrille, waltz, quadrille, waltz, in monotonous succession."

"I daresay Mr. Dalkey will find the Assembly Rooms as boring as you did, my lord, and so I do not yet despair of seeing him join this company. Gilroy's, after all, lacks a card room to hold his attention, and I do not think he is a man to be amused solely by dancing. He has often complained to me that the Assembly Rooms are a deadly dull collection of husband-hunting maidens and their scheming mothers."

"Oh, he seemed happy enough to me. The little Rattray girl was there, and you know the betting in my club is five to three that he declares for her before the end of the Season. A *quint*," said the Earl, showing a sequence of five cards.

Vivienne looked in dismay at her own hand, but she could not deny what it showed. "*Quatorze*," she said, and laid down the four Queens.

"By God, my luck here is worse than at hazard!"

"But here," Vivienne said, offering him the deck, "a man of your brilliance can easily recover from these small setbacks."

But in Torquhan's hands, the deal was honest and Vivienne had only her own luck to thank for an opening hand so brilliant that she would be hard put to it to lose to her opponent. She discarded her five best cards and received in exchange five more that actually improved her hand.

While Torquhan brooded over his own discards, pulling out first one card and then putting it back in favor of another, she listened for the sound of any late-coming arrivals. Surely Richert would not forego her company in favor of dull dances with girls whose only interest was to catch him as a husband!

And is that not your interest as well? whispered a mocking voice at the back of her aching head.

He and Kinross had both been well dosed last night. Why had the potion not drawn them both to her house? Had she erred in the compounding, thanks to Jenneret's interruption? Or – the more likely answer flashed upon her – perhaps when on a sudden inspiration she had divided the potion into two parts, giving each man half the dose originally prepared for Dalkey alone, neither of them had taken enough to ensure a lasting effect? Well, she had plenty left, and an ideal opportunity to test it right here.

In anticipation of that test, she played automatically and won far more handily than could please the Earl.

"Piqued, repiqued, and capotted!" he exclaimed, his brow thundery. "Mrs. de Larue, it is hardly feminine to play so extremely well!"

"Indeed, blame me not," Vivienne coaxed, "for I'm sure I have not the wit to defeat so skilled a player as yourself. 'Twas but that the fall of the cards was most unlucky for you. I vow, not the best gamester here could have won with the hands that you were dealt."

"It were time to change my luck, then," grumbled Torquhan. "Perhaps at another house…"

"You'll not leave here when you're angry with me?" Vivienne pleaded. "Indeed, my lord, it would break my heart to lose your friendship over such a trifling accident. Let you take a glass of wine with me, and I'm sure your fortunes will change."

Her luck did, at any rate, for after drinking the glass Vivienne had gone herself to procure – and to prepare – the Earl of Torquhan was full of compliments for her bright eyes and charming smile, and professed himself ready to lose at piquet the entire night for the sake of keeping her company to himself. "Besides," he said, "I have turned my coat inside out, and everyone knows that is the surest way to defeat a run of ill luck."

That, Vivienne thought, and his partner's full attention to the cards. Now that her potion's strength had been proved on the Earl, her mind was somewhat at rest. Clearly the doses she had administered to Dalkey and Kinross had been insufficient. She would do better next time… and for the present, she would make sure that the Earl of Torquhan won just enough to keep him cheerful. And while he was in this melting mood and desirous of agreeing with her, she could also make her case in favor of the Peace Party. What did Balcladich care whether she won over his four opponents by argument, debt, or ensorcelment? Results were all he cared about, and she still felt sure that she could deliver those results.

Chapter 13

The great ballroom of Gilroy's Assembly Rooms blazed with candles that Friday night, making a show as fine as anything I had seen in the theater. It was unfortunate that at the last minute, while I was having my hair dressed for the occasion, I had received a gift which I needed to think about, rather than being obliged to laugh and smile and mind my steps on the dance floor.

"And best of all," Izzie said as she seated herself by me with a little sigh of relief, "*here*, at least, unlike the Water Gardens, we know that the company is most select. Hussies like that de Larue woman will never get vouchers allowing them entry to Gilroy's!"

I winced at the reminder of my *faux pas*, and Izzie actually apologized after a fashion. "That was not meant to twit you on your mistakes, Elspet; I sincerely hope that business may be over and done with now. But as your chaperone, you must see how *restful* it is for me to go somewhere where I am not supposed to be shielding you from improper encounters!"

"You may have your work cut out for you here too," I said, scanning the throng. "Sophie Westlin's brother is here tonight, and so is Mr. Norval Petrie."

"Both of whom," Izzie said serenely, "are received everywhere."

"Well, if you *wish* me to dance with a gamester and gazetted fortune-hunter, or with an old roué who puts his hands all over every girl he gets close to, I suppose you need not worry!"

"Do not be so missish, Elspet. Considering your usual habits, you are the last person I should expect to hear preaching propriety! Ranald Westlin may dance with you, but he will hardly hang upon your skirts; your dowry would not even begin to cover his debts, let alone assuring him a comfortable life! As for Mr. Petrie… if *you* behave yourself, I'll wager he will not dare to go beyond the line. Not with a Rattray!"

I wished I could be quite as sure of that as she was, for Mr. Petrie showed every sign of having noticed our entrance and of approaching us from across the crowded room.

Izzie stretched out one foot and wriggled her toes luxuriously. "My feet hardly hurt at all in these slippers you stitched up for me. They are beyond anything comfortable – and light into the bargain! You are handy with your needle, Elspet, I must grant you that, even if I fail to agree that the results are positively magical."

I hardly heard the half-compliment; Mr. Petrie was coming closer. Damp hands, red face, and a habit of standing much too close – ugh! I'd as soon dance with the wicked Baron Jenneret, not that he was like to make an appearance in such respectable company. "Perhaps, if your feet do not hurt, *you* would care to dance with Mr. Petrie?"

"In my condition? Do not be ridiculous, Elspet! I am only here to look after you."

I could not help reflecting that 'looking after' me really should include finding a way for me to avoid Mr. Petrie's solicitation. At least the next dance was a country dance, and one whose figures hardly required us even to touch our fingertips. As we were first couple in the set, he was called upon to use both hands to turn the lady of the third couple and I did the same with her partner. That gentleman was young Mr. Coates, who favored me with a grimace that I took to be expressive of his sympathy. After that opening move, Mr. Petrie and I separated to lead down the set and never joined hands save in the circles left and right, which gave him scant opportunity to become over-familiar.

When I resumed my seat, I found that Izzie had deserted me to join a group of matrons whose heads and ostrich plumes were nodding as eagerly as their lips moved – doubtless retailing the latest *on-dit* about some lady's indiscretions and the probable parentage of her child. I had no desire to hear such gossip and was only happy that I could be sure Izzie's own behavior could never lead to her being pilloried in the court of censorious matrons.

Her place beside me had been taken by Dorothea Turvoll, who had evidently just arrived; at one moment she was all blushes and downcast eyes before the beaux who leveled their quizzing-glasses at her, and the next she was looking about her eagerly. "I am so happy to see you, Miss Rattray!" she exclaimed. "Aunt Turvoll has quite deserted me, and it is – not quite comfortable to be altogether alone on my first visit to the Assembly Rooms. I expect you know everybody here, so it is different for you."

I looked at Dorothea with satisfaction. Her blushes and excitement lent a becoming animation to her face which did much to improve her features; her hair was dressed with only two or three times the ropes of pearls that would have been appropriate; and best of all, the ball gown designed by Olympe showed off her charming figure and distracted attention from her long face. More pearls encircled her neck and dangled from her ears, but at least she was not decked out in all those sparkling rubies in their heavy, old-fashioned setting. Really, even without the aid of the charms I had stitched into her skirt, she could surely hope to attract a decent selection of partners.

I saw "Beau" Farquhar approaching and sighed inwardly. The Beau's attentions were invaluable to keep a young lady at the head of the fashionable set, but just now I had rather think about how to handle Patrice-Henri's surprising gift than make light conversation about nothing with that conversable gentleman.

Well, I need not have worried. Mr. Farquhar's eyes had been fixed on me when he approached, but when he was actually standing before us he blinked in surprise, looked at the embroidered hem of Dorothea's gown, raised his eyes to her face and solicited her hand for the next dance. Radiant, Dorothea rose and joined him on the dancing floor. Hmm. Had I slightly overdone the charms bespangling her gown? I could not even be happy to be spared the distraction of the dance, for Mr. Coates discovered me in time for us to join the same set as Dorothea and Mr. Farquhar. Between minding the figures of the dance and nodding in reply to Mr. Coates' disjointed remarks about hunting, I had no chance to think about what Patrice-Henri wanted of me, and which I could see no way to perform.

One did not, of course, come to Gilroy's Assembly Rooms to *think*. One came to see and be seen, to make valuable social connections, to compare one's dresses and jewels and partners to those of other young ladies – all the frippery stuff that I had until recently found so fascinating! Now, with a dark puzzle waiting for me at home, and with no hope of encountering Richert Dalkey here, I found that the Assembly had little to recommend it. Was I becoming so steeped in magic that I had forgotten how to enjoy life without it?

Dorothea was certainly enjoying life much more thanks to the good effects of my threadwork. She did not lack for partners after Mr. Farquhar; there was not a country-dance played in the next two hours that did not see her forming part of one set or another. She was not even condemned to sit alone during the waltzes which she had not yet been approved to dance; Major Maddox, whose war wound made him ineligible to dance, was eager to have her sit out those dances with him. Now that *was* strange. Why had Major Maddox decided to come to a place where the only entertainment was dancing? He could not have been allured hither by the light network of enchantments I had applied to Dorothea's gown, for observation had shown me that the charms' power fell off with distance. A gentleman had to be standing within a few feet of her to be affected.

It would have been most unmannerly of me to keep watching the door, rather than paying attention to my partners. Besides, I already knew that Richert would not trouble himself to make an appearance here. He was too well-bred to lounge around the ballroom without inviting girls to dance in a place where that was the only amusement, and too well versed in self-protection to put himself in a situation where he would be expected to choose from a bevy of marriage-minded young ladies. I had enough strength of mind to keep my eyes on the other dancers and my mind on the music, and so I was taken by surprise to hear Dorothea Turvoll's ecstatic sigh just as Ranald Westlin returned me to my seat after an energetic waltz.

"*Mr. Dalkey,*" she breathed.

Major Maddox, who had been sitting out this waltz with her like all the others, looked as displeased as I was surprised. But it was indeed Richert, his red hair shining in the candlelight of the entry way, his head raised as he scanned the hall this way and that. And Alastair – I mean, *Lord Kinross* – was with him. Dorothea sighed again, blissfully, when Richert led the way towards us as though he had found what he was searching for – and I felt a moment's horrid uncertainty. What if he, too, were affected by the stitchery I had worked on Dorothea's gown? Could I stage an accident and put my foot through the trailing rose silk to break the lines of the charm?

But he passed Dorothea with only a civil nod, and bowed to me. Of course – he was, as always, wearing the watch fob I had given him as a token of our pretended love. The slivers of rowan and the tangles of red thread concealed under the gold work were doing their job, protecting him against all enchantments.

Even mine.

And so, if he chose to come directly to me, to make his bow and ask me to stand up with him, it was all his own decision and a sign of how much he valued me.

Or, as he reminded me as we took our place in the next set, of how much he wanted me to protect him from Dorothea Turvoll's foolish, languishing ways.

"Mama has been giving me the rough side of her tongue," he explained when I expressed my surprise at seeing him there. "She said that after I had been paying you such marked attentions, it would be most unmannerly in me not to join you here; bad enough that I did not escort you and your sister here in the first place! And she was quite right," he said. "I should have thought of it myself."

I would have been happy enough if he had stopped there, but being Richert, he had to go on. "Can't expect the Turvoll chit to take my courtship of you seriously if I don't act more serious about it myself! So Kinross and I thought we'd just take a look-in here before the doors closed for the evening."

I thought that in that case, it was a pity he had not waited to solicit my hand for the next dance, which was a waltz. Not that I feared being without a partner, but I should have enjoyed being clasped in Richert's arms for the duration of the dance. Instead, we made our way through the figures of the country dance while I observed Dorothea's progress with Kinross through the second set. It would be a pity, I thought, if he were to become enmeshed by the little charms I had added to improve Dorothea's social success; I wished the girl well, but Kinross was far too good for her.

Besides – and this must really have been my first consideration, even if it only occurred to me second – once she formed an attachment to someone else, Richert would no longer trouble with even a pretense of courting me. It was far too soon for this to happen; I had not even begun to get his attention!

As the measures of the dance came to a close, we happened to be standing next to Kinross and Dorothea. Lady Dalkey swept through the hall, her tall headdress of ostrich plumes dancing to her graceful steps. She took Richert's hand and, with a cool nod to me, introduced him to Dorothea as a desirable partner for the next dance.

I thought the girl might faint from ecstasy. Her first waltz at Gilroy's – and in the arms of the man she imagined would be her own true love! I could not repress a slight pang of envy; how much I should have loved to have been in her place! But even though I had been given the nod to waltz some weeks ago, I had to watch my love dancing off with that silly girl and to settle for the brotherly partnership of Alastair... I mean, *Lord Kinross*.

Not that I had any grounds for complaint; although circumstances had all but forced Kinross to ask me for this waltz, he was too well-bred to show regret at losing his previous partner. It would, of course, have been as ineligible for them to have danced two consecutive dances together as for Richert and me to have done the same. And since I had better manners than to let my own disappointment show, I could hardly expect to read in Kinross' face whether or not he minded exchanging Dorothea for me.

I was, though, surprised into a stumble when, with the first bars of the waltz, he smiled down at me and said, "I have to thank you for my rescue!"

"I – I, my lord?"

"From the task of making conversation with Miss Turvoll. I wish Richert may not call me out for this turn of events; he is unlucky indeed, having to steer her around the ballroom while I enjoy your company!"

"A great many gentlemen have thought themselves fortunate to gain Miss Turvoll's hand for a dance tonight," I said, wishing that I dared ask him why he seemed so unaffected by the thread magic in Dorothea's gown. "Major Maddox is more like than Richert to call you out; until Lady Dalkey gave Dorothea permission to waltz just now, he had been sitting out all those dances with her!"

"Had he?" Kinross sounded quite indifferent. "Perhaps they will make a match of it."

"Would that please you?"

"It's nothing to me one way or another, but it would be a relief to Richert."

"Would it?"

His gaze seemed to sharpen. "Would it not?"

The music grew faster; we whirled, stepped back, spun in place. What had we been talking about? It did not seem to matter; I gave myself up to the pleasure of moving with a partner whose steps so perfectly matched mine. I had been foolish, trying to manage every last detail of the evening. I was happy to be dancing with Kinross now, and later on, no doubt, I should have the intoxicating pleasure of a waltz with Richert... but all that mattered now was this moment, this music, this waltz. As we spun round the ballroom I felt inexplicably happy, as though all the threads of my life were spinning harmoniously together –

"*Spinning!*" I exclaimed as the music drew to a close.

"I beg your pardon!" Kinross sounded startled.

"Oh... nothing. I'm sorry, it was just a stray thought, nothing important." Not to him, at any rate. But the inspiration left me jubilant. Of course! Threads – or anything else – that were too short to stitch, could be spun into something longer and stronger. Tonight – no, first thing tomorrow – I would have to see if Kirsty knew where the old spinning wheel was stored.

Chapter 14

"But, my dear Elspet, why should you want to use the spinning wheel *now*, of all times?"

Kirsty's bemusement was reasonable. In our schoolroom days, Izzie and I had vastly resented her insistence that spinning was one of the womanly arts which all females ought to master. Perhaps in the distant days of Kirsty's own youth that had been the case, but in the modern era, it made no sense. First the spinning jenny, and now the water frame, had rendered the laborious task of spinning one thread at a time obsolete. When the latter machine could create over a hundred threads at once, each one stronger than that produced by a spinster at her wheel – when the dizzying, clacking looms in manufactories such as that of Dorothea Turvoll's father positively demanded such a rate of production – what was a spinning wheel good for, and why should Izzie and I ruin our eyesight and blister our fingers in the effort to produce a single weak thread that would never have been acceptable in Mr. Turvoll's mill? The thing was nothing but a picturesque accessory for the antiquarian, the painter, or the teller of folk tales.

"My friends and I were talking over the olden days last night, at the dance," I began, feeling my way to a tale that would satisfy Kirsty, "and, and, ah, Sophie Westlin wagered me—"

"Elspet! I am shocked! A young lady should never *gamble*!" Kirsty interrupted.

"Oh, money does not enter into it," I assured her as my story came clear to me. "Say rather, if you like, that Sophie *challenged* the rest of us to a sort of spinning competition; we are each to see what kind of a thread we can produce without the aid of any modern machinery. And it is a pity that we did not bet money, at that," I said to further distract her, "for thanks to your tutelage, I am sure that I can outdo the girls who had not the benefit of such a conscientious governess!"

Dear Kirsty loved compliments as well as any other woman, and far too few of them had ever come her way. In between telling me where the spinning wheel was stored (the third attic over the housemaids' quarters) and pressing me to accept a bundle of unspun wool (unnecessary, but I could hardly refuse without calling into question my entire parcel of lies) she blushed, smiled, and thanked me with tears in her eyes for bringing back the memories of those happy days when she had overseen Izzie and me at the wheel. (Her memory was somewhat different from mine; I had not been happy at all about the spinning lessons, nor had Izzie.)

I left her with some degree of difficulty and a greater degree of guilt. Boring and tiresome though Kirsty's spinning lessons had been, she had taught us a great deal that was important to us now. French, Italian, German, the rules of aristocratic address and precedency, and the use of the globes might not be explicitly required of young ladies of the *ton*, but ignorance on these subjects would have been humiliating. For that matter, without Kirsty's intervention I suspected Mama would never have gotten around to hiring a music master; those lessons had been little use to me, but for Izzie they had been invaluable. Sir Joshua had first been attracted to her by the graceful attitudes and sweet, low singing voice that she demonstrated at the great harp. Indeed, Kirsty had put far more effort than anyone else in the household into seeing that Izzie and I were prepared to take our places in adult society. I vowed that I would visit her more frequently in future, would dedicate an hour or so to reminiscing with her; she deserved far more attention than that for the care she had taken of us!

For now, though, I was all eagerness to try the idea that had come to me the previous night.

The attic where I found the spinning wheel had clearly been used as a storage room for all manner of furniture which was too shabby even for the servants' quarters, or which needed repairs that no one had bothered to put in hand; not to mention boxes and trunks containing everything from winter cloaks to discarded masques from some long-past carnival. Scattered among the rubbish I glimpsed some things that members of my family had complained of missing since we removed to the town house this year: Mama's favorite silver infusing pot, Izzie's small Irish harp. Perhaps we girls should have paid more attention to Kirsty's strictures on the duty of a lady to oversee her household. I had no doubt that in a more well-regulated household the family's possessions would not be carelessly lumped in with rubbish for want of anybody to organize them. And Mama, of course, was the last person to organize anybody or anything. Kirsty had been right when she sought to train us to take over the burdens Mama never even recognized; certainly somebody needed to oversee the servants in this matter!

The long, low-ceilinged room was dim, and even after I squeezed past the table with the broken leg and dragged the wheel next to the one window, there was hardly light enough for me to see my work. Fortunately for me, Kirsty had been a strict task-mistress; I did not need to see, only to let the tips of my fingers feel what I was doing.

With trembling fingers I opened the small bundle which Patrice-Henri had conveyed to me when he came to dress my hair for the Assembly Rooms the previous night. I had, of course, already inspected the contents; that was what had set me in such a puzzle last night. Now I verified by touch what I remembered seeing. The crisply curling strands of golden hair were too fine for me to make out individual strands in this dim light, but I could run my thumb and forefinger along any one strand. The hairs were still far too short for me to work any thread magic with them in their present state; the longest was barely eighteen inches long, and most were less than half that length.

"I dressed Marguerite Fauchet's hair for her funeral," Patrice-Henri had said when he thrust the little bundle at me. "I saved these as – I don't know – a memorial, I thought; I would have somebody make me a mourning brooch from her hair. I loved her, you know. Oh, I knew fine it could come to nothing; she might not have despised me, but that sister of hers was determined both of them should make good marriages and rise in society. A mere hair-dresser would have been wholly contemptible in her eyes. And in any case..." He sighed. "Once she set eyes on Edouard de Larue, there was no hope for me or any other man! The two of them..."

"A sort of golden glow about them, my sister Izzie said."

Patrice-Henri nodded. "I told myself a hundred times to stop torturing myself, to tell the Fauchet girls to find some other hair-dresser, to leave Din Eidyn and emigrate to some barbarous colony where I need never hear Marguerite's laugh nor see her smiling at Edouard... but I could not do it... and so it was I who rendered her the last service that ever I could. Her tresses were so rich and full, and so curly, I had to thin them to make her look like a proper fine lady in the coffin. But I could not throw them away... I never did commission the brooch... and now..." He looked hopeful. "Olympe said that you knew a magic that you could work with threads. Perhaps you could do it with Marguerite's hair?"

"To do what, exactly?" I touched one of the shorn locks; it curled and clung to my fingers as if still alive. I shivered and withdrew my hand. "I am sorry, but these are far too short for me to stitch them into any kind of charm."

"There must be *something* you can do!"

"Patrick," I said, using his birth name instead of the assumed Lutécian version, "No one can bring Marguerite back to life – in any event, *I* could not, no matter how much of her hair you brought me. I only know a little thread magic for influencing how people feel. To revive the dead would take much more magic than I ever knew." I refrained from saying that even if I had the knowledge, I was not fool enough to dabble in such matters. Herb-witches like the Duchess of Quoy and Vivienne de Larue might think themselves powerful enough to meddle with the boundaries between life and death; I did not so overestimate my own capabilities.

Patrice-Henri nodded soberly. "I did not expect so much. But if I could but hear her laugh once more... if I could speak to her and know she forgives me that I was not there to save her from the stream..."

I shook my head. "Even that is beyond me." And I closed up the bundle and offered it back to him.

He put his hands behind his back. "No – no, keep it. Perhaps you will think of something. And in any case, I – I think it is better for me to leave it with you."

That, at least, was probably true. He could have done himself no good by brooding over this dead girl's relics for years. Perhaps, if he left the bundle of cropped curls with me, he would free himself at last from this obsession.

But what should I do with them?

Put the bundle away at the back of a drawer, and forget it.

But I had been teased by the notion that there was something I might yet accomplish with the pitiful relics. I'd meant to consult the Hob, but he had not made himself available after the dance last night. And this morning I had been in too much of a hurry to ask Kirsty for the spinning wheel to wait around for him to drop in on me.

Now I fed the curling hair through my hands and around the bobbin, creating a fine, bright, resilient cord while the turning of the great wheel kept all in motion. This much, at least, was working!

The room seemed even darker than before, though I could see bright sunshine through the small rippled panes of the window. Outside, sunlight sparkled on the rain-wet tiles of the roofs of the lower part of the house, slid down dripping gutters to dance in puddles and shoot back upward as reflected brightness. In this attic, shadows collected around me until I could barely see my own hands. Only the coiling mass of hair that was turning into a strong thread glowed as if with its own light.

The last tendrils of Marguerite Fauchet's hair slipped through my hands. My foot left the treadle and the great wheel spun to a halt. The bobbin was full of the eerily glowing thread of my spinning. I took the free end and gently transferred it to my fingers, drawing the cord free of the spinning wheel and around my own hands, and the back of my neck prickled with a cold chill.

There was ghostly music in the air!

And I had not yet fashioned the spun cord into any kind of a charm or pattern.

Was I listening to the song of a dead woman?

And where would it lead me?

Suddenly I could not wait to get away from this shadowy attic. I wrapped my skirt around the skein of spun hair and sidled back through the maze of furniture, only pausing to snatch up Izzie's small harp – she would be glad to have that back – as for Mama's silver pot, it was out of my reach and could wait for another day. A day with sunshine bright enough to penetrate that little window and dispel the gloom. Or a day when I would come here accompanied by a nice, stout footman to light my way with a branch of candles, some down-to-earth and commonplace serving man who had never in his life heard faerie music in the air.

The mirror atop my dressing table was swinging back and forth when I returned to my bedchamber.

"Hob," I addressed the air over the mirror, "what can I do with this?" Leaving Izzie's little harp on the table, I brought out the spun cord and held it up to show him. "It is too thick to stitch with." Now that I thought it over, I remembered that in all those boring lessons neither Izzie nor I had ever succeeded in spinning a thread that should be fine and smooth enough for stitchery, even woolen work on coarse fabric. We had never been permitted to waste materials in attempting to create a bright silken thread such as those I used for the Hob's patterns of thread magic.

"Leave it with me," said the deep voice emanating from just above the mirror. "You are wanted downstairs. Morning callers," he added. That was more of an explanation than he usually deigned to give me. That fact should have put me on my guard, but it did not.

"I had not realized it had been so late! Oh, will you *stop* swinging on the mirror for a moment?" I tried to brush the cobwebs from my sleeves and restore some order to my ringlets. How could I possibly have been so long in the attics? One of our old nurse's stories flashed through my mind: the gentleman who had been enticed by the music to enter the fairy hill, and who had come out in the morning to find his friends and family long dead, his lady love turned to dust, and no one at all left alive who knew him. Then there was the woman who had been called upon to midwife one of the Good People, and who had escaped a similar fate only by calling upon the Holy Name and by the fact that she was wearing a cross of rowan wood... But this was nonsense! I had not been wandering in enchanted lands, or consorting with the Fair Folk; I had only dawdled somewhat too long in a dusty attic.

"You have a smut on your nose," said the Hob helpfully.

I dabbed at my face and made my escape to help Mama and Izzie entertain our callers.

It seemed, that day, as though our entire acquaintance in Din Eidyn wished to call and talk over the events of last night's Assembly. Dorothea Turvoll's sudden popularity came in for much mention, as did the attentions paid me by Richert Dalkey and Alastair, Lord Kinross. I was hard put to it to keep my countenance when Richert was mentioned, but their coupling of Kinross' name with mine showed that my mother's gossips had no clue as to the real state of affairs; they thought Kinross' politeness as significant as Richert's much more marked attentions.

In a way, I suppose, they were right about that. Certainly Richert still showed no more signs of being really in love with me than did Kinross.

Last night, however, seemed to have awakened him to the importance of continuing our charade. Quite likely Lady Dalkey's somewhat high-handed action, in virtually forcing him to solicit Dorothea Turvoll's hand for the waltz, had reminded him that his supposed courtship of me was still his best defense against Dorothea's languishing. In any case, he sent round a very proper note entreating me to ride out with him. We had so many callers that I had barely time to slip upstairs and change into my riding dress before he was expected. The Hob seemed to have taken himself off somewhere, thank goodness, so Orrock was able to lace me up and smooth my hair under a nice, tight hat without distraction. I myself barely noted some slight change in the clutter upon the dressing table; all my attention was bent on making sure that Richert would notice that he was riding with a personable young lady, not with someone he still saw as his annoying little sister.

Orrock grumbled that lacing so tightly was pointless, for the cut of the riding dress would not change and would not show off the exaggerated curves so produced – and a good thing too, she pronounced darkly, for it would hardly have been decent!

The abominable thing was that she was quite right. There was no point in torturing myself to create such a feminine silhouette; it was only muffled by the cut and fabric of my costume. With a quiet sigh of relief I allowed her to loosen the laces. At least I should be able to enjoy my ride in comfort – and after all, it was not as if I really needed the tight lacing. A survey in the looking-glass reassured me that I did, after all, have curves sufficient to impress any man who had his eyes open, and that my waist could no longer be described in the unflattering terms Richert had once used. I was not *pudgy* or *dumpy* now, nor was my figure in the least *immature*.

But oh, if he could look at my unhandsome younger self with such clear eyes, why could he not see the slim, attractive young woman that my mirror assured me I had become? I might never be deemed an Incomparable like my great-grandmother, but surely I was worthy of Richert's affection?

Perhaps today would be the day when he finally did see me as I was now. The hope buoyed me up as I flew downstairs again, to find him and Kinross chatting with Izzie in the drawing-room. I made my apologies for being late, lowered my head and glanced up at Richert through the lashes that Orrock had just artfully darkened… and found him gazing out of the window.

Fool that he was, to be so blind! Fool that I was, to think anything I did could shake him out of his self-absorption!

Kinross, it was true, paid me the compliments I had hoped to hear from Richert, but that hardly improved my mood. Nor did the revelation that he meant to accompany us. Nor did Izzie's coy hints that the gentlemen were competing for my attention. After all, I knew how untrue that was. Neither of them cared a straw for me in that way!

On this fine afternoon the Park was crowded, and I was constrained to ride as decorously as even Richert could have desired. With Kinross attending us, I could think of nothing to do to compel Richert's attention. We all three chatted about trivialities and I returned home, if possible, more frustrated than when I had left. Caramella, I think, was equally frustrated; my spirited mare expected something more than a sedate walk along the riding path when I took her out. She would doubtless be happy when we returned to the country after the close of the Season, and I – well, I dared not think on that.

Even the pleasure of riding freely over the moors would hardly compensate me for the death of my hopes for Richert. For the first time, that afternoon, I began to fear that even this game of courtship that we played would not awaken him to my existence as a woman.

Upon my belated return home, I was pounced upon by Mama, Izzie and Kirsty all together. Had I forgotten that we were to dine early because Mama had decided to host a musical evening?

Well, yes, I had. There *had* been a few other things to think about that day, hadn't there? But I could scarcely excuse myself on the grounds that I had been frightened by spinning a cord of human hair that shivered with ghostly music, or that I had subsequently been cudgeling my wits to find some way of making Richert notice me. The first was scarcely something to share with the rest of my family, and as for the second – well, no more could I share the secret that Richert's courtship was still, disappointingly, only a charade to discourage Dorothea Turvoll from languishing after him. In my family's view, I had spent an excessively pleasant afternoon out riding with a charming young man who was inexplicably entranced with me, and had selfishly prolonged that afternoon to such a point that I would now have to choose between bathing and eating dinner.

Neither Richert nor Kinross had mentioned Mama's musicale to me, so I assumed they did not mean to attend; it was hardly the sort of entertainment to attract lively young men.

For that matter, it did not attract me either. I looked forward with little pleasure to an evening of pretending to listen to Izzie at the harp while trying to subdue the annoying complaints of my empty stomach.

I would have been fortunate indeed if that had been all I had to deal with.

Chapter 15

As for Mama, she was annoyed beyond measure that when she finally did exert herself to some social duties, I forgot the event and returned too late to dine with the family. She snapped that I would have to content myself with a cup of soup brought me by Orrock while I dressed. Of the three of us, only Izzie was in good humor enough to play the hostess gracefully.

She danced through my chamber while Orrock was arranging my still-damp ringlets. "These slippers which you made have done me more good than I thought possible, Elspet! Dare I beg you to contrive another such pair, or will you require that I pretend first to think the magic is in the embroidery and not in your clever fingers? Oh, and thank you for finding my small harp! Where was it?"

And she wafted herself out of the room before I could answer. Was that the difference I had half-noticed earlier about my dressing table – that the harp was no longer there? I closed my eyes and tried to conjure up a picture of the table as it was when I had dressed for riding. No, the harp had still been there. But – the broken strings were not. It had been new-strung... with bright, crisp wires made up of a hundred coiling strands of golden hair. Why had that not alarmed me? I must have been in too much of a hurry to dress.

And now, if I understood Izzie aright, she was in possession of that harp with its strings spun from a dead girl's hair, strings that hummed of themselves, that sucked out all the light and warmth from the air around them. What else could they do?

I'd been a fool to leave that cord spun from Marguerite Fauchet's hair with the Hob. And he, evidently, had been careless enough to leave the new-strung harp out on the table, where Izzie must have found it while I was wasting a golden afternoon in trotting sedately up and down the Park between Kinross and Richert.

I hastened downstairs to find Mama already receiving the first of our guests, while Izzie sat at the great harp and plucked its strings to make sure of the tuning.

The great harp – not the little Irish one. Good; the situation might yet be salvaged.

Just to make sure, I asked Izzie, "Did you find your Irish harp?"

She laughed at me. "Why, Elspet, you know I did! Have I not already thanked you for discovering my little harp and having it new-strung?"

"But you will not use it tonight?"

"Certainly not," said Izzie. "It is only a toy, suitable for nothing more than the simplest of folk songs. Our guests deserve more serious entertainment than that! Celeste has been invited to sing German *lieder* to her own accompaniment on the pianoforte, and I shall play a new Italian concerto for the great harp."

"That," I said with more enthusiasm than I could usually muster for Izzie's music, "sounds like a plan of entertainment that could hardly be bettered!"

And maybe, while Izzie was busy with the concerto, I could slip up to her room and steal back that little harp – no – there it was, sitting on the pianoforte. "I'll just put this away for you, then, shall I?"

But Mama's friends were already coming into the drawing-room. Even as we spoke, she was greeting the Duke of Balcladich with great pleasure and saying that she must make him known to her daughters. Papa and the Duke might disagree on some political issues, but ladies did not take account of mere politics, and to have attracted such a distinguished guest was a social triumph for Mama. No, it was too late for me to dispose of that ill-omened harp without being noticed.

A moment after the introductions to the Duke, Celeste Jamison and her tall, serious husband arrived and must also be greeted. Before I could get my breath a flood of other guests poured in, the servants were handing round light refreshments and I found myself trapped between Cecy Lauder and Sophie Westlin, with a plate of iced cakes in my hand.

Oh, well. The cakes were very tasty, particularly to someone who had been taking healthful exercise in the Park all afternoon and had barely tasted a cup of soup while dressing for this event. Sophie was her usual entertaining self, chattering away with the gossip of the day so fast that even I had trouble slipping in more than an "Indeed!" or "You don't say!" And Cecilia Lauder, who like Izzie boasted harp-playing as her principal accomplishment, looked with longing upon our ivory-painted great harp with its fluted column picked out in gold leaf. She hinted that should Izzie's condition make her too tired to sit long at the harp, she would be happy to help out. She had just been practicing a series of dances arranged for the harp by Boccherini...

All in all, things could be worse. When Celeste sat down at the pianoforte, of course, manners obliged Sophie and Cecy to fall silent. But I still had the iced cakes for entertainment – and, of course, Celeste's singing, though the scraps of the German language that Kirsty had managed to cram into my head were barely sufficient for me to follow the sense of the songs. There did not seem to be much sense to them in any case; all were the lovelorn complaints of some youth who appeared to be too unenterprising even to introduce himself to the object of his adoration. "I do not see," I remarked to Sophie during a pause between songs, "that he has much right to complain. How is his beloved supposed to remark his feelings, when she does not even know his name?"

"But it is so sad, and so beautiful!" Sophie said.

Celeste began another plaintive song, and I was cast back upon my own thoughts for company. I had, perhaps, little right myself to make fun of the lovesick narrator. What good had all my own enterprise done me? Richert knew my name, he had spent hours in my company – nay, at my elbow, or dancing or riding with me – yet he still did not know *me*, and I feared he never would.

It would have been expecting too much of Richert that he should subject himself to so tame an entertainment as this evening's little concert simply to bolster the pretense that he was in love with me; after all, he had already dedicated the afternoon to escorting me around the Park. I told myself it was a relief not to have to worry about finding or making another occasion to catch his interest.

That may have been true, but it was also uncommonly dull.

My spirits rose extremely when, in the interval of conversation after Celeste's songs, some late-coming arrivals were admitted. I saw Kinross' dark, serious face among the late-comers. Was it possible that he and Richert –

Well, no. Above the hubbub of genteel conversation, I could hear Kinross apologizing to Mama for his lateness. And in almost the same breath, he conveyed Richert's regrets – a prior engagement – he would be most sorry to have missed hearing Lady Herriot's harp-playing.

So much for Richert! All the same, I felt much more cheerful than I had at the commencement of the evening. I felt sure that Kinross would make his way to my side sooner or later, and he would be much more entertaining company than Cecy or Sophie. And Izzie was even now seating herself at the harp. There had not been even the breath of a suggestion that she might be more comfortable playing on the smaller instrument; it lay neglected on the pianoforte. We might get through this evening without disaster after all.

It might even be *fun*. Kinross was coming my way now. What a good thing I had already polished off the iced cakes! It might have been embarrassing to have greeted him with my mouth full... I felt a slight insecurity at the thought. It felt as though a flake of icing had adhered to the corner of my lips.

Even as my tongue darted out, I felt a broad finger just brushing across my face. "It is taken care of," Kinross murmured. His eyes sparkled at me; the laugh transformed his face. I could not feel embarrassed at my slovenliness, or annoyed that he was laughing at me. It *was* funny, wasn't it? And how like him to know exactly what I'd been thinking!

We listened to the first movement of the harp concerto in polite silence – that is, I assume most of the company was listening; my silence was definitely more polite than enthralled. But then, I had been privileged to hear Izzie practicing this piece for some weeks. As for Cecy and Sophie, they must have spent the entire first movement thinking of conversational lines to play off upon Kinross, for the closing notes of the *Adagio* had barely died away when they began competing for his attention. It was intensely irritating to listen to. As if Alastair had any interest in the latest suitors for some Incomparable's hand, or in the amount Ranald Westlin had won at faro immediately before losing a much larger sum to the bank! Oh, he answered them with all due civility, but his eyes frequently sought mine, and I could not but smile in response to the amusement I saw there.

I was almost relieved when the sweep of Izzie's fingers across the strings of the great harp announced the beginning of the *Allegro*, and put an end to the chattering of the girls.

Almost – but I had heard Izzie's practice of this movement, too, and I was painfully aware of the conflict before her. There were two brightly ornamented passages where she had two options, neither appropriate for public performance: she could continue playing at the vivacious speed with which she had opened the movement, or she could slow down and give herself time to perform the trills, quavers and turns that were the chief beauty of the passages. What she could not do was play through the entire *Allegro* at speed and as written.

At least, she had not been able to do that prior to today. Possibly she had spent the afternoon in practice – more profitably than I had spent it, to be sure – for she made it through the first difficult passage with only a very slight, hardly noticeable slowing of the pace to accommodate the brilliant sparkles of ornamental notes. I breathed more easily as she returned to the basic theme of the movement, and rejoiced in the murmur of appreciation I heard around me.

Once again I had relaxed too soon, for as the second difficult passage approached I could all but hear her beginning to fret. The tense regularity with which she plucked the strings was probably imperceptible to anyone who had not heard her practicing, but it warned me of the coming disaster just seconds before it occurred – just enough time to let me attempt a diversion.

As her fingers paused, trembled, and then swept a discord where she should have entered into the second series of ornaments, I was already making my way to her side. "Izzie, my love, I fear this piece is too stressful for you to attempt in your condition," I murmured over the exclamations of surprise from the rest of her audience. "Why do you not rest? Lady Cecelia Lauder is willing to entertain us with some dances of Boccherini's; you can play the third movement of the concerto after you have had a chance to catch your breath." The third and last movement, the *Largo*, was much easier than this one.

"Hand over my seat at the harp, in my house, to that insipid chit? *Never*," Izzie hissed. She stood with a celerity that belied my concern that her condition might be hampering her, and reached over to the pianoforte before I realized what she was about. Seating herself again with the newly strung Irish harp in her hands, she raised her voice to make a pretty apology to our visitors before saying that she hoped to amuse them with some traditional songs that were perhaps more within her capacities than the technically difficult work she had dared attempt for them.

"Izzie, *no!*" I whispered urgently. She had no idea what dangers she might unleash by touching the harp strings spun from a dead girl's golden locks. For that matter, no more did I – but that the harp was an unchancy thing to hold or to use, of that I felt sure. Already some of the candles in the wall sconces were guttering; shadows seemed to gather in the corners of the drawing room. And in those shadows, under the sound of our guests' conversation, I could hear a ghostly music that made the small hairs at the back of my neck prickle with apprehension.

She played three notes that echoed the fairy music; the candlelight sank lower, the shadows deepened, and I – I recognized the music that was insistently calling from the harp. That song of betrayal and death – I could not say how, but I felt absolutely certain that playing what the harp desired would be a mistake.

Perhaps it would not be so bad if only she did not follow the promptings of the harp strings. Izzie had never before been pliant, willing to accept suggestions, deferential to any authority save her own. It was vexing beyond measure that she should behave so *now*.

"At least," I pleaded, "do not play that song of all others!"

"Why ever not?" she laughed up at me. "Do you dislike it so? You did not dislike it when I played it for you and Mr. Dalkey, the other day!"

I could not explain my feeling of dread. And so I made no more objection as Izzie's white fingers called out the melody of "The Two Sisters" from the strings I had spun, the humming cord formed from Marguerite Fauchet's golden curls.

The shadows deepened and half-filled the room. The candles still burned, but seemed without power to spread their light in the part of the drawing room where Izzie sat with the Irish harp. The air around us chilled me; it seemed to come from some deep, cold, dark place that had nothing in common with the Din Eidyn summer evening outside the windows.

Words joined the melody; words certainly not sung by Izzie, but in a clear high soprano that had no resemblance to her voice. Even had she not, by now, been staring at the harp and at the movement of her own fingers with a slack-jawed look of fear and astonishment, I could not have mistaken the high, sweet music that sprang from the harp for Izzie's own singing.

"*Oh who has ta'en my golden hair,*" sang the voice over the plucked accompaniment,

"*Braemuirie, Braemurie.*"

There was a gasp from someone among the onlookers. Why had Izzie changed the place name? Or – no, that was certainly not Izzie's voice. But why was Celeste Jamison suddenly white as a sheet? In the dusky room her pale face stood out like a lighted lantern... or a ghost?

"*And made it a string to this harp here?*
By the bonny mill-dams of Braemuirie."

Braemuirie. Where had I heard that name before? It echoed in my mind like a sound of old sorrows. My knees were shaking; I might have fallen, but for a welcome hand under my elbow, helping me back to my chair. Nor did Kinross abandon me then; he stood behind me, one warm hand on my shoulder, an unspoken promise of support against what might come next.

"*And who will bid my mother farewell,*" continued the unearthly voice,

"*Braemuirie, Braemuirie,*"

A penetrating whisper cut through the music. "Was not Braemuirie where Marguerite Fauchet was drowned?"

"And her sister Vivienne there at the time," said another woman, with a nervous laugh.

"And tell her who has used me so ill,

By the bonny mill-dams of Braemuirie."

Why did no one interrupt! These society ninnies were all happy to whisper and titter while Izzie played for them, but now none of them had a word to say. By now Cecelia's cheeks were pale beneath her fair ringlets; Sophie's freckles stood out like spots of ink.

"I knew it, I always knew it!" Celeste Jamison exclaimed. "No, I will not be silent!" she told her husband, who was gesturing at her. "Did I not tell you so?"

"She swore that she'd reach to me her glove,

Braemuirie, Braemuirie,

If she could have my own true love

By the bonnie mill-dams of Braemuirie."

Kinross' hand left my shoulder and he took three steps through the shadowy room. He caught up the harp out of Izzie's hands, dropped it on the floor and broke the frame under his heel. The slackened strings were silenced, the song ended. The candles on the walls once more spread their light over a room full of white, shocked faces; everybody in the room spoke at once; and Izzie dropped to the floor, unconscious.

Chapter 16

Late, late that night I returned to my room. I desired Orrock to unfasten my dress and stays and then dismissed her to get what sleep she could in a household totally upset by this catastrophe.

My memories of that evening are not entirely clear. I remember that Kinross, after his prompt action in breaking the magical harp, had with equal promptitude lifted Izzie and carried her upstairs while I followed him and Mama received our guests' hasty farewells. Izzie's abigail was a useless fluttering piece of goods who only wrung her hands and made exclamations of distress; I turned to Kinross for yet one more service. He departed with a promise to go directly to Sir Joshua's personal physician, and bound himself that Izzie should receive medical attention within the hour.

He was as good as his word – at least, Dr. Wylie presented himself before we had had time to do more than unlace Izzie and revive her with an application of *sal volatile*. She was sadly confused, and kept crying out, piteously begging someone to take the charmed harp from her. I must have told her half a dozen times that Alastair had done that already, that the harp was broken in half and that she need never see it again. Finally Dr. Wylie administered a composing draught and she sank into a troubled slumber.

He shook his head over her. "She seems to have suffered a severe shock," he said with a look of inquiry at me.

"She has," I said without elaborating. Soon I would have to think of how to minimize the evening's events, how to quash the gossip even now brewing.

But tonight I could not bring myself even to discuss the matter. "Doctor, do you fear for her reason?"

"It is early to tell," he replied, and a chill of fear slid down my spine. What if, by my meddling, I had destroyed my sister?

"Keep her quiet, and do not let her worry," he instructed. "I shall call again tomorrow to see how she goes on."

I kept vigil by Izzie's bedside for some time, until Mama found me there. She was followed by Kirsty, who in turn led a servant with a basket full of little bottles and packets. Our mother had not, it seemed, spent the whole of the time since Izzie's collapse in reassuring our guests and attempting to suppress their conjectures; rather she had taken herself to the still-room, where she had provided herself with a wealth of remedies for whatever might ail my sister. I managed to dissuade her from attempting to dose Izzie with a violent purgative but had to admit that she seemed to rest better after Mama persuaded her to take a little syrup of poppies mixed with honey.

"Elspet, my love, you should rest now," Mama urged me after Izzie stopped thrashing and muttering in her sleep. "There is nothing so deleterious to the complexion as a lack of sleep."

As though that were important now! But I agreed to lie down for a few hours after Mama promised that Kirsty would sit with Izzie and that I should be called immediately if there were any change in her condition. Now that my immediate anxiety for Izzie was somewhat assuaged, there were certain other matters that required my attention.

I watched the mirror over my dressing table closely while Orrock unhooked my gown. It did not sway. Nonetheless, I felt quite sure that the Hob was in the room with us.

He had better be!

"You need not keep so still," I said in a low voice as soon as Orrock had left me, as she thought, alone. "I know you are there."

"O perceptive young sprout of the House of Rattray!" The Hob's ironic voice came, this time, from the corner behind the dressing table.

"You would be wiser to make yourself scarce!" I raged at him. "Look what you have done! Izzie in danger of her life, a scandal brewed in our drawing room that will engulf the *ton* – God and His saints preserve this house from any more of your *help*! How dared you!"

"I told you that you could leave the problem with me," the Hob said, sounding now more sulky than superior, "and so you did. Is it not a little late to complain of my solution? Besides, it has all worked out for the best."

I threw my hands up into the air. "How can you possibly claim that?"

"You complain of the scandal, but only think: it may have begun in this house, but it will end by destroying your rival. Was not Mrs. Jamison among your guests tonight?"

"You must know she was; you know everything that goes on in this house!"

"Thank you!"

"It was not meant as a compliment!" I snapped.

"Let us return, then, to the matter at hand. Celeste Jamison recognized the name of Braemurie and the voice of Marguerite Fauchet, as did a number of your other guests."

"And they will report that I – no, that *Izzie* – invented a way to disparage Vivienne de Larue, doubtless on my behalf. I can hardly thank you enough, you – you interfering idiot! Vivienne de Larue may have sought to ensnare Richert, but she did not succeed; he was going to cut the connection with her any day now; she was in no way my rival. You have elevated her to that position by your meddling. Oh, very helpful! Spare me from any more such aid!"

"A very little rational thought will show your guests that Izzie, whose own singing voice is much lower, could hardly have imitated Marguerite Fauchet's soprano; furthermore, they observed her at the time and know that her lips were not moving. As for you, you were never acquainted with Marguerite and could have had no knowledge of her singing."

"Someone could have told me." I shrugged off my overdress and sat down on the bed, too tired to stand and rant at the Hob any longer.

"And could you have darkened the room, chilled the spectators, and blocked the illumination from the candles?"

"Some of them may suspect that I have a little skill with thread magic."

"But not, I think, enough to create such dramatic effects. Rest, child. Your sister is too high-strung by half; I confess I did not anticipate such an ending to the scene, but it is for the best. Izzie will recover from her shock – and her fainting set the seal of authenticity upon the song."

"Oh, well then," I sneered, "everything is for the best, because I am happy to have hazarded my own sister's health upon the success of a magically stirred scandal-broth."

"You might be grateful for my help. Disposing of Vivienne must be a material improvement in your chances of catching young Dalkey."

"No such thing! And in any case, I neither want nor need your help with Richert! He will either come to see me as the woman he loves, or – or – or he will not, and it has nothing to do with magic – or with you either! If you even *think* of interfering again, I shall – I shall commission a suit of livery for you!"

The Hob went away at that insult, with a barely audible *pop!* of the air rushing in to fill the place he had occupied, and I was free to indulge my tears of rage and fear in private.

For several days after that my days and most of my nights were consumed watching over Izzie and waiting for Dr. Wylie's visits. Mama, after that first visit, declared that she could be of no use in the sick-room. It was true that her tendency to burst into tears over Izzie did my sister no good whatsoever, so it was rather a relief than otherwise that she occupied herself in the still-room, trying to find a tonic that would restore Izzie to her old self. It did, however, mean that I was more or less tied to Izzie's side, for her abigail – a poor, spiritless thing, the sort of servant you wound up with after summarily turning off several others for pertness – would meekly offer Izzie whatever potion Mama sent up without inquiring as to the contents or the intended effect. I, of course, accepted every one of Mama's offerings with thanks – and I was truly thankful that our mother did not come in person to see them administered. My own abigail Orrock, though disapproving, helped me to quietly dispose of the tincture of rhubarb in spirits of wine, the senna and coriander cordial, and other concoctions which I judged would act violently upon Izzie's digestion without relieving her oppression of spirits.

On one occasion these medicines were brought up by Kirsty, and to distract her from the fact that I did not mean to give them to Izzie at once I inquired as to the effect upon the *ton* of the terrifying scene that had brought our little musical evening to an end. She frowned and shook her head and said that she ought not to encourage discussion of these things... *but...* did I know that several people were claiming Izzie herself had sung?

"What nonsense!" I exclaimed warmly. "Anyone who was present could see for themselves that was not the case."

"Aye," said Kirsty, "but a vast number of people who were *not* present are now setting their tongues to click-clacking about the matter! Some say there was magic in it, others say that Lady Herriot is innocent of all such practices."

As was not I. But it was the Hob, not I, who ought to bear the blame, so I kept silent while Kirsty went on to tell me that most people felt Vivienne de Larue had been exposed as the murderess she was; others, however, argued that there was no evidence against her, only a repetition of the accusations Celeste Jamison had been making for years.

Kirsty did not mention, and I did not ask, what Richert Dalkey's reaction to the gossip had been. I feared I could guess that from the fact that he had not yet left his card to inquire after Izzie, nor had he asked to see me.

"Everyone with any sense," Kirsty said firmly when I hinted at the latter, "knows that you are completely occupied with Lady Herriot, and that this is no time to be pestering you with social calls!"

"Yes, but... Who *has* called, Kirsty?"

Izzie stirred then, complaining of thirst, and Kirsty made her escape from my interrogation while I was trying to persuade Izzie to take a little very weak chamomile tea. That might at least calm her, and at worst could do no harm. I wished I could say the same for all Mama's decoctions and tinctures.

Kirsty's account of the gossip worried me. Until now, I had felt it sufficient to protect myself and Richert against magical attacks from Vivienne de Larue. Despite the accident that had occurred to Kinross at the theatre, I did not think that he was in any great danger from the herb-witch. But now I wondered just what Vivienne had heard about the evening of the musicale, and whether she believed the wild tales that it was Izzie's own voice and words singing the damning ballad. Whether or not she thought that Izzie had been the singer, it was certain that Izzie had picked up the harp; her fingers had brought the strings to life; and most people would think that she had chosen the song.

After Izzie had drunk the tea, I took the rowan cross ornamented with red thread from my neck and slipped the chain over my sister's head. She lay quietly, but her eyes searched mine. "Still – playing with spells and cantrips, little sister?"

"There can be no harm in wearing a cross," I answered her, "and this is a very pretty one." And I should feel less concern about leaving Izzie to Orrock or Kirsty for brief periods, now that she was thus protected.

Chapter 17

Vivienne de Larue sat alone in her drawing-room, for once taking no pleasure in the gold-embroidered curtains, the gilded wall sconces, the chairs new-covered with straw-colored brocade or all the other evidence of wealth and luxury with which she had managed to surround herself since the untimely death of Edouard de Larue had left her with so much less of a fortune than she had expected to enjoy. As she shuffled and dealt a handful of cards, only to sweep them up unseeing and shuffle again, she reflected that Edouard had not, after all, been as great a skinflint as she had thought him after her marriage. His shakes of the head, his murmurs of protest at the bills he had to settle for her, had possibly been prompted not by meanness but by an awareness of how insecure his family's fortunes had become. She remembered that after the deaths of his parents, he had been greatly shaken by his interview with the advocat who had charge of the estate.

"More than I ever realized was lost without recompense when my parents fled Lutéce," he had told her after that meeting. "If they buried themselves in the country here, it must have been so that I would be able to draw sufficient income from the remaining property in Dalriada to support my life in the *ton* here in Din Eidyn – Oh, Papa! Papa!" he apostrophized his dead father in one of those emotional outbursts that Vivienne particularly detested. "Why could not you have told me how matters stood with you? Did you not know that I had rather share your cottage, earning my bread if necessary as a common laborer, than have you and Mama give up one comfort for my benefit?"

"Their country cottage was not so lacking in comforts as all that," Vivienne observed, "and as a common laborer you could scarcely have won *me* to wife!" But Edouard only gave her a hunted glance and took himself off to mourn in privacy. Really, the man had been ridiculously sentimental. Between his cheese-paring ways and his insistence on very public mourning not only of his parents, but of her sister Marguerite, she could not long have abided life with him. It was fortunate that her friendship with Ailsa of Quoy had shown her how to be rid of him in a way that, just to silence the skeptical, had demonstrably no taint of magic about it. The best physicians in Din Eidyn had attended Edouard during his brief decline and had unanimously agreed his illness to spring from natural causes. "A weakness of the heart, unsuspected in his youth," the great Dr. Wylie had proclaimed.

Vivienne had even won Dr. Wylie's praise for her devoted nursing of Edouard, for preparing with her own hands the gruels and panadas that were all the nourishment he took.

And much good all that anxious work had done her, when he was no sooner dead than a host of blood-sucking creditors besieged her! She had had no choice but to turn the de Larue town house into a sort of private gaming club. She began that venture with all possible advantages: a smart location, presided over by a beautiful and brilliant hostess boasting a name long honored in Lutéce, and very exclusive. Nonetheless, the fact of presiding over such an establishment had lost her all the social credit she thought to have gained by her marriage to a de Larue. Even after the whispers about Edouard's death, following so soon after the loss of his parents and her sister, had died down, she had had to scramble just to keep her present place on the fringes of polite society.

And now, thanks to a vicious little red-headed chit whom she should have crushed on their first meeting, she might have lost even that. She had had no morning callers these three days; her evening card salons had been so thin of company, the takings hardly paid for the wax tapers that blazed around the rooms; worst of all, she had received a stiffly formal note from the Earl of Torquhan, excusing himself from further attendance at her card-parties and claiming a need to retrench. Torquhan – whom she had thought bound to her by the love potion she had originally brewed for Richert Dalkey! But she had not seen Torquhan this se'enight, and had had no opportunity to renew the dosage.

She had already, with little success, been reduced to the stratagem of paying morning calls on the families of those most closely involved with her. She had left cards with Lilias Torquhan, with Innis Dalkey, even with Shona Rattray, only to be informed that none of the ladies were at home. Well, that had been an initial, panicky, miscalculation; houses where she had never been received socially were hardly likely to be open to her now. Folly! And worse folly to have called at the Rattray house three days running. It was high time she retired to consider the problem intelligently.

How could she have lost so much, so quickly? It could only be due to the machinations of her enemies. And isolated as she had become, must she rely on servants' gossip to find out what those enemies were doing? Perhaps she should drive out in the Park, where surely she would encounter someone eager to tell her the latest news of the *ton*.

But – what if that gambit, too, were to fail? Vivienne envisioned the haughty *grandes dames* whose barouches and landaulets filled the Park on every fine day. She could all too clearly imagine them turning their faces aside, affecting not to see her, deaf to her pleasant greetings. So public a humiliation would set the seal on the social ruin she feared was coming upon her.

She sighed, sharply; rang for a servant; and gave instructions to have the Rattray town house watched. She wanted information on all who came and went from there, and if possible, whatever gossip her agents might be able to pick up by infiltrating the servants' hall. Such information would be well repaid, she promised. She underlined the promise by tossing a purse of royals into her man's cupped hands as though she regarded it as but a trifle.

If she could not restore her standing in the *ton*, and that quickly, there would be no royals with which to bribe servants and precious few to maintain the household. Vivienne had always scorned saving as a petty bourgeois habit, an affectation which made Edouard de Larue seem more common even than her own family. Now she contemplated the humiliation of substituting tallow candles for wax tapers, and shuddered. It could not – *must* not – come to that.

Fortunately, she still had certain means at her disposal that were not dependent upon the approval of the *ton*. Vivienne rang again and ordered her phaeton brought round – but not for a pleasure drive in the park; her destination was the herb-gardens at Quoy house.

The young Duke of Quoy was, as usual, not in residence; he was so preoccupied with the effort to restore his family's lands to their previous good condition after the long period of his minority, when the Dowager Duchess had wrung every penny out of the land without returning anything to it, that even the height of Din Eidyn's social season saw him continually posting into the country to oversee some muddy matter of hedging or ditching. "And how Balcladich expects me to influence someone who is never in town—!" Vivienne murmured scornfully. She preferred not to think, just now, of the last few days' isolation, of the possibility that had young Quoy been in residence she might for the first time have been denied access to his mother's gardens. But that cold fear lurked at the back of her mind. She spent longer than she had planned in the gardens, collecting not just the herbs needed for her present plan but all those she might conceivably need in the future. She really ought to have taken cuttings and started her own garden years ago, she thought uneasily. But how could she have done that, when Edouard's town house had not an inch of land around it to support a garden? Was she supposed to have removed into the country, to have dwindled into a rural widow tending her little plants? And where, pray tell, could she have done even that much? Certainly not at his parents' cottage in Braemuirie! If ever a place was haunted, that grey cottage, dominated by the rushing sound of the river, must have been. She could not even sleep there; her fancy was tormented by the voice that seemed to call from the river. No, everything was against her and always had been. But she would rise above her circumstances and bend them to her will again, just as she always had done.

So vowed Vivienne de Larue, as she bent over the bushes in Quoy's gardens and worked with her gilt scissors, snipping nightshade and nettles, monkshood and mullein, and collecting her gatherings neatly in their separate little bags. There was more than enough here to induce the scrying trance, as well as for a great deal of other work that might be necessary in the coming battle to regain her status in Din Eidyn society.

***

Later that day, when I was resting in my room, Kirsty brought me a collection of all the cards that had been left upon us since the night of the ill-fated musicale. All the expected names were there, and some that I had never expected to see. But my attention was more on what I did *not* see. Not that there was any surprise in it, but I had hoped that Kirsty might have been mistaken. No; Richert had not called since Izzie's collapse, nor had he left any message for me. Did he, then, believe the worst of the stories circulating, and did he now condemn me for practicing the magic he so feared and hated? Surely Alastair would have spoken in my defense? *He*, at least, had called daily, not expecting to be admitted, but only asking for news of my sister's health. I should have thought Richert could do as much. But then, everyone knew how he felt about any practice of magic. In his ignorance, he lumped together everything from an innocent thread charm to the black arts practiced in the Mythic Society. I had thought to have educated him on this matter, given enough time, after he fell in love with me.

It appeared my time might have run out.

As I moodily stirred the cards with one finger, a single name leapt out at me. Vivienne de Larue! Her name, engraved in an elegant gold script, appeared no fewer than three times in the pile. I frowned over that. She had never been received here; did she enjoy the illusion that the acquaintance she had scraped in the Water Gardens would give her the entrée to our house? Surely not! *Certainly* not after the events of Saturday night! I could not puzzle out what her object had been, but I felt quite sure that it betokened nothing good. Well, if she meant to storm our very house, perhaps I ought to protect the entire household, not just Izzie, against magical malice.

A whisper of thunder rolled through the room, and the drawer of my work-table fell open. Skeins of red silk and wool fell onto the floor, followed by a small shower of twigs.

"Very subtle, Hob!" I filled my skirt with his gift of rowan twigs and added the skeins of red thread. I could work the protective charms that very night, while Orrock watched over Izzie's troubled slumber.

***

Once again, Vivienne's magical preparations were interrupted by a caller — but how different this occasion! The last time she resorted to the still-room, her days had been filled with visitors and her nights had been taken up by either her own card-parties or, on days when she did not entertain, with all the amusements offered by Din Eidyn's Season. Today, she had returned home with her baskets of herbs to a still, lifeless house where, by her own orders for the sake of economy, only one small fire burned and a single branch of candles fought the dimness of a cloudy afternoon. She had sent out no cards of invitation, for she dared not attempt another card-party until she had vanquished the foes who had so effectively spread evil tales about her. Nor had she any desire to show herself in public, inviting the cut direct from those most influential in Din Eidyn society, before those rumors had been dealt with and scotched for all time.

Exactly how she was to accomplish this, she did not know. The baskets she had filled outside Quoy House, added to her already extensive collection, boasted herbs enough for any magic she chose to use — but what witchcraft would be effective against words and whispers, glances and gossip? What exactly did the *ton* believe of her, and why had they turned against her so quickly and decisively? She needed to know *more*. No one would tell her exactly what had been said or sung; the few people she spoke to were in a hurry to change the subject, and even more in a hurry to break off the conversation.

And so she was more than happy to be interrupted in her bestowal of the fresh-cut herbs. Almost any caller would have been welcome, but a rich and influential one was best of all.

"Your Grace!" She swept her deepest curtsey to the Duke of Balcladich. "So happy to see you!"

But she was less happy when the footman who had summoned her had left them quite alone, and he explained the reason for his visit. The Duke had no interest in her difficulties except as they affected his own plans, but he was deeply perturbed that she had not yet secured the votes of the gentlemen of the War Party he had indicated for her attention. As he spoke, Vivienne understood he was even more concerned that in her current state of social near-ruin she would be unable to be of any use at all to him.

She reminded him of his promise to sponsor her for vouchers to Gilroy's, and generally to lend her his countenance in society, in return for those votes.

"That was to have been a reward for services rendered," the Duke said. "You have not yet turned the vote of any gentleman, nor do I see that you have any hope of doing so." He cast a despising glance at the dimly lit room. "This is hardly the atmosphere to attract men to your parties."

"With your support, I could do all that you have required of me, and more!"

"I beg to differ," said the Duke. "It seems in the highest degree unlikely that any of the *ton* will care to continue their acquaintance with you, after Lady Herriot's revelations."

"Lady Herriot! I had thought it was that spiteful chit Miss Rattray—"

"A sweet child," the Duke said, frowning, "and laudably concerned for her sister."

He proceeded to give Vivienne a first-hand account of the events she had only heretofore deduced from scraps of gossip: Izzie Herriot's reaching for the Irish harp, the cold and dark that concentrated around it, the damming words of the song.

"Vile rumors!" Vivienne exclaimed. "And are the *ton* of Din Eidyn so superstitious that they suddenly believe the same baseless lies that Celeste Jamison has always tried to spread? She must have persuaded her bosom-bow, Lady Herriot, to get up this mummery for no purpose but to harm me!"

Balcladich's massive white eyebrows drew together. "Lady Herriot has been dangerously ill since that evening. And I, who observed the whole, judged it not to be mummery, but true magic – *death* magic! I have since heard that the harp's strings had been spun from curls taken from your sister Marguerite after her untimely drowning."

"But, your Grace," Vivienne protested, feeling as if she were herself in danger of drowning, "*you* do not believe this calumny, else you would hardly have called on me today!"

The Duke's frown grew even deeper. "I know nothing and care less of your dealings with your unfortunate relatives – though I might be inclined to congratulate young Dalkey on his escape from what might have proved the *fatal* mistake of a mésalliance! My only interest is in scotching the so-called War Party, those young sprigs whose belligerence is like to cost Dalriada dear. This is a poor country; let Anglia bear the burden of repelling Lutécian aggression, if repel it they must. Our own historic ties to Lutéce assure me that Dalriada has naught to fear from that direction, and naught to gain by joining the Anglian adventure."

"As one whose ties to Lutéce are stronger even than the history you allude to, your Grace, I cannot but agree with you and reiterate my vow to serve you and the Peace Party in whatever manner I may."

"Hmph! Your usefulness is sadly diminished as a result of this week's events. But you do yourself no good by cowering within your house as though you believed yourself guilty of the accusations. I advise you to use your box at the theater tonight, to hold your head high and show yourself indifferent to popular gossip. Dress as though you expected to entertain the highest aristocracy – well – let us say, as though you expected to receive *me* as your visitor."

"And dare I indeed hope for such a signal honor, your Grace?"

"Hmph!" the Duke ejaculated again. "We shall see – we shall see. Convince me that you may yet recover from this setback, and perhaps I may help you to a position from which you can still influence my enemies."

Vivienne was hardly contented with this half-promise, but she understood that she ignored the Duke's advice at her peril. The remainder of the day was occupied with preparations for that evening; she demanded that her finest gown be adorned with an extra trimming of gold lace dripping with tassels, that her abigail apply certain creams and lotions to ensure that her complexion was a flawless white. She screamed in fury when Patrice-Henri sent word that he was unfortunately too much engaged elsewhere to dress her hair for that night, and broke a bottle of imported Lutécian scent over her abigail's head before reluctantly agreeing to accept the services of Din Eidyn's second-best hair-dresser.

The evening was all she had feared it would be: an exercise in public humiliation. Arriving halfway through the first act, she sat in her box alone save for the two footmen who had accompanied her there. She regarded the antics of the players with a stony face; with no admirers to laugh with, no chance to make *bons mots* at the expense of the milksop who played the foolish heroine, the play meant less than nothing to her.

The interval brought some slight relief, as the Duke of Balcladich visited her box and stood well forward, so that the *ton* could see he, at least, had not deserted her. But her knowledge of the payment he expected for this favor, and her new-born doubts of her ability to deliver that payment, made even that brief visit sour in her throat. Scarcely better was the championship of two young sprigs of the nobility who dared follow Balcladich, especially when the more verbose of the boys exclaimed, "I do not care what anybody says, Mrs. de Larue, you are as a goddess to *me*!" Only the habits developed through years of practice enabled her to laugh and smile and generally behave as though there were no sting in the speech he had meant as a compliment.

She left before the farce. Many people were in the habit of doing so; her departure could not be construed as any kind of flight. Could it?

Once safely home again – and just when had Edouard's cramped little town house become a refuge to her? – she dismissed the footmen and her abigail. She ordered candles and a fire for the still-room and gave orders that she was not to be interrupted. It was a bitter reflection that she hardly needed to work at night to insure privacy. No matter what the hour, there would be no callers, nothing to distract her from the concentration needed for successful scrying. But she could not bear to wait until morning to begin taking her revenge for the insult she had suffered.

If she had feared that the late hour would mean that there was also no activity in the Rattray house for her to spy upon, the first visions that appeared in the murky liquid in the scrying bowl reassured her. Shona Rattray was engaged in her own still-room, doubtless brewing up some tonic for her sickly daughter. Much good might it do her! Lady Herriot tossed and murmured on her bed, watched over by a hawk-faced abigail. Even that interfering little Elspet Rattray was awake, her hands busy and her needle flashing with some complex stitchery. The girl was working by the light of a single branch of candles, barely enough for her to see her own work, and not nearly enough for Vivienne to interpret it through the cloudy medium of the brew in the scrying bowl. No matter; she had seen enough to plot her revenge, and Balcladich had shown her the target.

Even as she framed this thought, the miniature Elspet Rattray in the scrying bowl rose and shook out the work she had been engaged upon… and the vision disappeared into a thick mist rising from the surface of the potion.

Thread magic! She should have guessed as much. No wonder her attempts to control Richert and to neutralize Elspet had failed; the little beast had been one step ahead of her. Was Lady Herriot also guarded by rowan twigs and red threads? She stirred the bowl, waited impatiently for the murky liquid to settle into a mirror-like pool and for the images to rise again. But there was nothing there, nothing but mist above the floating fragments of eye-bright and marry-gold, celery seed and coltsfoot that swirled in the troubled liquid.

Well, no matter. She had already given thought to ways of removing Elspet Rattray from her path that would owe nothing to magic and could not be stopped with childish tangles of red threads. And the brief success of her scrying had shown her an easy way to apply the same remedy to Lady Herriot, whose busy fingers had awakened the harp song to ruin her.

Vivienne put the silver bowl aside and rose to collect new supplies. Thorn apple and foxglove, laurel and oleander – the materials for this brew were even easier to collect than those for herb-magic, and would as certainly put a stop to Lady Herriot's troublemaking. As an afterthought, remembering the woman's condition, she added rosemary, pennyroyal and goldenseal to the concoction.

The only problem would be finding a way to introduce this potion to the Rattray still-room as another of Shona Rattray's medicinal mixtures, now that magical means of entering the house would be as useless as presenting her card at the front door had been.

Chapter 18

My own room was too far from Izzie's; I found myself unable to rest there after I had warded the house against magical attacks. In theory, of course, Izzie and all the rest of us should have been perfectly safe from any attempted revenge from Vivienne de Larue. In practice, I could not sleep in my own chamber for the consciousness of being too far away to hear if something untoward occurred in Izzie's. I removed myself to the chaise-longue in her dressing-room, and opened the connecting door a crack so that I should be warned if there were any need for me. Not that there should have been... Even if my wards over the house, hastily worked as they had been, proved to be lacking, was not Izzie still protected by my cross of rowan wood with its careful interlacings of red silk thread? But my mind ran uncontrollably upon the poorly understood interactions of magic and matter. If only the gentlemen of the Philosophical Society would deign to study the various forms of magic with the same attention they gave to the life-cycle of the wood-louse or the animalculae revealed by the Majuloscope, we might get some useful definitions. It might be generally understood why certain patterns worked in red thread could also work on men's emotions, and whether the repugnant practices of the Mythic Society truly added force to witches' spells or merely gave the practitioners a delicious *frisson* from the consciousness of doing evil...

The sound of an unfamiliar voice in the next room penetrated the uneasy slumber into which I had fallen. Like a swimmer coming up through deep water, limbs entangled with seaweed, I shook off a black dream in which witches danced round a taper made from the fat of unborn babes and rose into consciousness that a new day had dawned.

"It was your lady mother's wish that you should try this medicine, Miss Isobel."

"Lady Herriot," Izzie corrected weakly. "What is in it? It smells like ditch water – worse even than Dr. Wylie's nasty brews."

"It contains only what will do you good and help you to rest," said the strange voice. No – perhaps not so strange, after all. I gathered my wrapper about me and flung the door open to see a young woman in a servant's dark dress and white apron bending over my sister. She was urging Izzie to drink from the cup she held, speaking with more confidence and fluency than any housemaid could have brought to the task. And even as I watched, as the last veils of sleep fell from my eyes, the woman put one hand behind Izzie's head and pressed the cup to her lips.

"Izzie, no! Don't drink that!" I stumbled across the room and reached to strike the cup from the strange maidservant's hand. She whirled away from Izzie and caught me with an elbow into my throat, making me choke and gasp for air for a fatal movement before I could push her away. The dark beverage from the cup trickled into Izzie's half-open mouth before I recovered myself and slapped the cup onto the floor, where its foul-smelling contents stained the carpet.

"Mrs. de Larue," I said, standing straight and moving between her and Izzie. "I believe you are here without invitation." The brief tussle had disarranged her mob-cap. She stared at me, her black, bold eyes defiant. But her words were meek enough.

"I felt compelled to come, Miss Rattray, for it is a work of charity to comfort the sick. Since your servants denied me the front door, I was forced to employ what stratagems I might to reach your sister with a healing draught. Had she drunk it all, she would have found peace."

What sort of peace, I shuddered to contemplate. I rang the bell and requested the first manservant who presented himself to show Mrs. de Larue out.

"You will escort her to the front door, if you please," I specified, "so that in future she will know where a lady presents herself if she desires to visit us."

The herb-witch's expression promised yet another revenge for this humiliation, but she turned and left the room with apparent meekness. Evidently she was not yet so insane as to get into a brawl with the servants. I hoped that there would be someone other than street vendors and common working people in the street, some member of the *ton*; it would serve her right to have the report spread that she had been forcibly ejected from our house in the garb of a housemaid.

I rang again and dispatched a footman to Dr. Wylie's residence with a request that he would attend Izzie immediately. Then I was free to turn my attention back to my sister.

"How much of that stuff did you swallow?" I demanded.

She shook her head. "Not much," she whispered. "Burns…"

I urged her to rinse her mouth with the cold chamomile tea that had been left by her bed earlier. Perhaps it had been a mistake to spill most of the potion; Dr. Wylie might have been able to analyze the contents and deduce the best treatment for her. I could only hope that whatever was in Vivienne's noxious brew, Izzie had not taken enough to do her serious harm.

A few drops remained on the inside of the cup. I took one on my forefinger and just touched my tongue to it. It was a bitter-tasting drink; I thought, but could not be sure, that I recognized foxglove and… yes, that aroma was definitely rosemary.

Mama used foxglove sometimes in stimulating tonics, but with great care, and never in anything for old folk whose hearts might be affected by the herb. Izzie was young and her heart was strong, but a sufficiently strong decoction of foxglove might kill anybody. Thank the saints that she had not taken so much! As for rosemary… That was certainly not a poison, nor had it any magical uses that I had ever heard of. And if Vivienne had added it in an effort to make the potion taste better, she had been wasting her time; a little honey would have been far better to counteract the taste of foxglove.

Izzie was flushed now, complaining of the head-ache, and when I felt her pulse it was racing. *How much foxglove had she imbibed?* Ought I to administer an emetic to try and get the toxic drink out of her system? Or would that only add to the stress on her heart? Oh, if only Dr. Wylie would come! I did not know enough. Someone would have to wake Mama; we needed her still-room expertise.

I sent for Mama and got Kirsty, who sniffed the cup and frowned. "Not only rosemary, but also pennyroyal and goldenseal," she said.

I frowned. "Why would that herb-witch use *those* ingredients? Foxglove can be a poison, and I am sure that was her intent. But these other herbs…"

Kirsty touched my wrist and urged me to the far side of the room, out of Izzie's hearing. There she explained to me that the triumvirate of rosemary, pennyroyal and goldenseal could indeed be fatal – though not necessarily to the one who partook of them.

"Then what are they *for*?"

Kirsty sighed. "For foolish serving-girls who find themselves in trouble, you silly girl! Yes, and sometimes for careless young ladies as well. Do you remember when Sukey Webster left Town in the middle of the Season? No, I suppose you would not," she said when I shook my head. "It was put about that she had gone to the seaside to rest, that she suffered nervous fatigue from participating too much in all the gaiety of the Season. Well, it wasn't her *nerves* that had suffered… The silly girl had begged a potion from the Duchess of Quoy. And the herb-witch, fearing failure, had added much stronger ingredients to the packet of rosemary, pennyroyal and goldenseal that she sold to Sukey. She rid herself of the child, but it almost cost her life."

I gasped. "What else was in it? And do you think Vivienne put those stronger ingredients into this potion as well?"

"Let us hope not," said Kirsty. "The foxglove alone would have killed your sister, if she had drunk deeply enough before you dashed the cup from her lips. I hope the other herbs were but an afterthought of that harpy's malice."

Afterthought they may have been, but effective they and the other poisons surely were. By the time Dr. Wylie arrived, Izzie was writhing in pain and there was blood spotting her sheets. The physician, Mama and Kirsty banished me from the room, saying this was no sight for a young girl; I spent some hours perched on a stool in the dressing-room, listening to Izzie's cries

160

of distress, the doctor's barked commands and the hurrying steps of servants bringing whatever he required.

By the time dawn touched the rooftops of Din Eidyn the crisis was over. Izzie, so white and still I should hardly have known her, lay in a new-made bed where her slender body scarcely raised the sheets. Mama had ordered the room cleaned and the bloody sheets disposed of as though by fierce cleansing she could make the child that would never be disappear from my sister's memory. And Dr. Wylie, having ordered leeches and purgatives which I quietly countermanded, had gone home to take his own rest.

Over the next week I grew even more concerned about Izzie than I had been before Vivienne's attempt on her. Although she had survived the immediate effects of the poison, she grew no stronger and took little interest in anything around her. Dress? Go down to the drawing-room? Take a carriage ride to enjoy the summer sunshine? She received all these suggestions languidly. "You would think she did not *want* to regain her health!" I raged once at Kirsty, when we were safely out of hearing.

"Give her time. She is still grieving the lost child," said Kirsty. But she did not sound very sure of herself. We had both been alarmed by Izzie's continued weakness and passivity.

"It *cannot* be good for her to lie in a darkened room all day, weeping over her loss! And do you know what she told me this morning? She is afraid that Sir Joshua will blame her! In fact, she blames herself!"

"And you, of course, make no such error," Kirsty said drily.

"That is different. This whole affair is my fault; I should never have let Patrice-Henri persuade me into working something that bordered on death magic!"

Having burst out with that, I had no choice but to confess all to Kirsty. She pursed her lips and shook her head when I told her why I had really wanted the use of a spinning wheel, and looked deeply troubled when I recounted the eerie atmosphere that had invaded the attic where I spun the dead Marguerite's shorn locks into a golden cord. But she drew the line at letting me assume the guilt for all that followed. "You did not string the harp or put it out ready for your sister's hand. And more to the point, it was not you who brewed a poison for her, who stole into our house and set the cup to her lips. Izzie's trials are thanks to Vivienne de Larue alone."

"Do you know," I said, disconsolate, unable to take comfort from Kirsty, "she does not even care for music now? I tried to tempt her from her bed to hear Celeste Jamison playing the new work by that German composer, but she put her hands to her ears and said she could never hear music happily again. Oh, I *wish*…"

What did I wish? Only to have my sharp-tongued, bossy, musically talented sister back. Only to hear her annoying teasing about the thread magic she did not believe in, to have her twitting me about the baby fat I had been too long in losing, to hear her dire warnings that my hoydenish behavior would lose me the respect of the *ton*.

"Well, *I* wish," Kirsty interrupted my woebegone musings, "that you would set your sister an example!"

"How do you mean?"

"Instead of hovering over her sickbed, why do not you put on that shockingly over-decorated riding dress of yours and take your grey mare out for a turn around the Park?"

"It is not over-decorated," I said stiffly. "Alast – Lord Kinross said it was very becoming to me."

"It might have been just as becoming without being weighted down with a quantity of silver lace such that even a Hussar would be ashamed to put on his uniform," Kirsty said.

"Well, maybe so." It didn't matter. Why wrangle over the trimming of a riding outfit, or even point out that it was ornamented with silver braid, not lace? I would happily have unpicked all that silver braid and cast it into the fire, if the sacrifice made Izzie smile.

But when Richert Dalkey sent up his card with a plea that I would accompany him through the Park, I did as Kirsty urged and dressed to join him, and sent to have Caramella brought round for me.

Chapter 19

Somehow, Richert's call did not please and excite me as much as it would have only a few days earlier. I felt tired and listless; well, a brisk canter in the Park would take care of that. Kirsty was right, I had been within doors too long. As for Richert… well, I could hardly be overjoyed merely because he deigned to call after neglecting us for so many days.

The day was cloudy, with a misty hint of rain, and the Park was not overly full. I waited until we were riding abreast down the principal path before entering into anything more than commonplaces.

"We have not seen you for some days, Mr. Dalkey," I said.

Caramella splashed through a shallow puddle and Richert drew his own mount aside, fastidious as always at the risk of muddying his shining boots and perfectly fitted breeches. "I might say the same to you, Elspet, for you have been shut away in a sick room for far too long."

"Our *friends*," I said, "have called regularly for news of my sister."

"Yes. Kinross has conveyed the news to me daily."

All very well, but why had he not troubled himself to call in person?

I feared that I knew why.

"Were you afraid to visit a house where magic had run loose? And so you sent your friend to inquire on your behalf? I did not realize that was how soldiers dealt with their fear – by inviting someone else to take the lead! Perhaps you should rethink your ambitions for a military career!"

Richert colored. "You know my sentiments about that foulness, Pet! I could not believe my ears when I first heard tales of that – that accursed night. To think that Lady Herriot - your sister – someone so close to you – had toyed with witchcraft! Yes, I was shocked; yes, it took me some time to recognize that you could not be held responsible for her folly. For that I crave your pardon."

"Had you listened more attentively to the gossip, you might have known that what happened was as great a surprise to Izzie as to anyone else. And she has suffered for it more than anyone else, even though it was none of her doing." I could not – quite – bring myself to confess my own part in the misadventure to Richert. Not quite yet. Of course he would have to know eventually, but I had hoped for time to bring him to a more balanced understanding of the difference between harmless magic and black witchcraft before telling him about spinning Marguerite Fauchet's hair – which he might well think crossed the line between magic and witchcraft. Perhaps it would be better to leave him in ignorance.

"Someone must have planned it," he said obstinately. "Vivienne de Larue believes it was an attempt on your part to blacken her name."

"So you have found time to visit the widow, but not to leave a card with us!"

Richert's flush deepened. So red a face was not becoming to a man of his coloring. "I have not spoken to the lady. She wrote to me—"

"Did you know that Izzie's illness is her doing?" I interrupted, too angry to calculate the effect of my words.

"How can that be? She was not even present at your musicale!"

"No, but she stole into the house some days later, disguised as a servant, and tried to make Izzie drink a poison of her brewing. If I had not chanced to come upon her in the act, and struck the cup from my sister's lips, Izzie would be *dead* now, instead of only—" I bit my lip. Had I the right to tell Richert what was, properly, only Izzie's and Sir Joshua's business? "Instead of only too weak to lift her head, and too sad to make the effort," I concluded.

"Pet! You do not mean it! You're overwrought – I know this business has borne hardly upon you, but —"

"I am not," I said, reining in my temper, "in the habit of making false accusations. I tell you that Vivienne de Larue poisoned my sister, and that I was obliged to request the servants to escort her from our house. Perhaps you would like to ask the footmen who saw her out to verify my words?"

"No – no – I did not mean to accuse you of *lying*, Pet, but… I thought… If…"

Richert's disjointed words died on his lips, and we rode some distance farther in silence.

"If this is true," he said, "she is much worse than I thought, and I have you to thank that I'm well out of it and free of the lady!"

"*Are* you free?" It was most unmaidenly to question him so bluntly, but I found myself less interested than ever in Richert's approbation of my manners.

"She wrote to me," he said. "I answered as a gentleman must, telling her that I would treasure the memory of our association but that all things must come to an end. And I made her a handsome present, too. It is as well that I am about to win a monkey from Beau Farquhar and even more from my other wagers, or I would have had the devil of a time explaining my need for money to my father!"

I had never liked Richert so little as I did at that moment. He did not sound like a grown man, but like a sulky boy who resented being held responsible for his poor judgment. For a minute I almost thought that Mrs. de Larue was the one who was well out of the entanglement.

"Well, then. Believe what you like. But if you understand that the woman is a poisoner as well as a witch, then perhaps you will in time be able to believe that her murdered sister cried out for vengeance through the strings of Izzie's Irish harp."

"*Is* that what happened?"

"I tell you it is!" And would it be so very dishonest in me to leave the matter there, and put off telling him exactly what part my own actions had played in making that scene possible? It was not something I felt proud of… and anyway, it had really been the Hob's fault; if he had not meddled by stringing the harp and leaving it out for Izzie to find, nothing would have happened.

"I can only ask your forgiveness for not having communicated with you sooner," he said, still sounding rather sulky. "But you must admit, Pet, you haven't exactly been easy to speak to!"

That was true, and I supposed it would be mean-spirited to inquire how he would know, not having been bold enough to make the attempt in person. After all, he *had* known, through Kinross, of Izzie's illness and my own absorption in matters of the sick-room; and gentlemen do not like to know too many details of that sort of thing. I let the subject drop. After turning to return to the house, we chatted idly on indifferent matters for a few minutes. The days I had spent closeted with Izzie had left me badly out of date on the exciting topics currently exercising the *ton* – apart from the gossip about Mama's musicale, which Richert with rare tact did not bring up again. Instead he told me about the wagers that most interested the members of his club this week. Did the widowed Duke of Balcladich's sudden appearance in society signal that he was seeking another wife, or merely that he was gathering political support against the upcoming session of the Council? Would Major Maddox make an offer for the Turvoll heiress, and if so, how would her ambitious father respond to a prospective groom of the utmost respectability, but barely within the social class in which he was aiming to install Dorothea? And would Richert himself win what even his friends deemed an impossible marksmanship wager with Beau Farquhar and other members of his club?

This last, of course, he had mentioned already. I reminded him that he had seemed confident enough only a few minutes ago, to the point of already deciding how to spend his winnings. "Oh, I shall win," he assured me. "Truth is, Elspet, I am quietly trying to sow doubts among the members of my club, in the hope that a few more of them will be inspired to bet against me before the date. Trouble is, my current circumstances – I really spent far too much on the parting gift to Mrs. de Larue, but it was better than seeing her in person – urge me to hope that the coming full moon will shine in a cloudless sky, so that I can win Farquhar's money in time to stay out of Dun territory. Yet, if I can but put off my creditors for another month, that gives me time to try and place a few more bets before I demonstrate my skill and take all their money."

"Confident" seemed an inadequate description of his faith in his own marksmanship. I had half a mind to tell him he was odiously conceited; the trouble was, I suspected he was also correct.

"Then that is not what has furrowed your brow." For he had looked dark enough by the time he'd retailed all those wagers.

"No. It's the Maddox affair that worries me. The word is that Maddox would have made an offer already, but that the Turvoll girl is holding him off by chattering about how her heart belongs to Another."

"You?"

Richert nodded and scowled. "Not much I can do about it, though. As for my own wager, I practice daily; my eye is better than ever before. Whether this month or next, I shall certainly win. This month would be more convenient in many ways; Mama talks of making an excursion to the Spring of Ciarach in a day or two, so she will be safely out of town and not likely to hear anything about it. But if the present weather continues, there's not much chance of making the test this week." He cocked a gloomy eye at a sky that was scarcely less gloomy. Din Eidyn was certainly living up to its reputation as the city with the worst summer weather in the Anglian Isles.

"The Spring of Ciarach!" I had forgotten the summer festival at Ciarach. The water of that spring was believed to have healing properties all the year round, but they were doubled or tripled during the week of the festival, when folk from all over Dalriada gathered there to sing hymns to a Saint Ciarach (unknown to the Church; from most pulpits the week of festival was anathematized as a pagan gathering.) I had not been to church since Izzie fell ill, so I had some excuse for having forgotten about this upcoming gala.

Now a beautiful, bright idea blossomed in my mind. Ciarach was an easy half-day's ride north of Din Eidyn, not far from the country house on Loch Fàilte where my friend Sabira liked to spend the days around the full moon. The festival itself was a week of plays, concerts, informal dances and open-air sermons from any gentlemen of the church who were not overly disturbed by the absence of documentary evidence for "Saint Ciarach". (Or by the old songs in the Irish tongue commemorating a pagan hero also, purely coincidentally, called Ciarach.) On the one summer when our parents had tried the experiment of bringing their children to Din Eidyn long before any of us were ready for a Season, Tam and I had nagged unmercifully until Mama gave in and permitted Kirsty to take us to the fair for one day. I still remembered Izzie's grin after she had licked the gilt frosting off all three of the gingerbread poppets that we'd cajoled Kirsty into buying. The ear-splitting blasts Tam had produced on his willow whistle. Kirsty's shrieks of dismay when all three of us scrambled aboard the Spinning Cartwheel to be spun round and tumbled upside down by a rough ride that all but set my skirts about my ears.

Could a visit to this summer's fair possibly recapture the high spirits of that happy day? I glanced apprehensively at the lowering gray clouds. I remembered that escapade as a day of blue skies and golden fields. But then, I tended to remember my entire childhood as a time of bright unclouded sunshine, and reason argued it could not really have been quite so fine all the time.

And apart from the innocent excitement of a country fair, there were plenty of other reasons to go. The ride alone would surely do Izzie good; she would be more likely to regain her spirits, I thought, if she were outside in the open air instead of lying in a sickroom with the curtains drawn. And if all else failed, we could even go on to consult Sabira as to whether her salt magic could effect a cure for Izzie. I knew that she had left Din Eidyn for a few days. And since this was the week of the full moon, she would certainly be at their seaside country house on Loch Fàilte, only a few miles from Ciarach village.

It was even possible that the waters of the holy well would perform their healing magic. Energy and excitement surged through my veins; riding decorously through the Park was no longer an option.

"Richert, I have had an excellent idea, but you must race me to the gate before I tell you!"

Caramella responded to the slightest shift in my weight; she too must have been impatient at the dawdling pace Richert had set. The cool, slightly damp air rushed past my face, tugged at the ringlets confined under my hat; the blood thrummed in my veins with the sheer joy of speed and freedom. I did not pull Caramella up until we had reached the entrance to the Park, and even then I had my hands full to persuade her to go back to a decorous walking pace. We were almost at the house before I was free to turn my attention to Richert again.

"Well?" he drawled. "I trust this will not be like some of your earlier 'excellent' ideas, Pet! I've no mind to risk my neck birds-nesting off a seaside stack, or to explain to your brother how it was you happened to join us riding most unmaidenly astride his new horse."

I shook my head. "Richert, I'm not a child now; it is not fair to hold childish escapades against me!" Besides, both those little episodes had worked out perfectly well – if you forgot, as I preferred to do, the strapping I had earned from Papa for taking out Wildfire without permission. Well, no point in arguing about the past.

"This," I assured him, "is a truly excellent idea, and will serve both our purposes. You shall escort Izzie and me to the fair of Saint Ciarach!"

"Why cannot Tam do it?"

I gave him a pitying glance. Sometimes the man was extraordinarily slow. "Because," I said, "that would do you no good whatsoever! Look: it is like to be some time yet before Izzie is recovered, and I can scarcely go out raking every night when my sister is so ill. Already Dorothea Turvoll's hopes of getting you are rising. Escorting us to the fair will demonstrate to her that you have *not* lost interest in courting me, don't you see? And the outing is bound to be good for Izzie."

He gave me a reluctant grin. "And are you also plotting to get all the comfits you can eat?"

I laughed. "Quite likely I will treat us all to some gingerbread. *I* have taken enough exercise today to enjoy a comfit with no fear of putting on unsightly flesh, but I am not sure that you should take the risk!"

The groom was waiting to take Caramella back to the stables; I swung down from the saddle without waiting for a helping hand, laughed up at Richert and said, "Tomorrow, if it is fine? Or perhaps the day after!"

"Yes, but – Pet, we need to discuss – I can't—"

"No discussion is needed. On the first fine day this week, Izzie and I shall go to the fair of St. Ciaran. And you and Tammas shall escort us!" Now that

I was no longer mounted on Caramella, social concerns were obtruding. My hair was a tangled mess where the hat had not protected me, and the warmth in my cheeks made me worry that that last lovely gallop had left me unattractively wind-blown and blowsy. It could do me no good to stand talking to Richert in such a condition.

"You may call later," I told him, "but the decision is made!"

Later meant after I had had a chance to wash and change the riding habit for an afternoon dress, but there was no need to upset Richert by making this explicit. He had this vein of prudery; sometimes I thought he would be happier if I kept my eyes downcast and only spoke in monosyllables, like a child of seventeen newly freed from the nursery. That was another thing I'd have to work on… after he fell in love with me.

The prospect was not as exhilarating as usual, possibly because I was beginning to realize just how much work he was really going to need. After I entered the house, I paused a moment in the hall to close my eyes and remind myself of the day I fell in love with Richert: the sun and wind, the wild gallop over the moors, the sense of power when I realized I could indeed control my brother's steed, and – best of all – the laughing faces of the boys when I caught up with them and they realized that I, not Tam, was Wildfire's rider. Well, Richert at least had been laughing; Alastair had looked more horrified than impressed, but he soon got over it. But it was Richert's face I remembered most vividly, the sun striking bright fire in his hair, his face lit up with admiration and laughter.

Chapter 20

The memory of that glorious day, and the plan of an excursion to the fair, gave me all the energy I needed to impose this plan on my sister and brother. I fairly flew up the stairs to announce my plan to Izzie, and even her listless resistance did not slow me down... much. "Darling, I know it is hard to imagine enjoying yourself, but that is precisely why you must get out and about again!" I told her, whisking back and forth to plump her pillows, ring for fresh tea to replace the cold cup by her bedside, and loosen her braids to comb and plait them anew. "You have been frowsting in the dark for so long that you've forgotten how pleasant it can be to take a carriage ride on a sunny summer day!" And I explained, while making long smooth plaits of her tangled hair, how much she would be bound to enjoy the excursion, how I meant to commandeer our brother's light curricle, with Tammas and Richert to ride on either side and see to it that we encountered no obstacles along the way. "Remember when we cajoled Mama into letting Kirsty take us to the fair at Ciarach? And how much fun we had?"

Izzie gave me a tremulous smile. "Fancy you remembering that after all these years! And taking so much trouble to arrange the outing – I don't deserve that you should work so hard on my behalf, Elspet."

"Fiddlesticks!" I said, tying a new green riband around her head to confine the ringlets that were too short to be captured in the neat plaits that lay over her nightgown. "I shall vastly enjoy driving; I am simply, selfishly, forcing my poor older sister to come along to lend me countenance. But as long as we shall be so near the holy spring, surely you will not refuse to try the healing properties of its waters – to please me?"

"Only," said Izzie, "if you let me lick the icing off your gingerbread comfit."

I was so pleased that she managed a mild joke that I hardly cared that Richert did not, after all, call to confirm our arrangements. A quiet evening reading to Izzie was actually more to my taste than another tussle with Richert; the fact that he did not call, I reasoned, meant that on reflection he recognized the force of my reasoning and would cooperate with the plan without further argument. Such perspicacity argued well for our future life together.

I had chosen to leave the precise date of our excursion to be determined by the weather. Izzie would scarcely benefit by being dragged out on a day as overcast and gloomy as this one had been; where I found the cool air bracing, she would merely complain that her hands and feet were cold. For that matter, I was not myself over-eager to commit us to a longish carriage ride on such a day; sitting in Tammas' curricle, even if I did have the reins, would be completely different from riding my dear Caramella and enjoying the warmth that brisk exercise imparted. There was, of course, no question of Izzie's riding. Some carriage was therefore a necessity, and at least the curricle did not require that I saddle myself with a coachman. Oh, well. We would be out of the city, enjoying new sights and sounds, entertained by the fair; and there was always the hope that if the outing did not perk up Izzie's spirits, the waters of the holy spring would do so. And, of course, I would have Richert's company for the entire day... well, no need to worry about that. My duty was to Izzie; there must be no thought given to the task of making Richert *see* me.

That was almost a relief; I was growing tired of displaying myself to him with no reaction. The perfectly cut riding habit that I had donned for today's excursion, with its becoming trim of silver braid, had as little effect on him as the dowdiest last-year's round dress.

"What *ails* the man?" I murmured when, back in my own room before bed, I drew my night-rail close about me and inspected my figure in the mirror. A few years ago he had called me pudgy, but now the mirror assured me that I was as shapely as any young lady could desire to appear – with perhaps slightly more curves than some could boast. I could scarcely imagine that, alone of all the gentlemen I had flirted with, he found *that* feature unattractive.

"Maybe he really likes tall, languid females who droop like an elegant willow, and who have scarcely more shape than a willow either!" I proposed disconsolately to my mirror. That was a lowering reflection; I might have been able to slim myself into the preferred proportions for a young lady, but it was hardly possible to add six inches to my stature by taking thought.

"He has never shown any particular interest in your friend Sabira," croaked a familiar voice, as the mirror set to swinging on its pivot once again.

And Sabira was the very epitome of tall and willowy beauty. Whereas Vivienne de Larue, who had captivated Richert for a time, was a petite, vivacious brunette. I sighed. Vivienne's style of beauty was as beyond me as Sabira's, for I could scarcely dye my hair and go about with my knees bent. "And even if I did so," I remarked to the gyrating mirror, "I could never starve myself enough to look as tiny as Vivienne."

"No. You would merely look unattractively bony," the Hob, most infuriatingly, agreed. "And if you want my opinion—"

"What makes you think I do?"

"The young fool was not truly besotted with the Widow Larue either; he merely followed the fashion. Else he would not have dropped her for the sake of this pointless charade you invented."

"It is *not* pointless! Once he is in the habit of paying court to me, he will eventually observe that I am indeed worth courting, and then—"

"And just how long will that take?"

The cynical comment silenced me. We had been playing this courtship game long enough, Richert and I, had we not? And if no amount of calls, dances, midnight suppers and theater excursions had sufficed to make him see me as I really was rather than as the dumpy, dowdy schoolgirl of his memories, what good would more of the same do?

"The lout has never loved any female except Brown Bess," the Hob remarked sententiously.

I forced a laugh. "You are out there, at all events. Muskets are passé; the new rifles are his true love."

And as I could not, even in my wildest fantasy, assume the shape and semblance of a rifle, I put aside imagining and sought my bed.

The next day dawned brighter, but only insofar as the clouds had faded from steel-gray to pearl-gray; but by afternoon wisps of blue sky were visible as the wind far above the city harried the clouds and chased them south. Good, let them go and oppress the spirits of the Anglians; it was time for us in Dalriada to enjoy our too-brief summer. I occupied the day in arranging for the use of the curricle and Tammas' calmest pair of horses, and in making sure that Tammas understood he was to accompany us. He was not in general the most obliging of older brothers when it came to escorting his sisters, but the plea that it was necessary for Izzie's health worked powerfully upon him.

"And then," he said hopefully, "there are rumors that there's to be a mill at Ciarach tomorrow!"

I was puzzled. "Tammas, I do not think there are any factories in the village. Except for the week of the fair, it is a poor place and sparsely inhabited. Certainly I have never heard of any gentlefolk residing there! When we went ten years ago, remember, Papa commented that it was sadly run-down from the days when it was a prime halting-place for the coaching route north; three inns, and none of them with enough custom to maintain their owners!"

Tammas gave me an indulgent laugh and flicked my cheek with one finger. "Not a *factory*, little sister. A boxing match! Rumor has it that the Gentleman means to meet the Dago outside Ciarach tomorrow. 'Twill be a famous sight!"

"Then I hope that tomorrow will be fine," I said. And I privately hoped that we should see nothing of these oddly named characters. I had no real fear that we would; Tammas was always getting excited about rumors of some sporting event that never actually came off.

The morrow was all I could have wished, sending early sunlight streaming into the breakfast-room. After sending a man to remind Richert of his promise, I took coffee and sweet rolls up to Izzie. I nibbled on a roll while throwing open her curtains and persuading her into a new carriage dress with a bottle-green spencer that would both keep her warm and set off the flaming color of her hair. I had forced her to wash it the previous day, and had put up her ringlets in curl papers; her natural curiosity as to the results persuaded her to look in the mirror as her abigail and I dressed her.

"My hair is well enough," she sighed, "but oh, I am ashamed to show such a pale, thin countenance to the world!"

"Why, there are great ladies aplenty would be happy to have such white skin as yours, my lady," said the abigail. She went on at length about how pure white skin was the infallible sign of a true aristocrat, while I got out Izzie's new slippers and found a hat to protect her against the sun. Privately I thought my sister would look all the better with a little color in her cheeks; perhaps the day's activity and excitement, the fresh air and the novelty of being outside her sick-room, would accomplish that effect even if the holy water of the saint's spring did not.

Richert had still not presented himself by the time Izzie and I were dressed and the curricle was brought round, but Tammas engaged himself to ride by the Dalkey house and prod my laggard swain into joining us. "Depend upon it, Pet, he will hardly wish to miss the chance of seeing a mill!"

It would have been more tactful had Tammas said that Richert would not wish to miss an excursion into the country with me – but possibly less truthful. In any case, there could be nothing improper in my driving Izzie and myself unescorted as far as the Northgate. Tammas had promised faithfully to present himself and Richert there, and it seemed foolishly missish to insist on delaying our departure until he could bring Richert to our house. Fine days in Din Eidyn were not so common, nor of such long duration, that I wished to risk waiting out an hour of sunshine when one never knew when the rain might return.

Tammas's matched greys were showy animals and garnered much admiration as I took them neatly through the Langmarket and up the long hill to the Northgate. I myself would have preferred more spirited beasts like my own dear Caramella, but to most of the ladies we encountered these handsome, if slightly sluggish, steppers were all that could be desired. We were hard put to it to reach our rendezvous with Tammas and Richert within the half-hour, but I explained to our acquaintances that Izzie and I were desirous of reaching Ciarach that morning so as to return in good time before the weather could change and that we had no time to spare.

At the Northgate an unwelcome surprise greeted us.

Chapter 21

"Lady Heriot, Miss Rattray, your servant! Why these frowns, Miss Rattray? Do you object to my joining your excursion?"

I forced a smile. "Of course we are delighted to have your company, Lord Kinross!" But he and Tammas were the only two gentlemen at the gate. Where was Richert? Must we wait for him? I flashed an enquiring glance at my scapegrace elder brother, who appeared all unconscious of his failure to deliver Richert as promised.

"Dalkey is – indisposed," Tammas said. "I take it he made a serious attempt to drink up the proceeds of his wager last night." His grin made him look like the schoolboy who had played mad pranks with Alastair and Richert. "Though even one of Dalkey's capacity would be hard put to it –"

"Oh... the wager!" I had forgotten all about it. Of course! Not only this morning, but last night, had been fine; and it had been the first night of the full moon.

"It must have been a famous spectacle!" Tammas exclaimed, belatedly recollecting that it was scarcely proper to discuss Richert's subsequent overindulgence with us. "Kinross tells me that he shot through the wheeler's traces while the carriage was in motion, and by moonlight!"

"Such," Kinross said drily, "were the terms of the wager. Dalkey had only to repeat what he had already accomplished once – and this time he had the advantage of foreknowledge, not to mention having loaded his pistol with the expectation of taking such a shot. The only surprising thing is that he found a number of fools willing to bet heavily against him."

"All the same," grumbled Tammas, "I do wish you had told me, Pet! It is too bad to have missed such a feat!"

"Indeed, I had forgotten it myself." What a silly to-do over a shooting match! And what a flimsy excuse for failing to honor his commitments to myself! For a moment I was quite out of charity with Richert.

"Dalkey will be inconsolable at having let you down," Kinross said, "but I trust his grief, and yours, will be mitigated by my having dared to propose myself as his substitute."

I attempted to smile and to say all that was proper to the occasion. I fear I made a poor hand of it, for I was too furious with Richert to maintain the social graces. The drunken sot! How could he expect me to forgive a defection on such grounds!

Kinross directed his horse to bring him along the driver's side of the curricle. "I see you are not reconciled to the change of plans," he murmured. "There is, of course, no need for you to accept my escort if it is displeasing to you."

I mentally chastised myself for being as rag-mannered as Richert. It was hardly Kinross' fault that I had placed my trust in a young man as selfish as he was reckless.

"On the contrary, my lord," I said, achieving a somewhat better smile, "we can only benefit by the exchange, for I have no fear that you, at least, will be tempted to abandon us for some more exciting entertainment along the way."

It was easily said, for it was true. I could repose a confidence in Kinross that I had never been able to enjoy with Richert. And the recognition of that fact led me to some more serious contemplation which occupied me for the greater portion of our drive to Ciarach.

As we approached the village, the road grew much more crowded. Had I been riding, the increased traffic would have posed no difficulty; but I was not nearly so expert a whip as I was a rider, and all my concentration was required to guide the curricle through a throng of carts, carriages, riders and pedestrians in holiday mood. I could tell that Tammas wished he had consented to drive us rather than riding alongside, and he turned white to the lips when I turned the greys slightly to thread my way between a ditch and a slow, lumbering coach that looked vaguely familiar. But I had no alternative, not if we were to reach the holy spring in time for Izzie to partake of the healing rites and return home before she was quite exhausted by the outing.

After the near-misadventure of the coach and the roadside ditch, first Kinross and then Tammas shouldered their horses into the lead, where they kept the way clear for me. I was grateful, but what attention I could spare was directed towards my sister as we reached the outskirts of the village and the crowd of merry fair-goers surged about us. Izzie did not appear to be overset by the growing tumult of the crowd; although she was gripping the seat with both hands – an unconscious commentary on her opinion of my driving skills – she laughed at the antics of the amateur acrobats we passed, gave her smiles and a few stray coins to the urchins who turned cartwheels by the roadside for her delectation, and once nearly caused us to come to grief by grasping my arm to point out a gaily bedizened tent before which an iron-lunged barker roared out a promise to show us a dancing dog, a learned pig and an invisible girl.

"Yes, yes, Izzie, but do let me find the way out of the village first!" I implored. Kinross excited my gratitude yet again, this time by dropping back to ride beside Izzie and diverting her with a query as to how anybody could promise to *show* an *invisible* girl.

"Perhaps they mean to show the effects of her actions?" Izzie speculated. "Taking down a book from a shelf, for instance, or playing upon the pianoforte?"

"More likely a violin," Tammas put in. "Such an instrument is within the reach of any strolling beggar, whereas only gentlefolk are like to possess a pianoforte or a great harp. Look, Pet, there is the turnoff for the well!" He swept a careless arm forward, surprising the horses; the near grey flattened its ears and took two mincing steps sideways, and I was hard put to it to maintain my control through the subsequent sharp turn required to take us to the holy well rather than deeper into the village.

"Neatly managed!" Kinross voiced his approbation. "I see you are as competent a whip as you are a horsewoman, Miss Rattray."

Few of our fellow travelers had taken this turn; it seemed that most of them were more interested in the rope dancers, the learned pig, and other entertainments advertised by shouting barkers than in the healing properties of the holy well. In the comparative peace of this byway I had, finally, leisure to respond to Kinross and to entreat him not to offer me Spanish coin. "You must see that I have not your skill; I do not pretend to drive to an inch, to catch the thong of my whip over my head or perform the other tricks which, I am sure, Tammas is itching to demonstrate. Indeed, had I guessed there would be such a crowd in the village, I should have entreated my brother to take the reins."

"But your instinctive understanding of and sympathy with the horses has stood you in good stead," said Kinross, his voice still warm with an approval that put me to the blush, knowing how undeserved it was. "With a little more practice I believe you would drive quite as well as any of the young fools who play at shaving one another's carriage wheels."

"At least I know better than to attempt such unnecessary feats!" I laughed. "And after today, Tammas is hardly like to invite me to take the reins of his curricle again. He was quite white with fear for his horses in that crowd!"

"He appears," said Kinross drily, "to have conquered that fear quite handily." He gestured behind us, and for the first time I realized that Tammas had missed the turn-off for the holy well.

"No, he is not lost," Kinross said before I had more than frowned in concern. "He has charged me to inform you that the promised prize-fight is to be held beyond the village, and since he knows you ladies will be safe under my escort, he is just taking a little detour to view the field."

I sighed. "Of course he is! Tell me, Kinross, do you think there will really be a fight, or is Tammas merely chasing another rumor?"

"The size and the mood of the crowd suggests that he is correct this time," Kinross said.

"Leaving all the responsibility to you!" My cheeks flamed with embarrassment. "Really, Tammas is as bad as Richert! It is too bad that you should be saddled with us like this!"

"I have endured worse hardships than being permitted to escort two lovely ladies on a fine summer's day," Kinross said.

We were scarcely alone on this by-road to the well, but most of the rowdier elements of the crowd had, thankfully, followed Tammas' lead, going on to the delights of the taverns, the raree-shows and the promised exhibition of fighting. Our companions on this road were quieter and, I thought, more sensible of the holy nature of their pilgrimage. I saw a man bent and withered with age being helped along the way by a much younger man, probably his son. A young mother bent anxiously over the wailing infant in her arms. A boy on crutches swung himself along with a merry whistle. And some distance behind us, the coach I had passed labored on its way.

"I do not know if you had leisure to recognize that coach at the time?" Kinross inquired with a glance to the rear.

"Indeed, no. But I have an exceedingly vivid memory of the ditch on the other side, in which I so nearly overturned us!" I confessed with another blush.

"You were in no danger," said Kinross. "But – if I do not mistake the arms, that is Lady Dalkey's coach."

"Indeed!" If Richert had abandoned us not because he was in a drunken stupor, but because of his mama's prior claim, his defection was more excusable.

"No, he is not with her either." It was beyond annoying that Kinross could read my face so easily.

"It is of no matter," I said, and felt the truth of the words as I spoke them. Richert could not be relied upon. I had never been able to rely upon him, even when I was helping him to play this charade of courtship. Unlike the man who rode beside me, who had ever been my aid and support in so unobtrusive a way that I had been able to remain unconscious of all I owed to him, Richert had no more stability than the colored illuminations that burst over the Castle on holidays. Like those illuminations, he caught the eye; and like them, he was without substance.

This new understanding of mine demanded serious thought. But we were within sight of the holy spring now, or rather, of the ferns and other foliage ringing the water. The thorn trees on either side of the road were gay with the fragments of garments and the shiny trinkets left by generations of supplicants. After I drew up the curricle alongside the other carriages – there were not many - Kinross gave Izzie his arm and assisted her to the fern-bordered brink of the water. I followed after them. Izzie's steps were shaky and she leaned heavily on Kinross' arm, but that, I hoped, could be accounted for by the natural fatigue resulting from this morning's exertion after her prolonged illness and inactivity. Twice I heard her laugh in response to some sally of our escort's, and the sound raised my hopes. Could it be that fresh air and new sights were working their cure upon her already, even before we solicited the intervention of the saint?

It certainly seemed so. Just as I joined them at the brim of the spring, Izzie politely declined Kinross' offer to borrow a cup from one of the other supplicants with which he might dip up her draft of the healing water. "All the tales say that the healing properties are strongest if one takes up the water in one's own hands," she declared, kneeling with surprising alacrity among the green ferns. I knelt beside her, thinking to support her should the sudden motion render her momentarily giddy. She turned her head and whispered in my ear, "Besides, one cannot know how many have already used a common cup, and what diseases afflict them!" She stifled a giggle. "I had far rather trust my own hands, which I know to be clean!"

While Izzie scooped up the water three times, each time taking a sip from her cupped hands, I gazed into the green depths of the spring. Around the edge worshippers dipped into the spring and created little circles of spreading ripples, but in the center the water was so still that it perfectly reflected the blue sky overhead. I knew not whether 'twas pagan magic or Christian holiness, or merely that greatest enchantress, Nature, that affected me; but a sense of great age and great power emanated from the entire spring. I cupped my hands to take my own sips of the sacred water. It seemed to me that it bubbled with energy that penetrated my body and elated my spirits. Richert, I thought, with his rooted dislike of the supernatural, would have laughed at me and told me that I was suffering from the hysteria of the crowd, and that the only wonderful property of the water was that it was so cold as to constitute a shock to the body.

But Richert was not here, nor did I miss him.

All around the pool I saw the changed faces of the others who had knelt to taste the healing spring for themselves. A light seemed to play upon the features of the young mother who had dipped her ailing infant's feet into the water; the babe was bawling lustily enough now, in all conscience! If the lame boy did not spring to his feet and throw away his stick, at least he stood more easily than when he had flung himself down to drink, and I thought the lines of old pain patiently endured had somewhat been smoothed away from his face. Beside those two, a pretty country girl in apron and kerchief leaned perilously out over the pool and chanted in a half-whisper,

"Water, water, tell me truly,
Is the man I love truly
On the earth, or under the sod,
Sick or well, – in the name of God?"

Everyone around the pool stilled their whispers and movements for a long moment while the girl stared anxiously into the water; then, like an answer to her query, a flurry of bubbles arose before her, breaking in the air and, it seemed to me, releasing rainbows that danced over her face. Laughing with joy, she rose from her knees and exclaimed, "Oh, I can be happy now!"

I glanced towards Izzie, but she had retreated from the verge while I watched the girl and the answer – if it was truly an answer – that she received. My questioning eyes met Kinross' grave stare. "And you, Elspet, do you wish to ask the pool anything?" he inquired in an undertone.

"All I ask for is my sister's health and happiness."

"But there may be other matters that you wish to learn."

"Nothing," I said, rising from my knees and accepting the help of his proffered hand, "nothing that I am not capable of sorting out for myself."

Chapter 22

That was at least half true. I had no more desire to enlist the aid of the holy spring, or of the Hob, or of my own thread magic, to win Richert. I had come to that much acceptance and clarity on this morning's journey, and the water had cleared my vision once and for all. Richert would never truly court me, nor did I wish him to; the dreams I had enjoyed these ten years past were of no more substance than the rainbow bubbles rising to the surface of the pool. I had remembered childhood happiness, had attached those feelings to a remembered face that had nothing to do with the grown man. How could I complain that Richert never saw me as I was? I had refused to see *him*; I had kept trying to force him into the mold of the immature dreams and inchoate longings of the child I had been. Now I could consider the actual young man: lively, irresponsible, occasionally petulant, military-mad, and firmly opposed to anything that smacked of the supernatural. That young man, I saw now, would never court me; nor could I wish him to. My only problem relative to Richert now was how to put an end to our charade of courtship without leaving him vulnerable to the languishing of Dorothea Turvoll – and I now perceived that she had been no sillier, no more deluded by romantic phantasies, than had I myself. It was not even beyond the bounds of possibility that Dorothea and Richert might eventually, especially if encouraged by Lady Dalkey, make a match of it and fare no worse than many another couple.

What I did not know, and might have asked the holy spring had I enjoyed privacy, was what to make of the grave looks that Kinross bent on me. With him, half unnoticed as I pursued Richert, I had enjoyed an easy companionship and shared laughter. He showed a gentlemanly concern for my safety tempered by the recognition – which Richert had never granted – that I was in general quite competent to look after myself.

And he had never, not once, stepped beyond the line of what was pleasing and socially acceptable, nor had he forced his addresses upon me. When I looked back over our happy interactions this summer, there had been words and phrases and looks that *might* betoken a deeper, more personal interest than he had explicitly avowed – or they might have been mere casual courtesy.

I began to know my own heart; but I had no clue as to the state of his own.

"We should make room for other supplicants," he prompted gently, and I realized that I had been standing for too long, silent, and searching his face for I knew not what.

A silvery laugh, too long unheard in our house, came to my ears, and I saw that Izzie had retreated as far as the line of carriages drawn up at some little distance from the pool. She had walked that far without the support of Kinross' arm? Not only that; the animation of her countenance and the vivacity of her gestures all bespoke a return to the lively, if sharp-tongued, sister I had been missing since the miscarriage. She shifted her position slightly as she spoke, and I caught my breath in surprise as I recognized her interlocutor. It was none other than Richert's mother, Lady Dalkey. And now I saw that the heavy Dalkey coach had finally joined the other carriages. As they chatted in the sunshine, Lady Dalkey raised a heavy silver cup to her lips, then handed it to the waiting footman. The draught of the holy waters did not seem to have benefited her as it had Izzie; she appeared as languid as ever. Perhaps – but no, of course Lady Dalkey would never have demeaned herself to kneel at the muddy edge of a pool and to drink from her own cupped hands.

"Elspet, I have had a famous notion!" Izzie called as Kinross and I approached.

"You seem so much recovered, that I dare not speculate as to what that might be! Do you wish to go and watch the rope-dancers? Or to partake of too much hot gingerbread with gilt icing?" I thought that I should happily accede to any plan she desired, so delightful it was to see her animated and taking a lively interest in her surroundings again.

"No," she said, "I fear I am far too exhausted from our journey to enjoy the rowdy delights of a fair. Lady Dalkey has very kindly offered to take me up in her coach and convey me home. If you do not object, we two invalids shall make our way back to the city and leave you to enjoy the fair. I need have no fears for your comfort and safety, seeing in whose hands I leave you." Her smile flashed for Kinross, and her green eyes searched mine with some unspoken message.

"But – but, Izzie," I stammered, "you seem so much better!"

"Nevertheless, I am much too tired to remain in Ciarach," she insisted.

"Shall I take you home at once?"

She shook her head. For someone who claimed to be so fatigued, she certainly looked healthy and decisive enough. "No, for you must wait for Tammas. And as it would be quite improper for him to leave you here alone, Lord Kinross must wait with you. I shall do very well in the care of Lady Dalkey and her servants, Elspet. And while you are awaiting Tammas' return, why do not you and Lord Kinross enjoy the delights of the fair? You can tell me all about it tonight."

"But – but –"

As you know, I had had some thoughts of going on from Ciarach to visit my friend Sabira, who was making her usual monthly visit to the country house on the shores of Loch Fàilte. If the spring of Ciarach failed to cure Izzie, I might implore Sabira to try what she might achieve with her magic based on the sea and salt water – powers I did not fully understand, but that seemed to be much stronger than anything I could achieve with my little tangles of thread.

But Izzie, whatever she might claim, seemed far livelier and more cheerful than before; I had not even dared to hope that the holy spring would achieve such speedy results. It must have been the relief I felt on her account that made the day itself seem brighter now, the scene around the pool so beautiful and – yes, I had to admit it – the sights of the fair so tempting.

I could scarcely interrogate her about her true reasons for insisting on a speedy return home, not before Lady Dalkey. And if I had learned one thing in my life with a sharp-tongued, sharp-tempered older sister, it was that disputing her wishes was only too likely to cost me dear. I could not guess why she had taken it into her head to endure the slow coach ride back to Din Eidyn with a languishing, invalidish woman old enough to be her mother, but neither could I oppose the decision.

And for some reason, my heart was too light to bear overmuch concern. Yes, let Izzie return to Din Eidyn if she thought the fairgoers would be too common and too noisy for her. Kinross and I could easily while away an hour or two until Tammas was ready to join us. And there could be no impropriety in his escorting me alone in such a public setting!

When I made my adieux to Izzie, she surprised me very much by embracing me. Had the healing waters not only cured her ailments, but made her into a sweet and loving sister?

Not precisely, no. The purpose of the affectionate gesture was to allow her to whisper a parting injunction to me, to the effect that I was a greater fool than she had hitherto supposed if I continued to languish after a ne'er-do-well like Richert Dalkey when such a man as Lord Kinross was dangling after me. She hoped I was properly appreciative of her arranging to give me this day at the fair to fix his interest, and she would be very much disappointed in me if I failed to do so.

If that wasn't Izzie all over, covering me in confusion and blushes just as I needed to express my gratitude to Lady Dalkey and to appear unmoved by the turn of events which had pitchforked me into a lengthy tête-a-tête with the one man whose presence was like to overset my hard-won calm! Somehow, I know not how, I said something of what was proper to Lady Dalkey; Kinross, ever ready with the right words, covered some of my stammering embarrassment. We waved farewell for what seemed like hours while the coachman turned his great clumsy vehicle and finally took it back toward the main road.

Kinross proposed that we wait a few minutes to avoid overtaking the coach and being forced to prolong our farewells through the window of a heavy moving vehicle that was bound to splash up mud on my skirts.

"To say nothing of your top-boots!" I added with a laugh that was but slightly forced.

Kinross surveyed the state of his boots and pulled an exaggerated face of comical dismay that forced a more genuine laugh from me. "I fear there is little more damage that can be done in that quarter. My man will rate me finely for having defaced his handiwork by carelessly riding through these muddy lanes."

"What, are gentlemen as much at the mercy of their valets as we ladies are of our abigails?" I asked. "I have never heard Tammas to express fear of his manservant."

"Jem, not being cut out for a soldier, attached himself to me during the Galician campaign," Kinross said absently, "and I have heard enough of his strictures on mud, blood and garlic-eating peasants to have a most hearty dread of incurring his displeasure! Still," he finished with a slight bow to me, "far be it from me to complain that the game is not worth the candle. Will you take my arm up the hill, Miss Rattray?"

"On our last meeting," I said, "it was Elspet."

"And on that occasion," riposted he, "you promised to drop the 'my lord' which still causes me to look round in anticipation of seeing my father's frown. But perhaps you feel that our present situation requires a degree of formal distance?"

All I could say to that was to express my perfect confidence in him and in the propriety of our visiting a crowded country fair in full view of more than a hundred folk. "But though I thank you, I am not so weak as to require to lean upon your arm while traversing the gentle slope back up to the village!"

There might be no impropriety in it, but I feared there was some danger to myself in accepting the proffered support. Feelings long denied and as long suppressed had been leaping to life within me since that cold draught from the spring of Ciarach. I knew not whether the water had laid some bewitchment over me, or whether it had – as was more congruent with its reputation – liberated me from a spell. Was it possible that I had, all unawares, in those long-ago days, charmed myself into a phantasy of love for Richert Dalkey? I could not now imagine why I had been so desperately set on getting his notice and becoming his lady – any more than I could understand why I had been so oblivious to the fact that our third playmate had grown into a man infinitely superior to Richert and far more deserving of any lady's appreciation.

Not, I reminded myself, that there was any reason to hope that I risked other than heartbreak by an attempt to fix Kinross' affections. Having wasted a lonely ten years and one busy summer by attempting to give my heart to a man who had no desire for it, I should be a very great fool indeed were I to immediately transfer my longings to another old friend. No, I would not think of Kinross in any light other than that of a dear friend of long standing whom I could trust absolutely to – to – well, never mind. We had the gift of this afternoon at the fair; I resolved to enjoy it for what it was, and abjured foolish daydreams of an unlikely future.

My resolve was not, alas, nearly as strong as had been my headstrong insistence on winning over Richert Dalkey. I blamed Kinross; he was so pleasant a companion, his manners and address all that any lady could have desired, that it was all but impossible for me not to keep hoping for just that shade of additional warmth that would have fed my new dreams.

My new, foolish, totally unjustifiable dreams. I would *not* be another Dorothea Turvoll, perpetually imputing love where the gentleman proffered only common courtesy.

Well, common courtesy and long-standing friendship.

Common courtesy, long-standing friendship, and a warm recollection of happy memories.

Blast the man! Did he *have* to make it so difficult for me to maintain my façade of amiable but impersonal manners?

An impertinent vagabond of a piper spied us strolling up to the village and promptly serenaded us with a variety of what I supposed must be traditional Irish airs, though the hideous squealing of the instrument was reminiscent more of the death of a pig than of the sweet melodies Izzie had coaxed from her small Irish harp before… But I would not think of the last time she took up the harp, save to be grateful that Kinross had broken it!

"Oh, pray, make him go away!" I begged Kinross.

"What, do you not care for traditional music?" he said, or rather shouted, over the caterwauling of the pipes. But without waiting for an answer, he flipped a silver mark to the musician and told him there would be another when he finished his impromptu concert... so long as he played from the far side of the holy spring.

"I understand the Irish people who inhabit the hills north of us are quite fond of the instrument," I said with a gasp of relief as the squealing noises faded into the distance, "though I have never understood their taste."

"Ah," said Kinross gravely, "but that is because you have never experienced an expert playing the pipes in their natural environment."

I looked my bemusement.

"The piper stands on one mountain," Kinross explained, still maintaining a preternatural gravity, "and the audience on a different one. I am given to understand that, just as distance lends enchantment to the view, it lends – well, endurability – to the music."

I sputtered with most unladylike laughter as he led us to a suitable vantage point for observing the antics of the rope dancers.

After the death-defying tricks of the lady who danced upon a slack rope on her tip-toes, a handful of sugarplums, the sight of the Learned Pig completely failing to recognize the subtle hand gestures with which a showman attempted to guide its answers to arithmetical inquiries, a platter of roast pork accompanied by ratafia (Kinross tried the locally brewed ale, and assured me that I had the best of the bargain) and a half hour of laughing at the two Dancing Dogs' acrobatic attempts to chew off their ruffs and escape the rest of their costumes, I became belatedly aware that Kinross' attention was neither on the dogs' antics nor on me. He kept looking past the entertainers with a frown of concern, which he hurriedly disguised as laughter when he saw me observing him.

"I wish you will tell me what is troubling you!" I said. "For I do not think it is merely pity for those poor confused animals and their struggles with knee-breeches and stockings."

Kinross flipped the last morsels of his roast pork to the dogs, effectively ending the act, and tossed a handful of silver to the dogs' master before taking my elbow and steering me out of the crowd. "I had expected to see Tammas before now," he said with a last worried glance at the sky.

I had scarcely given a thought to the passage of time, but now I too looked upward. Clouds streaked the sky, obscuring the sun. Still, "It cannot be much past noon?" I ventured. It seemed to me that we had hardly begun to taste the delights of the fair.

"I make it past three of the clock," said Kinross, consulting his watch, "and 'twas said the prize fight would begin before ten."

"If those heroes of boxing have been belaboring one another for the past five hours –"

"They cannot have," said Kinross. "I laid fifty guineas that by the third round the Gentleman – ah, that is—"

"Tammas," I said, casting my eyes down and wishing I had the ability to blush at will, the better to appear properly maidenly, "has made me acquainted with some of the slang of the sporting world. I take it that you do not believe the person called the Dago would have been able to stand up to his opponent Gentleman Jenkins for long?"

"For five hours? Impossible!"

"Perhaps there were other matches?"

"None that I heard planned. But stay – let me find you a place to rest, Elspet, and I shall inquire as to what has happened and try, if I can, to discover when we may hope for your brother's return to the village."

But all three of the taverns on the main (and only) street of Ciarach were filled to the brim with roaring-drunk sportsmen and fairgoers, and quite ineligible, as even I had to admit, as resting places for a gently bred lady. In the end Kinross deposited me on a shaky bench that formed part of a traveling sweet-stall, and, commending me to the beribboned dame who guarded her stock of peppermints and gingerbread, went off into the crowd to make his inquiries.

Feeling guilty for taking up space that might otherwise have been filled by paying customers, I bought the proprietor's good will by making several purchases, one after another, from her stock. The first bag of gingerbread figures came fresh from the oven in the bakery behind the stall, and with a glass of cold tea, served to fill up the corners left after that nuncheon of roast pork. The second bag was not quite so attractive as the first; I tucked it into my sleeve to take to Izzie. And after that, I felt it would be wise to confine my depredations on the lady's stock to nibbling peppermints. Besides, I was running out of small change.

Kinross was still not back when I finished the last peppermint, and I was beginning to feel chilly after sitting still so long. Thoughtfully, remembering how Izzie had served me on a previous occasion, I took out the bag of gingerbread I was saving for Izzie and carefully licked off the icing on the figure of St. Ciarach.

Even revenge could not give me appetite to continue attacking Izzie's gilt gingerbread figures. With some regret I did up the parcel again. A brisk walk or, better, a canter through the countryside would have been ideal to settle my stomach after the day's indulgences, as well as warming my limbs. But Kinross would be displeased and, worse, worried, if he returned to find me gone, and I had no dependence on the keeper of the stall to convey a spoken message to him. Perhaps I could leave him a note which she would have only to hand to him? And then take some exercise? A walk back down the hill to where our horses waited would be delightful. And then I might make so bold as to saddle Kinross' horse and take a turn about the outskirts of the village – even going so far as to meet him on his way back from the scene of the prize-fight. It would be a tame adventure compared to some of my childhood escapades, but perhaps it might put us back on the easy terms of those days. Especially if he lost his temper!

This plan, however, failed. I did find something to write on – the back of a printed flyer advertising the fair - but there was no such thing as ink or a pen in the gingerbread stall. Of course not. I was still considering where to procure writing materials when he returned, looking warmer and more disheveled than I had seen him since the long-ago day of our bird's-nesting excursion. "The mill was delayed several hours due to the tardiness of the principals," he informed me, "and the stage taken over by some vagabond players whose production is not yet finished."

"Oh! I should like to see the players!" Truth to tell, I was quite ready to see *anything* other than the slice of Ciarach village that was visible from within the gingerbread stall.

"Not these players," Kinross said gloomily.

"Oh… are they vulgar?"

"In the extreme. And what's worse, the mob in attendance is divided between those who wish to see more horseplay and more boys dressed as girls attacking one another with bladders, and those who are demanding the bloodletting they were promised with this prize-fight."

"And which side is Tammas taking?"

"I was unable to find him in the crowd," Kinross said. "I can but hope that he has sense enough to get out of there before the argument turns into a riot." He cast a worried glance at the sky. "And before the storm is upon us!"

I realized, tardily, that the chill in my limbs was not solely caused by sitting still for so long. The sun that had made the morning so pleasant was now quite hidden behind layers of gray-black clouds. And when I stepped out of the gingerbread stall and gazed down the street at the distant hills, I could see the soft gray of rain falling over them. Was the storm moving this way?

"You must have better shelter than this," Kinross muttered, and taking my arm, made his way towards the largest of the three taverns along the street.

We were quite out of luck, for not only the Savage's Head, but the Victory Oak and the Woolpack were completely filled with lively gentlemen who had come for the prize-fight and intended to stay the night. Not a few of them, I thought, would miss the fight that had attracted them, for they were so deep in their cups already that they would scarcely be able to stagger to the mill – and Heaven help the fairgoers if these drunken dandies tried to drive their carriages to the scene! But this, Kinross remarked in disgust, was no help to us, for they were too inebriated to recognize their duty as gentlemen to give place to a lady in distress.

"But I am not distressed," I told Kinross, "and I do know where we can find shelter! Let us go to Loch Fàilte, and quickly, before the storm breaks!"

"To Iveroth's country house? But if he is not in residence—"

"Yes, yes, I know; it would be pointless to beg lodging there if the house is shut up. But I happen to know that *Lady* Iveroth is there."

Kinross bent a sharp glance on me. "I take it she informed you of her intention to visit Loch Fàilte."

It was not precisely a question, so I did not feel obliged to admit that we had not discussed the matter. But Sabira's nature required regular visits to the sea which she assuaged by visiting the country house on the shores of the sea-loch of Fàilte; the longing was strongest at times of the full moon; and she was certainly not resident in Din Eidyn this week, so where else could she be?

"Very well," he said, requiring pen and ink, paper and sand from the landlord of the Savage's Head. "Your brother can scarcely expect you to wait for him in such inclement weather. I shall just leave him a note giving our direction, then let us be off and attempt to outrun the rain."

I rather thought that Tammas *would* expect me to sit in a stuffy tap-room, surrounded by drunken fair-goers, until it should be convenient for him to return and collect me. Not only that, but – not knowing that Izzie had found her own way back to the capital – he was doubtless expecting my poor sister to undergo the same ordeal, regardless of the consequences to her health! Well, so much the worse for him! He might get himself drenched while waiting for a prize-fight that I suspected would never happen, given the sudden inclemency of the weather; Kinross and I should be safe and warm at Loch Fàilte, welcome guests of Sabira. Tammas might ride through the rain and mud to find us there. The passing inconvenience would serve him right for being so thoughtless!

Chapter 23

We were on the treeless high road to Loch Fàilte when the threatened storm broke with a flash of lightning and a thunderclap that so startled Tammas' greys, I was hard put to it to prevent them from veering off the road altogether. As the rain drummed down upon us, Kinross dropped back to ride beside me and leaned over. "Shall I take them?"

"No, I can manage!" I shouted back. Already I was a sad excuse for a fashionable young lady. My bonnet had been so soaked in the first burst of rain that it fell about my face and made me feel like a horse wearing blinkers. I wrenched it off and screwed up my eyes against the pouring rain. I could feel that some of my hair had come loose with the bonnet; the damp locks clung to my neck like seaweed. At least my carriage dress was of sturdy material and, no matter how wet, would not make me look like a lightskirt who damped her petticoats on purpose to reveal her form – or so I trusted; I could pay little attention to anything but the absolute necessity of keeping a firm hand on the reins.

If I asked it, Kinross would tie his horse to the back of the curricle and take over the driving. I did not wish to ask that. Not only would it be humiliating to admit I had taken out a pair of horses that I could not control, but making the changeover would necessarily delay our progress by several minutes – and all I wished, just now, was to reach the shelter of Sabira's house as soon as possible.

I might also have wished to look something less like a drowned rat, but I was too busy with the horses to consider my bedraggled appearance. It was not until we pulled up at the door of the Iveroth country house that I had leisure to regret my discarded bonnet, disheveled hair and soaked dress. While Kinross pounded on the door, I put up one hand to smooth my hair and decided that it was quite beyond help.

The door opened just far enough to reveal the figure of a stooped, elderly man who scowled at us without speaking.

I was not minded to sit in the rain until he made up his mind about us. Without waiting for Kinross to help me out, I put one hand on the side of the curricle and scrambled out. As I stepped to the ground I heard an ominous ripping sound from my skirt. As if there had not already been disasters enough!

"Pray announce us to Lady Iveroth at once," I said, trying to infuse my voice with the commanding hauteur that my mother and Izzie employed when speaking to the lower sort of persons.

"Not at home!" the old man announced with an air of triumph. He would have swung the door shut in our faces had Kinross not interposed one booted foot.

"Oh, do not be ridiculous," I said, sweeping forward and trying to ignore the dripping of my hair and dress. By now I had recognized Iveroth's elderly retainer. "I happen to know that Sabira left Din Eidyn for Loch Fàilte two days since, and I am far too wet and uncomfortable to be kept standing on the doorstep while you correct your error. Let us in at once, Clydie!"

My use of his name had sufficient good effect to make him back away, mumbling some nonsense about m'lady's absence from home, while Kinross and I entered the gloomy hall. I looked about me in some consternation. Clydie held a single taper, but the candles in the hall were all unlit. This did not look like a house with a wealthy lady in residence, but like one shut up except for the minimum requirements of a caretaker.

As I debated what to do next, Kinross took the lead. "I trust," he said with the natural hauteur that I had attempted with little success, "that you will not even think of turning away a gentlewoman, not to say a good friend of your mistress and master, in such a storm as rages now. As you can see, Miss Rattray requires immediate service. Pray call your wife - or whatever domestic is in charge of the household arrangements – to wait upon her immediately. We shall require, at a minimum, a bedchamber for Miss Rattray, a can of hot water, a change of clothes, and a dish of soup to be served her immediately."

His list of minimal requirements sounded like Paradise to me – with one significant omission. He had commanded nothing for his own comfort.

Fortunately for us, Clydie's near-senile mutterings of protest were interrupted by the entrance of a liveried servant – a youngish man, dark-featured and handsome, whom I recognized immediately as Sabira's groom and a favored servant of hers. Meldun, I felt sure, would supply my every need – and Alastair's as well.

So it proved. Mrs. Clydie escorted me to a bedchamber where dust-sheets had been hastily removed from the furniture and where a beautiful fire was already burning. Less than an hour later, I emerged rosy and quite blessedly warm from the hip-bath that had been brought together with multiple cans of hot water. I made shift to drink a bowl of steaming broth while Mrs. Clydie worked around me, complaining under her breath about the necessity of ripping the seams in one of Sabira's garments and cobbling the dress together again around my somewhat more generous shape. I myself was in no mood to complain; dry clothing was at that moment a luxury beyond words. Even if the gown was of a dull, dark color that suited no coloring less fair than Sabira's ivory face and silver-gilt hair, even if Mrs. Clydie's hasty stitching left the garments too tight in some places and so long that the hem of the dress puddled around my feet – what did it matter? I was warm and dry and had already partaken of something more sustaining than gingerbread comfits. Under the circumstances I would be quite content to await Sabira in the small drawing-room downstairs where, Mrs. Clydie assured me, a fire had been lit for us.

Kinross was already there, warming his hands before the fire. Iveroth's borrowed garments fit him far better than Sabira's did me; for the first time I regretted the awkwardly altered gown in its unbecoming color. I must appear a figure of fun to him! Still, I told myself, better to look a scarecrow than to succumb to the lung-fever.

It was hard for me to smile at him when he greeted me with a frown. "That fool Clydie is still mumbling and muttering that he is not supposed to let anyone into the house when the master and mistress are away. Elspet, it does seem very much as though you were mistaken in believing Sabira to have come here; if she left Din Eidyn, it must have been for some other destination. What are we to do now? It is quite ineligible for you and me to stay here with no lady to act as chaperone."

I glanced at the windows. The storm was raging with renewed fury outside. I could see no help for it; I had no intention of putting either myself or Kinross at the mercy of the elements. Gossip might sting, but it could hardly kill us.

"Perhaps," I suggested without really believing it, "the storm will pass before long. We may yet be able to set off by moonlight. Or perhaps it's Clydie, not me, who is wrong about Sabira. I am quite sure that she intended spending several days here. And you must admit that the old man seems three parts senile! Let us inquire of Meldun as to Sabira's plans. I feel sure he would not be here were he not in attendance upon Sabira."

"The rub is," said Kinross gloomily, "that, at least according to Clydie, he is no longer here."

"Why, where could he have gone in such weather?" But even as I spoke, I recalled Sabira's nature, and the hints that Meldun was not merely a servant but her companion in the realms under the water's surface. However, it would hardly do to mention my suspicions to Kinross; I had no right to betray Sabira's secrets. Besides, the explanations would be tedious. "Clydie must be mistaken."

"I hope so," said Kinross, "for I can scarcely search this house for your friend or her servant."

"Well," said I, "the case is not yet desperate. Mrs. Clydie promised to prepare a proper meal for us, or at least, to do as well as she could under the circumstances. We would both be the better for some hot food. And very likely, by the time we have dined, Sabira will join us, or the storm will abate so that we can be on our way again." Not to mention that I myself was taking an unladylike interest as to what exactly Mrs. Clydie would produce for us. A cup of broth sipped while I dressed, while cheering, would hardly sustain me through a moonlight journey back to Din Eidyn. Even a tough fowl new-killed from the henhouse, or a dish of turnips in cheese, would be a material improvement over the returning emptiness in my midsection.

In the event, Mrs. Clydie did better than I had imagined possible. Indeed, the dinner she eventually set before us, consisting of two removes and a selection of sweet pastries, went some way to confirm my belief that – regardless of what the servants claimed – the lady of the house was in residence, or had been so until quite recently. I could not imagine the elderly housekeeper preparing such dainties as sweetbreads in cream and scalloped oysters for the delectation of herself and her bad-tempered husband – much less a compote of strawberries served up in a turreted pastry castle. "Sabira *must* be here," I said finally, after Kinross and I had exhausted the topics of the festival, the holy well, Izzie's departure and Tam's untimely disappearance in the direction of the prize-fight.

"Either that," Kinross agreed, "or Iveroth's servants eat uncommonly well. Still, I can hardly imagine that she has casually stepped out of the house on a night like this."

"Can you not?" I was tempted to tell him that water was no enemy to one of Sabira's nature, but rather the reverse. I reminded myself again that Sabira's secrets were not mine to tell. Purely to give myself time to think, I took another generous helping of the strawberries in sugared pastry, while Kinross poured himself a glass of what he was pleased to tell me was excellent port.

What with waiting for our dinner, and lingering over the dishes, so much time had passed that by my calculations we should hardly reach Din Eidyn before midnight even if we left straightaway. And alas, the rain had not abated yet. Well, I mused as I chased the last crumbs of pastry to catch the thickened juice left by the strawberries, Kinross would just have to reconcile himself to a night spent under slightly improper circumstances. It should not be beyond my ingenuity to come up with a convincing explanation for our overnight absence; after all, I would have the rest of the night and the whole of our return journey on the morrow in which to think up something. At present, listening to the rain as it thudded down on the house like the blows of some enraged giant, I was frankly more concerned with Mrs. Clydie's ingenuity in finding me something to sleep in. Perhaps Sabira's night-rails were cut on more generous lines than her fashionable dresses; I certainly hoped so, for it would be all but impossible to sleep in something as tight as this dress was on me.

The thudding noise increased, and I was almost frightened until I realized that the drumming of the rain had been supplemented by the sound of someone pounding on the front door. Even as I recognized the familiar rhythm of that knocking, Clydie shuffled in to inquire as to whether he was to open to the visitor. Evidently he had decided that in the absence of Sabira and Iveroth, we were gentry and entitled to give him orders – anything, I supposed, was better than making decisions on his own!

"Of course you shall open," Kinross snapped, "would you deny any man refuge from this storm?"

"There be strange creatures hereabouts," Clydie quavered, "and 'tis not men only who may come." But he shuffled off again, this time in the direction of the front hall, and I relaxed slightly. If I had recognized that rhythm aright, it was indeed a fully human man at the door, and one to whom we could scarcely deny entrance. Besides, I had a bone to pick with this particular visitor.

Chapter 24

Moments later, my brother Tam burst into the dining parlor. Water dripped from his shirt and darkened his reddish hair; his boots were soaked and probably beyond repair, and a stray lock on his forehead sent a periodic drip of cold water onto the bridge of his nose.

"Elspet!" he exclaimed, pushing the offending lock of hair away from his face. "I might have known as much." He swept a censorious eye over the litter of dishes and the open bottle on the table. "Was it not enough for you to com... compromise my sister by bringing her here, Lord Kinross, but you must also include her in your drunken carouse! Faugh! Don't attempt to deny it; I can smell the wine from here." That last statement was truly amazing, considering that he himself had brought a cloud of beery fumes into the room.

"Tam, are you mad?" I demanded. "You should be apologizing to me, rather than insulting the gentleman who took care of me when you disappeared to amuse yourself with your coarse sporting pursuits!"

"*Took care of you?*" Tam repeated. "Is that what you call it?"

"What else?"

The wet hair fell forward over his face again, and he brushed it away again. "First," he said, raising his open hand as if to count on the fingers, "first he disposes of our sister, whose first task it should have been to protect your virtue. Next he... what? Oh, yes. He brings you to a deserted house, for Clydie tells me the master and mistress are not here." The diatribe was momentarily interrupted by the need to push the wet hair out of his face yet again. "And to crown his infamy, he plies you with wine, doubtless to render you incapable of resisting his designs!"

"You *are* mad," I said with resignation. "Tam, sit down, have something to eat – let me see, there is some of the beef left, sadly cold by now, as well as a dish of neats' tongues which neither Kinross nor myself fancied. I regret that there is nothing left of the strawberry castle, but then you never did care for sweets."

"Elspet is quite right," said Kinross calmly. "You must be chilled, Rattray; will you take a glass of wine with me? Then, if you like, we shall see what Clydie can do in the way of dry clothes for you while you enjoy your dinner."

"I do not drink with seducers and vol- volup- "Tam gave up on the last word and glared at me instead. "And *you*, Missy, should come with me on the instant, unless it is already too late to save your virtue! Where had you that dress, and why? Did he tear your own dress from your body?"

By the last word he had advanced to the table and, bending over me, was all but shouting in my face. The smell of his breath went some way to explaining his ravings.

"Tam," I said, "have you been drinking cheap ale ever since you abandoned me in the village? You had better sit down and eat something; perhaps the food may clear your head."

"*You*," Tam said, swaying slightly, "had better consider how we may clear your name."

"There will be no clearing to be done if you will but hold your tongue!" I snapped.

"What, and connive at my sister's shame?" Tam pulled himself upright with a jerk and directed his fulminating gaze upon Kinross. "I see she dares not answer me. It is already too late, then. Nothing will answer but an immediate marriage."

"Your senses are disordered," said Kinross coolly, "and so, it would seem, are your wits. How dare you insinuate that Miss Rattray is anything less than you would believe her?"

"How dare *you* attempt to evade your responsibilities as a gentleman?" Tam riposted. "If you will not wed her, Kinross, you shall meet me on the field of honor!"

"Gladly," said Kinross between his teeth.

"Oh, you are both mad!" I snapped, jumping up to stand between them. "Kinross, if you duel with Tam I shall never forgive you. Tam, there is no shame and no cause for concern. Clydie may have told you that Sabira was not here, but he is an old man and sometimes loses track of the truth. Neither my reputation nor my virtue are endangered here. Or do you not consider Lady Iveroth an acceptable chaperone?"

"I require to sh-see Lady Iveroth for myshelf," Tam said thickly. I saw with resignation that he had profited by my interruption to drain the glass of wine he had earlier refused and to pour himself more; the bottle was half empty now.

"She has retired for the night," I said.

Unfortunately, at the same moment Kinross said, "She has stepped out to visit a neighbor, but we expect her back at any minute."

Tam's beady-eyed, accusing stare moved from Kinross, to me, and back to Kinross.

"I shall shee for myshelf!" Tam repeated, and calling loudly for Lady Iveroth, left us to pound up the stairs. Doubtless he meant to inspect the bedrooms. I feared that the sight of my discarded garments would further inflame his imagination. Oh well, maybe he would pass out in a drunken slumber before he got that far.

Kinross moved around the table to stand beside me. "Do not concern yourself," he said with his usual calm. "There will be no duel, nor shall you be forced into a marriage against your will. It's the devil of a tangle, my dear, but I engage to bring you off safely yet."

The words *my dear* warmed me better than the crackling fire in the hearth. But at the same time it was clear to me that he wanted nothing less than to be forced into marriage with me by my idiot brother's overheated, drunken hysterics. Who could blame him? It was hardly a situation that any man would relish. And yet – and yet –

I was ashamed to feel my lashes wet with silly tears. What was wrong with me, that no man wanted my hand? First Richert, now Alastair…

"I *promise*," said Kinross, and I blinked away the tears so that I could force a convincing smile to my lips.

My acting skills were not to be unduly strained at this moment, for we had a most welcome interruption. Sabira flung open the door and stood poised on the threshold, taking in the scene. Her hair was darkened with water and pulled back from her face, and her dress was ever so slightly untidy, as though she had dressed in haste and without the help of an abigail. Neither minor factor detracted from her unearthly beauty; her pale face seemed to illumine the room like a candle behind a screen of pearly shell.

I was of course happy beyond anything to see her, but a tiny, silly corner of my mind was so low as to wish that my friend were not quite so beautiful. I knew from that last hasty inspection of the mirror in my bedchamber that I looked like a young woman who had been dowsed in water and subsequently dragged through a hedge backward. Sabira, by contrast, looked like a magical being whose element was water.

Of course, that was a completely accurate description of her, and I realized after that first moment of surprise that this was simply what she looked like when she had been following her true nature rather than deliberately playing it down so as to blend in with us common creatures of earth. The deluge of rain might have made me look like a half-drowned orange cat; Sabira's dampness sprang, I surmised, from a refreshing dip in the salt sea water that was the source of all her strength and powers.

Kinross, so far as I knew, was not privy to her secret. I glanced at him and was somewhat surprised to see that he did not show the goggle-eyed devotion common to men who were surprised by exposure to Sabira's shimmering, lustrous face and form. I supposed he had been so accustomed to seeing her in town that even the added glamour which now clothed her with an otherworldly radiance was not enough to stun him.

Then, too, he had an impressive ability to conceal his feelings and control his countenance.

All this flashed through my mind in the split second before Sabira drew breath and spoke, at once welcoming us and apologizing for her brief absence.

"I had merely... stepped out... for a moment, and I returned as soon as Meldun apprised me of your arrival," she said, and tilted her head slightly as though listening to the crashes and thuds of Tam's progress through the upper story of the house. "He did not mention any other visitor?" she said with a faint questioning intonation.

I sighed. "My brother. Who appears to be the worse for drink, though that hardly excuses his behavior," I said over the sound of Tammas shouting for Lady Iveroth to show herself if she were indeed in the house.

Sabira nodded slightly to Clydie, who had been hovering just outside the room. "Find Mr. Rattray and invite him to join us," she said, and, moving into the parlor, seated herself on a backless chair on the far side of the table from the fire.

"Lady Iveroth, you are wet from the rain," said Kinross. "Will you not sit on this side of the table? Miss Rattray and I are perfectly dry and comfortable now and do not need to monopolize the fire."

Sabira inclined her head with a slight smile. "Thank you, but I am not in the least cold," she said. Kinross had amused her, I thought. How was he to know that she was really a finwife, a creature of the sea who swam in its chilly northern waters as naturally as a human child played in a sunny meadow? Nor would it be *convenable* for her to explain that her anatomy, with the broad tail that sprung from her lower back and that was currently wrapped around her legs like a shimmering petticoat, made the stool she had taken more comfortable for her than any chair designed for human beings. The thought of Kinross' probable reaction to such explanations made my own lips twitch.

"But now," Sabira said, "if you are indeed quite comfortable, perhaps you will tell me what impelled you two to brave the storm? Delighted though I am to see you, Elspet, I can hardly flatter myself that this is a purely social call. There must be some desperate emergency to have brought you out in this weather."

Kinross explained that the storm had surprised us at the festival of Saint Ciarach, and that the public houses in that village had been so crammed with drunken fair-goers and sporting men that I could hardly have taken refuge there. I was attempting to tell of Tam's arrival and his idiotic suspicions when my sot of a brother crashed into the room. "She'sh not here!" he shouted. Then, comically, he registered Sabira's presence and attempted to make a leg. "That ish – I – Pleashed to s- see you, Lady Iveroth! Shervant, ma'am!" The deep, sweeping bow with which he finished was too much for his equilibrium; he swayed, staggered, and collapsed without further ceremony into the chair which Kinross had vacated upon Sabrina's entrance.

"Please forgive Mr. Rattray," said Kinross. "Not having had the pleasure of being greeted by you at the moment of his arrival, he harbored some suspicion – I cannot imagine why – that you were not here at all, and that I had brought his sister here unchaperoned in pursuit of some sinister plan of my own."

Sabira's brows arched. "Indeed!" she said icily. "I am sorry, Elspet, to hear that your brother thinks so little of you as to assume you would lend yourself to such an improper arrangement."

"Not – not *her*!" Tam protested. "It'sh *him* I don't trust!"

"I collect," said Sabira, "you mean that it is to Lord Kinross you should apologize, having leapt to conclusions and accused him of the basest treachery."

Tam subsided into incoherent burblings while Sabira dominated the room with her clear voice. "Mr. Rattray, the most charitable explanation for your behavior is that you have partaken far too freely of ale while enjoying your sporting pursuits. Despite your manners, the barest courtesy towards yourself, together with my friendship with your sister, dictates that this house shall offer you shelter for the night, and, if possible, a change of clothes. Perhaps Clydie or Meldun can find something," she added with a glance at Tam, who was both shorter and thicker than the dapper Iveroth. "Or if not…"

Tam interrupted her musings. "Yesh – yes – but Pet told me you had retired for the night, Lady Iveroth! Wha' should make her tell me such a bouncer, if she were not hiding something?"

Sabira favored him with a cool – not to say freezing – smile and a quelling glance from her sea-green eyes. "A natural misunderstanding, Mr. Rattray. You yourself have just experienced the power of this storm; surely you understand that, having been caught out in the rain on my way back from visiting a neighbor, I was soaking wet and required to change my clothes immediately. Since I had already eaten, I told Mrs. Clydie not to set a place for me at the late dinner which she was preparing for Lord Kinross and your sister. She must have taken that to mean I had no intention of returning downstairs tonight, and so she misinformed Elspet."

"W-w-what neighbor, I sh'd like to know!" Tam exploded. "And why should you go visiting just when your guests are arrived?"

Sabira arched her fair brows. "Mr. Rattray," she said, icicles dripping off every word, "you forget your position and my own. If courtesy to your hostess is not enough to mend your manners, let me explain that I *am* Lady Iveroth and that I feel no obligation to explain my behavior – in my own home, no less – to a Rattray!"

"If you hope to claim shelter for the night, Rattray," said Lord Kinross, "I strongly suggest you apologize to Lady Iveroth at once!"

"I – *I*! – apologizhe!" Tam was indignant. "*I'm* not the one trying to conceal my havey-cavey doings with some cobbled-together string of lies! Yesh… yes… and another thing, Clydie told me that Lady Iveroth was not even in residence! How d'you explain *that*?"

"I have no intention of doing so," said Kinross. "Clearly, in your confused and drunken condition, you misunderstood the man. I would offer you a glass of port to clear your head, but that you have obviously taken on more liquor than you can carry. Are you a silly schoolboy, to become so castaway on village ale?"

I thought that his challenging tone was a mistake, but only for a moment. Tam's head came up, he glared at Kinross and said, "I'll match *you* drink for drink any day, Alastair!" He seized the open bottle, tilted his head back and drained the contents. Scarcely had he relinquished his grasp upon the bottle when he swayed in his chair. He rested his arms on the table and laid his head on them. "Momentary – dizzy – don't signify!" he mumbled, and his whole body relaxed into unconsciousness.

"I may have timed that little provocation poorly," commented Kinross, "But it seemed the best way to stop his blustering before he managed to say something I could not ignore."

"He has not done that already?" I asked over the increasing rumble of Tam's drunken snores.

Kinross favored me with a wry smile. "Your brother, Elspet, would have to be far more outrageous than that before I would truly take offense at him! But it did seem almost as though he was determined to provoke me, did it not? I wonder…."

He paused, contemplating Tam's sleeping form.

"You wonder?" I prompted after it seemed that neither he nor Sabira was minded to break the silence.

"Oh. Well. He was half-sprung, to be sure."

"More than half, I should say! You might as well say it: he was totally foxed," I exclaimed before remembering Kirsty's objection to my knowledge and use of slang terms.

"Indeed. And yet there are several steps between having taken too much to drink, and accusing a friend of trying to seduce one's sister! I cannot help but wonder if someone had been working on his mind, feeding in filthy insinuations under cover of sympathy."

Now that Kinross mentioned it, I wondered the same thing. "But surely Vivienne de Larue would not have been among the sporting crowd? And who else would be so malicious?"

"I saw Baron Jenneret riding that way," Kinross said.

Sabira gasped. "I never told you, Elspet, but last year the Baron did his best to destroy me, first with vile gossip and then with an attempted abduction – and in that last, Vivienne de Larue helped him!"

Kinross nodded slowly. "It is not beyond belief that he would seize any opportunity to help her, in return."

"And just how," I enquired tartly, "would it help her to make us two miserable?"

"Malice," Kinross said. "Revenge. Jenneret will surely have known that Vivienne would be pleased, should he succeed in goading your brother and me into a duel; more pleased yet, should he raise such a scandal-broth as would force you to marry me!"

Silly tears filled my eyes, and I brushed one hand across my lashes.

"Don't look so sad, my dear," Kinross said. "The scheme, if such it was, was hastily conceived and poorly executed. And in any case it could not have succeeded, for I have no mind to be forced into taking an unwilling bride!

Your freedom and reputation are alike uninjured by this tawdry plot."

I wished that I might say the same for my heart. But how could I tell Kinross that the unwillingness was entirely on his side?

Chapter 25

After the previous day's drama, I found life after my return to Din Eidyn curiously flat. No one there had been so foolish as to be alarmed over my night's absence, for Izzie had assured my parents that Kinross and Tammas between them were perfectly competent to look after me.

Well, she had been half right at all events.

Kinross did not call in the days immediately following our excursion to Ciarach. I supposed that was only reasonable. He had probably had a surfeit of my company and he had certainly seen more than enough of my idiotish brother! Quite likely he feared that even a courtesy call to inquire after my health would start Tam's melodramatic fantasies off again. On that subject at least I could have reassured him. Tam had still been asleep when Kinross and I set off from Loch Fàilte early on the day after the storm, but he had turned up in town that evening, with a splitting headache and spilling out sheepish apologies for his behavior. He did not seem to remember very much of his wild accusations, but he feared that something he said might have offended Kinross.

"Do not concern yourself," I said, "he holds no grudge. *I* found your manner offensive in the extreme, but that is unimportant, since I am merely your sister."

Tam stammered, hemmed and hawed, and finally asked me outright just what he had said at Loch Fàilte.

"If you cannot remember," I said, "Kinross and Sabira and I all choose not to remember, so let that scene pass into oblivion!"

I did wonder about the notion Kinross had raised, that Tam's strange behavior had been occasioned by something more than an excess of ale. But my brother did not recall having spoken with Baron Jenneret before his arrival at Sabira's house – or rather, he was not sure whether or not he had seen Jenneret at the prize-fight. Such vagueness might have been ascribed to the ale. Or it might not. I was left uneasy, but with no ground for firm suspicions.

I had, in any case, little leisure for brooding upon the matter. Kirsty had seized upon Izzie's absence as a chance to set the servants at work to give her bedchamber a thorough cleaning. Being Kirsty, once started, she went on to afflict the entire house with a cleaning and sorting-out such as had not been performed since before we took up residence there this year. I found myself fully employed in getting to various rooms of the house before Kirsty swept through them, so that I could salvage any small possessions that Izzie and I had left out before she put them away where we would never find them again. I rescued a sheaf of music from the drawing-room and put it in a drawer of Izzie's dressing table, found my embroidery projects and stuffed them into one of my own drawers, and thought myself well ahead of the cleaning frenzy when the Hob gave me one more thing to secrete.

"I thought it was broken beyond repair," I said, stupidly, when Izzie's little Irish harp came sailing through the air to rest on my dressing-table. Oh, I knew it wasn't really wafting itself towards me; the Hob was carrying the thing. But its passage through my bedchamber did look most uncanny.

I suppose, to people who are not accustomed to having a small invisible being involve himself in the housework, the floating harp really would have been an eerie sight. I, however, ought to have taken it for granted; perhaps my nerves were a trifle disordered after the alarms of the past weeks.

"Nothing is beyond repair to those who will take the trouble," the Hob's voice rasped from about the height of my waist. The dressing table shook slightly, the swinging mirror quivered, and when next the Hob spoke his voice came from above the mirror. "A certain degree of skill is of course required.'

"I think," I said, fingering the pattern of new wood inlaid and matched to the old frame, "that some things cannot be repaired so easily." Like my summer's insanity, trying to make over Richert Dalkey into the romantic hero of my schoolgirl dreams! If Kinross had ever had the slightest of preferences for me, I had surely killed those feelings by my foolish pursuit of Richert. But then, probably he never had felt anything for me, so it did not matter. "It does not matter," I said aloud, firmly. It was not as though I *needed* to marry. I felt sure that I could always have a home with Izzie, and I intended to be an exemplary maiden aunt to her children once she produced them.

The prospect made me feel like the poor harp, smashed to splinters and repaired with an infinitely painstaking inlay of new wood and glue. I wondered if the harp felt a stabbing pain where each new sliver of wood had been inserted.

"Repairing that harp was not easy," the Hob grumbled.

"And I wish you had not troubled yourself to do it!" The thing was still strung with the golden wires I had spun from Marguerite Fauchet's hair. I thought I ought to remove it... but when my fingertips just brushed the taut strings, a whisper of unearthly music filled the air and the room began to grow darker and colder. A shiver ran down my spine. I opened the top drawer of the dressing table, dropped the harp in and shut the drawer with a slam. I would take the thing apart some other time, preferably when the Hob was not watching to complain that I failed to appreciate his work. Also, preferably, at high noon on a very sunny day.

He leapt from the top of the mirror – I could see it swinging in response to his violent shove, and heard the soft thump of his bare feet hitting the floor – and said, "Do not be all day mooning over that harp. You have work to do!"

"I have?"

A stiffly interlaced tangle of threads, threaded through two wooden beads, appeared to float across the room to me. I recognized one of the small charms I had made from red threads and rowan to protect the house. "That Woman," said Hob, his usual style of referring to Kirsty, "has cleaned away the wards you put on the back door! And who knows what else she will cause the maids with their mops and buckets to destroy?"

"Oh." I had placed my wards hastily, fastening them to the walls above doors and windows with drawing-pins. In my defense, it was hard to know exactly how I could have persuaded people like Mama, Kirsty and Izzie to consider these little tangles of thread and wood as important as physical locks and latches. But I had not even tried.

I looked into Izzie's room first, since that was where the great cleaning frenzy had begun and since my greatest fear was that Vivienne de Larue would attack her again. My heart sank. The curtains had been removed for cleaning, the windows sparkled in the morning sun; there were no dusty corners now, nor was there any place for a thread charm to lie unnoticed. I would have to work them all over again.

Izzie was seated before her mirror, twisting and tweaking a new bonnet.

"You're going out?"

I was delighted to see that she felt well enough to make the effort. I was also pleased to think that I should have a chance to be alone in her room while I renewed the protections upon it.

"Yes, I feel it my duty to visit poor Lady Dalkey. She is quite overset by young Mr. Dalkey's behavior, and as she was so kind as to take me back to town from Ciarach, the least I can do is sit with her now and try to ease her fears!"

"What fears?" I demanded a trifle sharply. "What has Richert gone and done now?"

"Oh, I don't know," Izzie said, waving one hand vaguely. "There was that scandalous wager, of course, and now she says that he... Do you think the trimming on this bonnet is too much? Seeing that I am visiting an invalid?"

"I fancy Lady Dalkey's constitution is strong enough to sustain the sight of a few silk roses," I said, but then I was distracted by another feature of her costume. "Izzie, what have you done with the cross I gave to you?"

"Oh, that... Elspet, it was kind in you, but nobody except servants wears wooden trinkets like that! To be sure it was a vastly pretty little cross, and I shall treasure it always for the giver's sake, but it would not be at all suitable with this walking-dress."

"Where did you put it?" Without waiting for an answer, I yanked open the small drawers at the top of her dressing table, one after another, until I found the cross with its winding of red threads. "Izzie, you must not go out without this!"

Izzie sighed. "Elspet. You cannot seriously expect me to go to Lady Dalkey's looking like a country lass whose only adornment is a wooden fairing from her sweetheart? Sir Joshua would be mortified to hear that I had made such a show of myself!"

"Tuck the cross under your fichu," I said, "but for love of me, Izzie, please, please continue to wear it for a few days! I do not know what new malice Vivienne de Larue may be plotting, but I beg you not to go out without me – or if you must do so, at least accept what protection the rowan wood can give you!"

Izzie gave vent to another long-suffering sigh. "Oh, very well, Elspet. You were so good to me during my illness, I suppose I can bear to go about like a dowd if that is all that will please you! But mind, I will not do this forever!"

The cross was small enough to disappear behind the lace folds of her fichu, and there was nothing amiss with the fine gold chain from which it was suspended. I thought that Izzie's reputation as a well-dressed young matron would not suffer unduly from humoring me this once. "I do not expect you to do it forever," I promised her, "only until we have found some other way to neutralize that herb-witch's attacks!"

But what that might be, I could not begin to imagine.

I had meant to spend a quiet hour alone in Izzie's room, renewing the thread magic that would protect her, but before she had even finished adjusting her bonnet I was called downstairs to receive another visitor.

I felt quite unreasonably let down to find that my caller was only Dorothea Turvoll. It was not as though I really expected Kinross to bother with me again after all the problems I had caused him, and I had quite gotten over my childish fantasies about Richert Dalkey. But... *Dorothea Turvoll?* A nice girl, yes, and it was not her fault that she was scarcely needle-witted. I supposed that I had better accustom myself to a social life consisting of platitudes and prattling from unmarried girls and superannuated maiden ladies; that was how most unwed aunts lived, was it not?

After a few minutes of social chitchat I discovered the reason for Dorothea's sudden friendliness. It was not, as I had snobbishly feared, that she was under the illusion that we were kindred spirits. Not exactly.

She believed herself to be commiserating with me over a humiliating defeat.

It seemed that Richert Dalkey, not content with setting the *ton* by the ears over his reckless shooting wager, not content with gloating over his winnings, had promptly expended most of those winnings on purchasing himself a commission in the army over the objections of his mama.

That, then, was why Izzie was hastening to Lady Dalkey's side. I had no doubt that the lady was enjoying a protracted attack of her favorite palpitations. I was only surprised that our mama had not gone along to ply her with remedies from the stillroom.

Dorothea showed a gleam of sly triumph when I confessed that I had not heard her news already.

"Oh, I thought sure Mr. Dalkey would call upon you, if only to take leave!" she said, attempting to look concerned for me.

She did it very ill.

"But then," she went on after I shook my head, "young men are so wanton, so fickle, are they not? I know Mr. Dalkey was considered the catch of the season, but for my part, I much prefer a mature man who is not so volatile in his preferences."

"Like Major Maddox?" I hazarded.

Dorothea smiled, tittered, and prayed that I would spare her blushes.

She went on, though, as though everything were completely settled; pluming herself on having made such a good match, and pretending to commiserate with me over my failure to do the same.

I had previously thought Dorothea a sweet girl, if not overburdened with intelligence. Now I was constrained to revise my opinion. As a wallflower she had put on sweet airs as a disguise; in the triumph of her engagement to Major Maddox, and once assured that Dalkey had neglected me as totally as he had her, she exuded a poisonous superiority.

As if marrying a half-pay officer with no prospects were such a success to boast of!

I supposed I should have to grow used to that. In the eyes of the *ton*, any respectable marriage was better than none at all.

Perhaps I should begin immediately to put off my fashionable dresses for the caps and demure styles of a lady who admitted she was no longer in the marriage market. Oh, dear. I was not ready to cover my hair, to dress in sad, sober colors and to eschew the pleasures of silver braid and Venezian lace. Would it not be possible to advertise that I had no intention of marrying without condemning myself to such a lackluster life?

As Dorothea prattled on, I accused myself of being irredeemably frivolous. With my life in ruins about my feet, how could I mourn bright colors and fancy trimmings, or the delights of the ballroom? But I did love life and color and movement, and if I could not have the man I loved, it did seem hard that I should have to give up all the little delights of life as well.

Better that, though, than to have chits like Dorothea thinking they had triumphed over me. I knew now that I could never settle for marriage to a man I did not love; and since I had assuredly given the man I did love a disgust of me, it was best to make a clean break with the fripperies of society and assume my maiden aunt status immediately.

Even if I did not, as yet, have any nephews and nieces to give me the title of "Auntie Elspet." I felt sure that Izzie would supply that lack, once Sir Joshua was returned to this country.

I could not repress a start of surprise, nor a rising blush, when a second caller was announced. Kinross! What brought him here?

His grave face caused me a momentary concern. I was relieved to discover that the cause for his serious looks was only that he thought himself to be breaking the news of Richert Dalkey's imminent departure.

"Oh, Miss Turvoll has been before you with that news," I said cheerfully. "I am sure we both wish Mr. Dalkey every success in the military career to which he has so long aspired!"

"And for my part," said Dorothea waspishly, "I think Din Eidyn will be better off to have that young man safely abroad, rather than indulging his penchant for pistol-shooting in the streets of the city!"

Not a very charitable comment, considering that Dalkey's skill with a pistol had saved her from a humiliating abduction by Baron Jenneret. But I had to admire the speed with which she had switched from Dalkey's lovelorn admirer to Major Maddox' happily affianced bride. She might after all have the adroitness, if not the wit, to do well enough in Din Eidyn society – not, I reflected, that marriage to the Major, a kind man but neither rich nor titled, was exactly a key to success in the *ton*.

"I am… happy," said Kinross slowly, looking quite the reverse, "to hear that you are not distressed by the news."

"It was very wrong indeed in Mr. Dalkey to depart without taking leave of Miss Rattray," Dorothea opined, "after his attentions to her had been so *marked*." An air of triumph invalidated the pretense of concern in her words. I favored her with my best smile.

"If *you* do not take offense at his celerity in taking up a military career," I said sweetly, "how then shall I, one of his oldest friends and who has been like a sister to him, object?"

Kinross looked desperately uncomfortable, as well he might. No man could be expected to enjoy witnessing the increasingly barbed fencing between Dorothea and me. I wondered he did not make his excuses and withdraw, having performed his errand – or rather, having discovered that it was unnecessary. Instead he kept glancing at Dorothea and then back to me, as if he had some message he wished to convey in secret.

"Perhaps, Miss Rattray, you will permit that I call again later? There are certain other matters which I would bring to your attention, family matters I might say, which can be of no interest to Miss Turvoll."

It was an uncharacteristically broad hint for someone as suave as Kinross to drop, and for a moment I actually hoped that Dorothea would not take it. For what could Kinross wish to say to me privately? Did he think it necessary to explain once again that he had not the slightest desire to treat me as anything other than a sister? Surely he had made *that* clear enough at Loch Fàilte! I certainly did not need to hear it again!

But with her usual talent for doing the most annoying thing, this once Dorothea understood and acted on his hint. With apologies for having trespassed so long upon my time, she took herself off. Kinross and I sat in tense silence until we heard the front door close behind her. That is, I sat, hands clasped before me and my knuckles white with tension. Kinross rose, paced the length of the room and back, and took up a position behind my chair where I could not see his face.

The silence stretched out intolerably.

"If you have come to explain once again that our misadventure at Loch Fàilte does not require us to marry," I burst out at length, "your assurances are entirely unnecessary! In any event, Tammas is now quite ashamed of having indulged such distempered fantasies. He owes you every apology, but in his absence, let me apologize for him and let us agree to consider the matter at an end!"

"I had not thought," said Kinross, "to revisit that unhappy episode. Or, at any rate, only to make it clear that my objections were to taking an unwilling bride. I had believed your affections fixed upon our friend Richert, and I would not have allowed chance and circumstance to ruin your life by my coming between you two."

"You said... you *had* believed that."

"On that day in Ciarach, yes. You will allow that I had every reason to think so."

I suppose he had. Certainly I had taken no care to conceal what I believed to be my sentiments while I was still enjoying the fantasy of a storybook romance between Richert and myself. And there had been no time at Ciarach to explain to him the magical speed with which those illusions had faded or the reality which had supplanted them, my realization of all his patient care and affection had meant.

But now, I hoped, he understood that matters were entirely different.

"If ever I still cherished a childish infatuation with Mr. Dalkey," I said slowly, "I trust you can see that it is entirely a matter of the past. I am not in the least overset by his departure for the army; quite the reverse! I wish him well *exactly as a sister* might do, and believe that he will be both successful and happy in his chosen career."

"The *ton* will think that he has slighted you sadly by abandoning his mad pursuit of you without so much as the courtesy of a farewell visit."

"Oh, as to that," I said, "you may with my good will put it about that he did indeed tell me of his intentions, and that I sent him off with my blessing

– as I should have done in fact, had he but had the grace to call!"

"*Should* you, Elspet?" Kinross came around the chair and stood looking down upon me with a gravely questioning face.

"I was never in love with Richert," I said. "I was, I think, in love with the idea of love. Such idiotish fantasies, relics of childhood, do not long survive contact with reality."

"And yet," said Kinross slowly, "my own sentiments have been unchanged by the events of this Season."

My heart leapt. Could he mean— ?

"Do you remember, Elspet," Kinross said in a cooler, almost conversational tone, "when you confessed to having thrown a love spell over me on the night of our visit to the theater?"

"It was only – only an attempt to break the power of Vivienne's enchantment over you," I stammered, "and I *have* already apologized."

"And do you remember," he went on, "that I told you my sentiments towards you were entirely unchanged by that spell? It was not that it failed, Elspet; it was that I was already—"

At that untoward moment the front door slammed again, and I stiffened. Surely Dorothea had not returned on some silly pretext?

No. Not Dorothea.

And this time she was not disguised as a servant.

Vivienne de Larue swept into the drawing room, unannounced and decidedly unwelcome, and dressed to outshine any other female in Din Eidyn.

My first thought was to be thankful that Izzie was from home; my second was the sinking understanding of how she had gained entrance. *Kirsty had cleaned away all my house wards.* I wondered if she had killed the servant who made the mistake of opening our front door, or merely paralyzed him.

Then I wondered if I would have a chance to save that unlucky footman. For – my own ward, the rowan cross wrapped in red thread, was about Izzie's neck. At my own insistence I had stripped myself of protections and in my folly, I had allowed Dorothea and the news about Richert to distract me from adding so much as a minor thread tangle to my dress.

But Vivienne's snapping black eyes were fixed not on me, but on Kinross.

Who was equally unprotected, though he did not realize his danger. Even now he had moved to place his body between Vivienne and me.

"You lost no time finding a substitute for your former lover, did you?" Vivienne taunted me. "But I fear this one will serve you even less well than Dalkey did."

"Madame, you –" Kinross began, and then his voice seemed to be strangled in his throat. I looked up in alarm and saw him begin to claw at his immaculately arranged cravat. His clutching fingers disarranged the perfect folds, then slipped limply down as if they had lost all power of motion. Even as I watched, his face became suffused with darkness and I could feel, as though in my own body, his struggle to draw breath.

"No man will risk being close to you," Vivienne jeered, "when they learn that the cost is death! I had rather make you pay thus, slowly and over long years, than grant you the merciful release which *he* will soon enjoy!"

I had only seconds to act, and no idea what to do. The slow patient working of thread magic, even had I my needle and threads ready to hand, could hardly free the breath in Kinross' chest in time to save him. I should have – should have –

The door swung open again, this time without the help of human hands; a ghostly chord sounded, and the sunlit windows dimmed. Unbelieving, I saw Izzie's Irish harp hovering in mid-air and, to all appearances of its own volition, moving towards me. The Hob still did not permit me to see him, even while he brought what might be our salvation.

I had not Izzie's skill with the harp, nor her fine true singing voice. But did that matter? When Izzie touched those bright strands spun from a dead girl's hair, the harp had made its own music, had sung with Marguerite Fauchet's voice. Would it not do the same for me, if I could but awaken the strings with the touch of my living hands?

I would have to move before it occurred to Vivienne to paralyze me as she had done in the Park. Her attention, though, was all on Kinross' darkening face and his convulsive struggles to breathe. I opened my hand; the harp was pressed into it, and with one quick movement I swept my fingers across the taut strings.

What should have been a vile discord was turned, by the death magic in the harp, to a line of melody that brought Vivienne, whirling, to stare at me in shock.

"*To my love I'll leave my golden hair,*" sang a high, clear voice over the rippling music called from the harp strings,

"*Braemuirie, Braemuirie.*"

The shadows circled around us, hungry, chilling; it seemed to me that they reached cold fingers towards Vivienne in her sumptuous dress.

"*You!*" she screeched, and drew something bright from her sleeve as she leaned towards me.

Kinross still was not breathing. I passed my fingers over the harp strings again.

"*That he may string me a harp so fair,*
By the bonnie mill-dams of Braemuirie."

Vivienne struck at me with the dagger she had concealed in her sleeve; I dodged to the side and it parted my dress, left a bright line of pain along my right arm, but that was all.

The shadows were thickest and darkest right around Vivienne now; I felt their cold edges like ghostly knife cuts, hurting me and then withdrawing as Vivienne struggled to keep her balance. The harp thrummed in my left hand. Moving my right arm hurt, but not enough to stop me passing my fingers over the strings yet again.

"*And a knife I leave to my sister Vivienne,*
Braemuirie, Braemuirie."

The shadows coalesced around Vivienne and it seemed to me that she was struggling against their invisible hands. Her own right hand was slowly forced back, away from me. The cold was so intense now that it almost burned.

"*For it was she who threw me in,*
By the bonnie mill-dams of Braemuirie."

Vivienne's arm twisted horribly, pointing the dagger at her own breast. Her own hand drove it home, and the shadows swirled and fluttered around her in a macabre dance of triumph. As she slumped to the floor, my cold-numbed fingers let loose the harp. It too fell to the floor, and I heard a cracking sound as light flooded the room again. And, most welcome of all, I heard Kinross' indrawn breath rasping in his throat. A moment later, and he was breathing freely again.

Vivienne was not breathing at all.

And the harp, its work done, lay shattered into a hundred scraps. As I watched, the bright crisp strings spun from Marguerite's hair shimmered and disappeared into the morning sunlight.

Chapter 26

I have, as you may have observed, never been overly deterred by considerations of mere propriety from doing what I felt was necessary. You must allow, however, that it was hardly possible to continue that fascinating, tantalizing conversation with Kinross with a corpse at our feet on the drawing-room floor. And, missish though it might have been, I actually felt myself quite faint in the moments following the shattering of the harp; I was more than willing to sink back into a chair and to allow Kinross to make the arrangements for notifying the authorities and removing the body.

We had no more to fear from Vivienne de Larue's malice!

And I was nearly as relieved to feel that the matter of Marguerite Fauchet's vengeance upon her sister was also at an end.

Izzie, when she returned from consoling Lady Dalkey, was gracious enough to make little of the shattering of her smaller harp. To be sure, she had been unaware of the Hob's role in mending it, so from her point of view the breakage had occurred some time earlier and nothing more need be said about it. She declared that she had never cared for the instrument anyway, that it was a device for common folk singing vulgar songs and that in future she intended to dedicate herself entirely to playing classical music on the great harp. For my part, I intended never to touch her great harp and certainly not to meddle with its strings.

Vivienne de Larue's suicide in our drawing-room was, of course, a nine days' wonder in the *ton*. Izzie and I both became quite fatigued with explaining that we had no idea why she had chosen our house as the place to accomplish her own death; we could only surmise that her reason had been disturbed and that she had not really known what she was doing.

Izzie, at least, was speaking the truth, which made the explanations somewhat easier for her.

And Kinross?

I could only surmise that in the days immediately following Vivienne's death, he too had been completely occupied in doing his part to damp the more unpleasant rumors about that event. Certainly he had shown no desire to reopen the subject that had been under discussion when we were so rudely interrupted. But when I considered the matter, I realized that there was another reason why he might not have called. Who would want to be allied with a girl who could call death-music from a harp, who could turn a room dark and cold with wraiths called out of the grave, who could compass a rival's death by such magical means? I might have done what I did only to save Kinross; no matter; he could easily combine gratitude for his life with a desire never to risk such an experience again. He might not be as prejudiced against magic as Richert, but the most broad-minded of men might well balk at courting a girl who had made music from the strands of a dead woman's hair, and who had used that music to turn a living woman's dagger back upon herself.

And even I was not so lost to propriety as to go out to social events immediately after what folk termed the tragedy in our drawing-room; far less could I contemplate being so forward as to write to Kinross desiring him to complete that conversation. Unmarried and already followed by whispers of impropriety, I should have sunk myself beyond reproach were I to enter into secret correspondence with a gentleman – *particularly* with a gentleman who showed no sign of desiring to renew his addresses!

If I spent more hours than usual alone in my bedchamber, dismissing Orrock, that was nobody's business but my own. And if I covered a few – well, all right, somewhat more than a few – sheets of paper with my poorly worded explanations that the death-music had been no part of my plan, my requests that Kinross call and complete the thoughts he had been about to express when Vivienne interrupted us – well, that too was strictly my business. It was not as though I had any intention of *sending* any of those notes; if I had, would I not have borrowed Kirsty's Dictionary and checked the spelling? Instead, those scribblings went uncorrected into the same drawer where I had once attempted to inter the Irish harp. Their sole purpose was to relieve my mind of the thoughts that continually raced through it, to express those thoughts and feelings once and for all so that I could stop mentally repeating them.

It was not working.

I had to acknowledge my failure on the day when I could no longer cram another of my blotted, ill-spelt scribblings into the drawer. In less than a week I seemed to have used up as much paper as would have made a good start on the first volume of a novel! I could not even shut the drawer. Irritated, I pulled out a handful of the letters I would never send and rang for Orrock. She could turn them into spills for lighting the fire; a fitting end to my romantic fantasies.

I was draping a square of lace over my head and twisting it this way and that, trying to find some version of a maiden aunt's cap that I could wear without casting myself into a melancholy, when the violent swinging of the mirror distracted me.

"You," the Hob informed me, "are a fool."

I leafed through the discarded letters lying before me. "I know that."

"Succumbing to missish propriety!" he jeered.

"Coming to my senses," I replied. "Cast these into the fire for me?" There was really no point in the very minor economy of recycling the letters as candle-lighting spills, and some danger. Orrock did not read with ease, but she might well be inspired to make the effort, presented with papers that contained the secrets of my heart. Better to destroy them immediately. As the Hob removed the collection of crumpled notes with invisible hands, I resumed trying to fold the lace into some semblance of a cap. Perhaps, trimmed with emerald ribands, it would not be *too* bad...

"What *are* you doing, Miss?"

Orrock's shocked voice broke into my depressed soliloquy. I looked in the mirror to see my room, not merely my own reflection. The fire burned no brighter, but the letters were not to be seen. Neither, of course, was the Hob; but since the mirror was no longer swinging, I presumed that he had taken himself off after burning my papers. At least there was now no risk of Orrock's attempting to decipher them.

Orrock received my explanation that I was trying to design a fetching cap for myself with the scorn she felt for such a notion. Why would a young lady voluntarily consign herself to the shelf in such a foolish way?

"Better," I said glumly, "than waiting for the *ton* to laugh and say I had put it off too long. I shall never marry, Orrock."

"Nonsense, Miss. Just because you have been disappointed by that young Mr. Dalkey—"

"I have *not*," I said, "been disappointed. There was never any possibility that Mr. Dalkey and I would make a match of it."

Orrock did not actually say so, but her face expressed her feelings: she believed that statement no more than she had my assertion that it was time for me to retire into settled spinsterhood. A new bonnet? she suggested. Call Patrice-Henri and desire him to find a new way to dress my hair? A visit to Olympe to commission a new dress for what remained of the Season?

She was more certain than I that renewed attention to such fripperies would refresh my flagging spirits enough to send me back undaunted into the small cruelties and smaller joys of the Marriage Mart. Still, her suggestions reminded me that Madame Olympe should by now have completed her commission to transform my Indian uncle's amber silk into a new ball gown. I would go for a fitting that very day. And when the dress was completed, perhaps I would embroider charms against melancholy around the hem. For Orrock had made me aware that for my own pride, I must finish this Season with my head high and with every appearance of gaiety. Otherwise I was like to suffer the crushing humiliation of being supposed to have been disappointed in love by Richert Dalkey.

"Very well," I said. "You may accompany me to Madame Olympe's."

I was pleasantly surprised to find that while I had been occupied with Izzie's illness and subsequent events, Olympe had taken it upon herself to create a new ball gown from the amber silk without waiting for my orders. There was not even any need for last-minute adjustments, for she knew all my measurements from her previous work. The shimmering gold and amber silk floated over a simple slip of ivory crape in a fashion I could not but find enchanting. The only point in which Olympe's taste and mine diverged was in the use of decoration; had I been thinking about it, I should have commissioned a trim of gold lace about the hem and some discreet gold braid emphasizing the neckline. Olympe was more conventional than I. In this one case she might have been right. The Indian silk required no ornamentation to set it off, and for once, I had to allow, masterful simplicity was better than generous decoration.

"You will turn all heads in this," Olympe promised me, "even without your usual *aids* embroidered about the hem!"

She might be right. But there was only one head I wanted to turn, and I thought that no quantity of India silk, however fetchingly made up, would compensate for the dark memories of that day when the music I drew from a harp caused Vivienne de Larue to turn her own dagger upon herself.

"It will look better, of course, with jewels," Olympe said.

"Yes. My pearls…"

"I hear that the Kinross emeralds are always given to the new bride," Olympe said, a teasing note in her voice, "and what better than emeralds to strike a spark from your pretty eyes and complement the warm tones of your hair and dress?"

My pretty eyes filled with foolish tears.

"What, indeed," I essayed to say lightly, "but you forget that I am a Rattray, not a Graeme. The Kinross emeralds have nothing to do with me."

Olympe surveyed me through narrowed eyes. "If you say so, Miss Rattray. If you say so."

I had thought my only ordeal upon reappearing in Society would be the malicious whispers that I had been disappointed by Richert Dalkey. It would be a thousand times worse if gossip had already linked my name with Kinross'. Nothing could be more certain to give him a disgust of me – but then, my own actions had apparently done that. At least, I thought bleakly, matters could hardly be worse.

That thought was cold comfort for the walk home, already made dreary enough by tiny winds that tugged my hair into tangles, spatters of rain that damped my dress and muddied the streets. I was in no mood to pretend a lightness of spirit I did not possess when Izzie intercepted me in the hall.

"The new dress?"

"To be sent," I said wearily.

"You must try it on for me when it arrives! But for now..."

She was blocking my way upstairs, trying to push me into the drawing-room.

"Izzie, I am much too tired to visit with whoever has called upon us."

"Don't be silly," Izzie said, her eyes dancing, "he has waited a weary time for you while you have been prinking it at the dressmaker's. The least you can do is give the gentleman the favor of an audience now that you have finally returned home!"

All the breath seemed to leave my body at once. I swayed, feeling giddy, and plumped myself down on the bottom stair before I should fall. "Izzie, not—"

"Yes," she said, grinning like an urchin.

"But – why now?"

"Go in there," she said, taking my hands to pull me upright again, "and find out!"

So, all wind-blown from the walk home, with my curls dampened by rain, and in an old walking dress whose hem was soiled from the muddy street, I was pushed into the drawing-room with no chance to protest.

"Miss Rattray," Kinross said. "Elspet. I came directly I had your letter. Letters, I should say."

"My *what?*" Had I gone mad? I had burned those foolish effusions, not sent them to him.

Oh.

No.

I had not exactly burned them; I had requested the Hob to do so.

Could he have —?

Yes.

Would he have —?

Oh, yes.

The letters may not have burned, but my cheeks certainly did.

"Lord Kinross," I said in a desperate attempt to retain my dignity, "those scribblings were never intended for any eyes but my own. If you are a gentleman, you will not read them."

"I am afraid it is too late for that," he said.

"Then – if you are a gentleman – you will, if you please, forget what you have read and throw the pages into the fire, where I intended they should go!"

"I should be sorry to do that."

Somehow, he was standing very close to me; far closer than propriety dictated. I could feel the warmth of his body. He was smiling down at me.

"The creativity and originality of your spelling alone –"

"Oh, spare my blushes!"

"I am afraid," said Kinross, "that I am not as much of a gentleman as I always believed myself to be. Miss Rattray – Elspet – on the unhappy occasion of our last meeting, I was about to discover something to you. I know that you must have been quite overset by the tragic conclusion of that meeting—"

"I am not," I said through a throat unaccountably constricted, "so fragile as all that. But I quite understand if *you* would rather not revisit the subject. After what I did you can hardly have any desire to maintain a connection with me – and so, if you please, give me back those letters!"

"After what you did?" Kinross repeated. "You mean, after *saving my life*? Elspet, you can hardly have thought me so gross an ingrate!"

His hands had closed over my elbows, and he held me so close that I could not escape him.

Not that I desired to do so.

"Elspet, you thought once before that I would cast you off, just because you employed a thread magic to break the spell that Vivienne de Larue had set on me. I told you then that your magic had no effect on my sentiments; do I really need to explain why?"

I gazed up at him, speechless.

"I was already in love with you, long before you threw that silly tangle of threads over my sleeve. I have been," said Kinross, "in love with you since I saw you, a child of twelve, fearlessly bestriding your brother's new horse."

"You never said…"

"A gentleman," Kinross said, his voice harsh now, "does not make love to a little girl. A gentleman waits for her to grow up. A gentleman does not seek to bind a girl to him on the eve of his departure for the war… and when I returned, I found that the reward of all my patient waiting was to find you in love with my best friend!"

I could not speak for a moment, but he seemed to find my headshake a satisfactory response.

"That was a childish dream," I said when he freed my lips, "from which I have long since awakened."

"By God, you'd best have put it aside now," said Kinross, "for, Elspet, I have done with playing the gentleman!"

And so, to my great satisfaction, he demonstrated until my mother interrupted us.

"*Elspet!*" she gasped as the door opened to reveal us locked together in a decidedly improper fashion.

Kinross raised his head. "Mrs. Rattray, I intend to marry your daughter."

A gentleman would have asked her permission, and my father's. My mother gasped again.

"I should, of course," he said belatedly, "prefer to do so with your approval…"

"I, I, I shall send Mr. Rattray to you," my mother said.

I turned my head and saw that she was beaming approval despite the unorthodox manner of my love's wooing.

"A dining hall filled with fairy music," she said as if to herself, while leaving the room. "Yes, a great improvement on a mere Hob!"

"*No* one," said a gruff voice from the region of my waist, "can improve on *me!*"

"Of course not, dear Hob," I said. "But would you please go away now?"

Also by Margaret Ball:

Regency Fantasy series:

Salt Magic: Regency Magic Book 1
A beautiful young widow with a deadly secret... monsters (and other creatures)
from the depths of the sea... An accusation of murder... and six aunts telling her
what to do, as if Sabira doesn't have enough problems already!

Applied Topology series:

A Pocketful of Stars: Applied Topology Book 1
A quiet math major has to fight in the magical realm for her life and those of her
friends after the CIA decides to make use of her paranormal abilities.

An Opening in the Air: Applied Topology Book 2
When a rival mage attacks, Thalia needs wits as well as magic to save the Center
for Applied Topology. And the defense may cost her the man she loves.

An Annoyance of Grackles: Applied Topology Book 3
It's bad enough when a rival mage tries to destroy you. When he turns out to be
a god, that's worse. And when the god teams up with the most notorious contract
bomber in America? If Thalia can't outwit the duo, she may wind up scattered
across the campus in tiny pieces.

A Tapestry of Fire: Applied Topology Book 4
Saving her best friend from life as a fish is difficult. Rescuing the man she loves from a past era of fire and fury ought to be impossible, so it may take Thalia a little longer.

A Creature of Smokeless Flame: Applied Topology Book 5
When CIA officers' children are kidnapped for revenge, Thalia and her colleagues follow the trail across the continents to an African terrorists' camp whose leader has the help of his own personal genie.

A Revolution of Rubies: Applied Topology Book 6
When the CIA sends Thalia and her colleagues abroad, they should have realized the diplomatic consequences could be explosive. Can Thalia stop the revolutionaries in Central Asia before all of Taklanistan is under water?

A Child of Magic: Applied Topology Book 7
When their son Aleksi is kidnapped, Thalia and Lensky are left wondering if the reason is ransom (bad) or revenge (worse). It'll take all Thalia's genius for applied topology (aka magic) to retrieve their baby - and she has yet to discover the consequences of having used applied topology (aka magic) while she was pregnant...

Harmony series:

Insurgents
The colony world of Harmony established its own separate colony to which everybody who disagreed with the government was banished. Now they're surprised that the exiles want to run their own country.

Awakening
Being a good citizen was never easy. It got harder when Devra realized that it was incompatible with being a decent human being.

Survivors
The pampered life of a holostar is no preparation for surviving the collapse of a country.

Earlier books:

Disappearing Act
Duchess of Aquitaine
Mathemagics
Lost in Translation
No Earthly Sunne
Changeweaver
Flameweaver
The Shadow Gate

www.ingramcontent.com/pod-product-compliance
Lightning Source LLC
Chambersburg PA
CBHW022010170626
46808CB00001B/348